THE BIG DAY

Ruth Harrow

CONTENTS

SEVENTEEN

EIGHTEEN

NINETEEN

TWENTY

TWENTY-ONE

TWENTY-TWO

TWENTY-THREE

TWENTY-FOUR

TWENTY-FIVE

TWENTY-SIX

TWENTY-SEVEN

TWENTY-EIGHT

TWENTY-NINE

THIRTY

THIRTY-ONE

THIRTY-TWO

THIRTY-THREE

THIRTY-FOUR

THIRTY-FIVE

THIRTY-SIX

THIRTY-SEVEN

THIRTY-EIGHT

THIRTY-NINE

FORTY

FORTY-ONE

FORTY-TWO

FORTY-THREE

COPYRIGHT

ALSO BY RUTH:

PROLOGUE

He is after me.

The house is eerie and silent. It is dead, like the people inside it. I know he has killed everyone else.

Even the baby's screams have been silenced now, too. And he never stops crying once he has revved up. He certainly had been worked up as my fingers had tried and failed to free him from his highchair straps. The stupid things were jammed as they have done lately. I thought I had almost done that magic trick the clasp requires to make it function, but not quite. Then it was too late. I heard him coming for us.

In the end, I turned and left the baby. Even if I could have escaped this, there is no way I will ever forgive myself for that.

I'm so sorry, little angel. I didn't want to leave you. My feet did it by themselves. My brain forced me to turn and flee. The front door was locked anyway so that it wouldn't have mattered. I should have stayed with you until the end. I'm so sorry.

I'm so sorry.

The shot rang through me as I dodged from the room and ran up the broad staircase instead. Everyone is gone. It's just him and me now that he has dispatched everyone else.

It's my turn now.

Recent events have led us here. Who would have thought things would end like this?

I shake violently in my hiding place like a five-year-old.

I've wedged myself beneath my bed. I'm a sandwich made with luxurious damask bedding and plush wool carpet. If only the king-sized mattress was enough to protect me. There is nothing else to stare at but the quilted underside inches from my face.

I remember there being a disagreement when it was purchased. There was an eagerness for the space above me to be occupied by the best money could buy.

It seems so futile now. I'd give up all my worldly possessions to be anywhere else but alone in this house with him.

I shrink into the thick carpet pile, willing it to swallow me up.

My breath catches as I hear his footsteps on the stairs. It will be over soon. Isn't that what Mum always says?

'Nothing bad lasts forever,' she always says. 'Just brave it for a little while. Even unpleasant things aren't endless.'

Poor Mum. My lip trembles as I consider

her sprawled and lifeless on the marble tiles downstairs in the kitchen. A look of shock fixed permanently upon her face. I want her up here with me. She would put her arms around me and tell me everything was fine, just like she did when I was little. But she won't. She never will again.

She was right. It's all over now. Any second. Will he drag me out of my hiding place, or will he simply shoot the visible bit of me when he inevitably crouches?

Under the bed was a stupid place to hide. It's too obvious. Isn't that where all the silly bimbos run to in movies? Now it has come to this I fear I'm one of them. And it will have been my last act too, far from my finest moment. I wonder what people will think when they discover this scene.

Something catches in the back of my throat —smoke. Like that time when Uncle Derek's barbecue got out of control. I can smell it now. He is burning our beautiful house to the ground, ensuring I can't escape. Either the smoke will get me, or he will.

My eyes sting—my tear ducts overflow, running down my cheeks. My chest muscles contract, trying to force a cough from me. I wrap my arms around my ribs and will myself to stay still and silent.

Then I hear him calling out my name.

How long will it take for other people to stumble upon the scene? Our home is detached.

Are our nearest neighbours too far away to hear the shots?

The other bedroom doors are being banged open, one by one. He will find me any second.

Maybe it will be a delivery man who stumbles upon the scene. Or a friend popping by for a surprise visit. They would be the ones getting a shock.

I screw up my eyes as the door to the bedroom bangs open, trying not to imagine the horror some unsuspecting person will stumble upon. The future is challenging to imagine for one reason: I don't think I have one.

He has finally found me.

ONE

I used to think happiness was for other people. That was until I met Scott. Then everything changed. Does describing him as the man of my dreams sound like a cliché?

Probably, but I don't care because that is precisely what he is. Not that I ever dreamed of such a man. Dreaming was for other women. Love found me.

I've spent my life with my eyes open for the next disaster, the one little thread that could unravel and ruin everything. It takes just a little lifted edge of the page to turn into a tear so big your whole life gets sucked right through it. I should know.

So whenever something good happens to me, I start looking over my shoulder, wondering what will come along and take it away.

Especially now, when I am the happiest I have ever been. I have never had so much to lose. I'm engaged to a man who is so wonderful, so it is hard to conceive he is real. Yet, he is. I can't believe I'm saying that after all these years of being single, interspersed with one disastrous relationship after the other.

It's two weeks until the big day, and I couldn't be happier. Excitement buzzes right down to my fingertips and toes whenever I think of my wedding day. I haven't felt like that since I was a child, before my life went disastrously wrong. I feel I need to pinch myself at increasing intervals. The fairytale is happening. I've found a happiness I never could have imagined, and in a fortnight, it is being made official.

Are you ready for another cliché? Every day is an exciting adventure with Scott. I can't believe I finally understand what people mean by this. My fiancé makes me glad I wake up in the morning. I couldn't be farther removed from how I was in the past. I've had some pretty dark days.

This evening's adventure: a quick solo shower that has turned into a romantic bath for two, complete with chocolates. Seriously, I only popped upstairs to refresh before our dinner party.

Now, the two of us are in the curvy freestanding tub together. I cradle Scott's head as he leans back and rests on my shoulder, sated in the warm bubbles. We both bask in the late afternoon sun streaming in through the tall window beside us. It's warm on our faces. When I open my eyes again, the glossy marble tiles of the bathroom have a fleeting greenish tinge.

I love these moments the best—the ones

where we don't have to say anything. We just know how we both feel, and our actions speak for themselves. I've never had this with anyone else, apart from my best friend, Sara, but that's a different thing.

Scott's wet arm stretches to the window ledge. He retrieves the box of chocolates and selects the raspberry panna cotta for me and the billionaire's shortbread for himself.

I giggle through a mouthful of creamy filling. 'I won't fit into my wedding dress at this rate.'

He shrugs, crunching up his shortbread pieces. 'I don't mind. You can get it adjusted or something. I love you no matter what.'

'That's not the point. I want to look nice for you on our wedding day.' I try to say it casually. My appearance has always been in the back of my mind, bugging me and gnawing at my self-confidence.

To other people, it's just some scarring up my arms. To me, it means not having the confidence to wear anything other than long-sleeved tops all year round, even when it's a heatwave and I long for the summer breeze on my skin. Scott has never asked me about my scars, which is another reason why I love him.

All my other partners have posed the question early on. It's usually in the first or second post-coital comedown of the relationship, and we lie naked together. They always worded it casually as we lay in bed or on a sofa afterwards, as though my not explaining it sooner was simply because it slipped my mind, not because it's a constant reminder of a past I would rather forget.

It gets tiresome repeating over again, 'Firework accident in my teens. It's what happens when you play with fire.' And for the brazen one or two that questioned further, 'A group of friends decided to launch some in a park one night. I was stupid enough to go with them.'

My last relationship was with Adam. He practically gave me an interview over the whole thing. I even momentarily wondered if he was with the press for the level of detail he requested.

I'm ashamed to say I didn't give him the boot right then and there. Many times since then, I have fantasised about throwing his sorry behind out of bed and into the street without so much as his underwear. As it happened, his stay lasted four years. The worst of my adult life.

At least Adam is firmly in the past now. Scott has restored my faith in men. He hasn't asked me to recount my painful life history either. He has been happy to take me as I am ever since we literally stumbled into each other in a coffee shop after I finished work one day.

This was back in January. Scott had to rush off to some important business meeting with coffee on his designer suit as I apologised profusely. But only after we exchanged numbers.

After my disastrous dating history and its effect on my confidence, part of me wondered if he wanted my number to send me the dry cleaning bill. He didn't. He asked me out that very weekend.

It's now May, and we will be getting married in fourteen days. I'm so excited. We jet off a week on Monday to settle in and soak up Santorini before our destination wedding in the sun. We have both taken time off work. There is nothing left to do but enjoy each other before the wedding.

Scott stretches his neck back, and his lips brush my jawline tenderly. Things start stirring again. I can see where this is heading.

'I think we need to get dressed.' I pull away with regret. 'Our guests will arrive soon. I dread to think what condition the roast will be in. It's been in the oven way too long already.'

'Roast dinners take care of themselves.'

I grin. Scott barely knows his way around the kitchen. 'They seem to if you aren't the one cooking them.'

'I don't know why you have put the pressure on yourself to do a full meal. We could have ordered all the food in. It's too hot for a roast dinner anyway. You shouldn't have dismissed my idea of a barbecue so quickly.

He gestures to the glorious sunshine outside. The window is open, and hot summer air does nothing to cool the steamy bathroom environment.

'I told you I don't like barbecues. I hate the smell.' I shiver internally as I think of searing flesh over naked flames, the outside of the meat becoming irreversibly charred and black. I can't stand it. I shiver again.

The last thing I want to do is drag myself out of this perfect moment with my fiancé to check on the food. I explain this to him as I stand up.

'Then don't,' he says, taking my hand. His steel eyes have a dark ring around the iris. They unabashedly take in every detail as I extrapolate myself from the bathtub. 'I'm sure your friend will enjoy whatever we serve. It's you she is coming to see, not a plate of food. It's our pre-wedding dinner. You can give yourself some time off cooking.'

'I know. But it's a traditional thing we do. We always make a roast dinner whenever we get together. Sara's mum did the most legendary ones when we were growing up. I'm not joking. Her Yorkshire puddings were a meal in themselves. No matter what was happening in our lives, it was the one thing we could rely on. You always knew you could sit down and enjoy that meal together. Patricia was so welcoming to me. Since she developed early onset dementia, her recipes are lost with her. She never wrote them down or told anyone. Sara and I have had to piece it together ourselves over the years. It's not a patch on Patricia's, of course. But it's the thought behind it that's important, you know?'

Scott smiles. 'That sounds nice. My mum was never a cook. If we ate at home, the au pair did all the cooking.'

'That explains your lack of skills in the kitchen.'

Scott aims a playful slap in my direction as he lounges back in the bubbles, but I dodge it. 'Cheeky!'

Laughing, I wrap a fluffy grey towel around myself. Then the doorbell rings, and my face falls.

I look at Scott with wide eyes. 'Is that a guest? People can't be arriving this early! What time is it?'

He looks just as surprised as he sits up straight. 'No idea. But if that is a guest, they are unfashionably early. It wasn't five thirty when I came up here. I thought we told people seven?'

'We did! It can't be Sara. Her train doesn't get in until twenty to seven.'

'Maybe she got an earlier one?'

'I hope she didn't. I was supposed to pick her up from the station. My phone is downstairs. Has she been trying me, do you think?'

I rub the towel over myself frantically. I'm soaking wet and naked, and thanks to Scott, my clothes are strewn along the landing and stairs. I only meant to pop up here briefly for a quick shower. I haven't applied any makeup yet, either.

Scott stands up and steps out of the bath. 'Relax, Sam. I'll go and get the door. It's probably an overzealous guest. Take your time.'

He kisses my cheek and wraps a towel around his waist.

I watch him leave through the crack in the door. As he goes, he leaves receding wet footprints on the landing carpet. Scott is likely right about our early visitor, I think as I dry myself and move along the landing, gathering my clothes. The only person in my life other than my fiancé is Sara.

I have my colleagues at the school where I work, but we rarely see each other outside the grounds, fraternising in the staff room instead.

I've always kept a certain distance with my fellow workers. You could say I've moved around a lot in my life. I've never got too close to anyone for very long. Sara is the only constant line that exists in everything I do. She has been my rock. It's not her voice, which I hear trailing upstairs as I near the top of the statement staircase.

It is a woman, however.

Curiosity lifts my head. I peer through the glass balustrade, where Scott talks to a woman I've never seen before. She is beautiful; that is my first impression. Based on the obvious familiarity between the pair, I assume she is a guest of his.

Something doesn't seem right, however.

The fist Scott grips his towel with is tight

and white. He doesn't make any attempt to invite this mystery woman in. His broad shoulders fill the front door frame as though trying to block her from seeing inside our home.

Now, I spot the suitcases through the tall glass panel beside the front door. At least three are peppering the driveway tarmac beside this visitor.

Scott's voice is angry. I hear him muttering through gritted teeth. I pull my towel tighter around me and abandon my discarded clothing upstairs.

I take a tentative step towards the walnut staircase. The woman notices me now. She turns her glossy head, peering at me from between the modern orbs of the staircase chandelier.

'Hiya,' she says brightly. 'You must be Scott's fiancé?'

'Yes, hello,' I say uncertainly, looking at Scott for confirmation.

The woman glances at Scott, too, piercing him with bright green eyes. She nods at him and looks back at me. 'He hasn't mentioned me, has he? I'm Dawn. I'm Scott's wife.'

TWO

Scott is married. My brain should be buzzing with this new fact. Instead, it is just numb. I must look like a right fool standing halfway down the stairs with my mouth agape, wearing nothing but a towel.

My fiancé has a wife. This must be a mistake. One look at Scott tells me it is not. He doesn't rush to deny it, nor does he make a move to comfort or reassure me. Instead, he looks furious.

I have flashbacks to Adam all of a sudden. My ex-boyfriend was a University lecturer. I'd returned home from a girl's weekend with Sara to find him attempting to rush out one of his students from our flat.

It turned out he had overslept and hadn't managed to clear up the evidence before my return. At least I was the one who left him in the end. I wouldn't have wanted to clean up the scene of the crime. It looked like they had quite the weekend together. The bed sheets were smeared with used condoms and melted chocolate.

I'm grateful to that girl for hammering in that relationship's final nail in the coffin. She pushed me into doing what I should have done much sooner, and I was pleased to move on after the initial shock had worn off.

I can't say the same now. Scott was the one. I just knew it.

'What's going on?' I say into the awkward silence. I bite my lip and stare at the nearest suitcase, a plastic magenta one on wheels. Anything other than letting this woman and Scott see my watering eyes. I said I would never let a man get the better of me again.

Hadn't I done my due diligence on Scott? He may believe our meeting was purely by chance, but it could have been more spontaneous. I researched him on a dating app before taking the plunge. His profile said he had never been married, but all his other details have proven correct. He is six-foot-two, has pale blue eyes, an athletic build, and dark hair.

While I haven't seen his financial statements, I've seen enough to believe his claimed income range. We live in this detached Didsbury house worth over a million. We have taken several expensive vacations together, and Scott often spends on me.

So why would he lie about being single?

I should have known I couldn't bag a man like Scott—not for real. He is too handsome, refined, and sophisticated for me. He knows fine wines and has insider knowledge of the best restaurants. I've always been content to drink a decent bottle of Sauvignon Blanc from Aldi to pair with one of their ready meals. That was before I became teetotal, however.

Scott was raised in something short of a stately home, by the sound of it. He doesn't know my troubled childhood history. Yet. He doesn't know I spent my teenage years in various foster homes whilst he was being waited on hand and foot, enjoying lavish parties.

Frozen fish fingers would seem like an alien concept to him. To me, that was a treat as a teen. The only thing my fiancé has in his freezer is ice and vodka.

'I'm Scott's wife,' the woman repeats, glancing at my towel and then back at my face.

She seems pleased to be delivering this news. Her pretty green eyes are alight, and her full lips are drawn in a small smile.

Scott shakes his head as he turns and looks at me imploringly. 'It's not what you think, Sam. Yes, Dawn was my wife. We haven't been together for years. I filed for divorce ages ago. It should have gone through by now. I believed it had.'

I blink. 'You didn't tell me you were married.'

Dawn grimaces. 'Didn't he? Oops. Sorry. This is probably a little awkward, then. Sam, is it?'

I nod, feeling underdressed. Dawn is beautiful and glossy, every bit the attractive partner I've always thought Scott would look good with. I'm highly aware my wet hair hangs limp around my face. I have no makeup on. I don't believe Dawn can see my scars from her position on the doorstep. Still, it doesn't stop me from wrapping my arms around me, shrinking into the Egyptian cotton fibres of the towel.

Scott must sense this. 'Look, Dawn. It isn't appropriate for you to be here. We are having a dinner party tonight.'

She cringes. 'Yes, I know. A little send-off before your wedding in sunny Santorini.'

Scott frowns. 'How did you know that?'

'A little bird told me, Scotty.' She tilts her head to one side. 'Remember, your friends are still mine. Even if you pretend otherwise these days.'

'So what are you doing here?'

'I have nowhere else to go, I'm afraid.' She gestures at her suitcases around her feet. 'My landlady kicked me out.'

'What are you talking about?'

'The landlady is selling the flat. I had to leave. And since I still legally own half this house, I thought, why not stay here?'

'You don't own anything. We are divorced.'

Dawn smiles. 'No, we are not. You might want to check your paperwork. Our divorce was never finalised. I checked.'

'That can't be right. I had my solicitor handle everything. He told me a while ago that the divorce would be over soon. That was months ago.'

Dawn seems exasperated. 'Listen, I don't know what's gone wrong, but we are still legally married, okay?'

'We can't be.'

'We are, Scotty,' she purrs. 'I don't remember agreeing to any divorce. Don't you need my permission or something?'

'We didn't need it. You left me well over two years ago and we've had no contact since. That counts as abandonment.'

'Whatever. I've checked the legalities in the last few days. I promise we are still married. Look, I need somewhere to stay and this is legally still a place I can call home.'

'Your landlady can't just kick you into the street,' Scott protests impatiently. 'She has to give you two months' notice to find somewhere else by law.'

'Yes, she did. That was back in March. I haven't been able to find anywhere suitable. Yesterday was officially my last day in that flat. I've been wandering the streets lugging my stuff around with me.'

Scott stares. 'You can't be serious.'

'I am.' Dawn presses her fingertips beneath her eyes. I assume there must be bags beneath them, but I can't see from this distance. 'I honestly have nowhere else to go. I've been awake all night, moving between coffee shops and restaurants.'

'What about your car?'

'I let go of it ages ago, before I left the country.'

'What about friends? Why not stay with one of them?'

'I can't. Most of them are jetting off shortly for your wedding.'

'You must have other friends.' The doubt in Scott's voice is audible.

'Of course I do. But none of them can put me up for one reason or another. Don't you think I've tried?'

'What about a hotel, then?'

'I don't have the stacks of money you do, darling. I can't just burn through my savings until I find somewhere suitable to live.'

'What happened to your job?'

'I'm between jobs at the moment.'

It's hard to imagine what employment Dawn might have had looking at her delicate, manicured hands. Now isn't the moment to ask.

Scott sighs impatiently and shifts his weight from one foot to another. 'You can't be here.'

Dawn grits her perfect white teeth. 'I don't like it any more than you do, Scott. Trust me, I would be there like a shot if I had anywhere else to go. But I do have a legal claim on this house. I have a right to be here.'

Scott looks sceptical. He has lost the verbal tennis match. I can tell if either of us was wearing more than towels and we weren't hosting a dinner party in an hour or so, my fiancé might put up more of a fight. He glances up at me as though asking the question.

'It's okay,' I say. 'You can't leave her out in the cold.'

I realise it's late May and sweltering hot outside, but it's the principle. 'Our guests are going to be here soon anyway.'

Scott seems defeated. I think he wanted me to say no, protest so he didn't have to. Perhaps I was supposed to conjure an ironclad excuse as to why Dawn would have to gather her things and turn back.

I'm not cold enough to turn someone in need away. I don't know Dawn, but I hate the thought of anyone having nowhere to go, having exercised all her resources.

Scott reluctantly opens the door wider and stands back to let Dawn in. He doesn't help her with her bags, however. 'You can stay tonight. But just for the night. Then you have to find somewhere else to go.'

'Brill.' Dawn reaches down for the nearest magenta suitcase. I realise there is a lampshade and a plant on the tarmac behind it. 'You won't even notice I'm here.'

THREE

I trot back up the stairs as Dawn shuffles her things into the house. Scott closes the door behind her. I'm eager to be dressed. I feel way too exposed.

I leave the pair to it and slip into the bedroom. There isn't a door lock and I hope Dawn won't come in when I'm getting dressed. I assume she knows this is the master bedroom since it turns out this was her marital home.

I hear her moving back and forth on the landing to one of the other bedrooms, shouting casually to Scott as she goes. I retreat through the glossy sliding door of the walk-in wardrobe for some semblance of privacy.

The bedroom door flies open as I slip my knickers over my damp skin.

My stomach drops through the floor before I realise it is my fiancé.

He looks flushed and uncharacteristically stressed. 'You okay, Sam?'

'Sure.' I nod stiffly.

I'm not all right, of course. I've had a shock. Our pre-wedding alone time has been shattered, and I've just found out my husband-to-be has lied to me about being single.

Okay, so it's a legal technicality. Dawn and her ex are clearly not together, but Scott didn't mention he had been married. What else is he hiding from me?

His dating profile had said he had never been married. Now, his wife is in our house, moving her belongings into the spare room.

It wasn't supposed to be this way. It should have been just the two of us at this special time. We were supposed to cherish these moments before we officially tied the knot and became man and wife.

Will there even be a wedding at all? How can my fiancé get married if his divorce isn't yet legal?

I voice this to Scott as he joins me in the walk-in wardrobe. He hastily pulls on some underwear and jeans too. 'Don't worry about that. I'll make sure it is sorted before the wedding.'

I stare at him. He is always self-assured but can't expect to get out of this one so easily. 'How? We get married in fourteen days!'

'It will be all right, babes. I promise. Any decent solicitor can fix this fast. I've got the best one too, remember? He has got me out of worse scrapes before, honestly.'

'I don't think forgetting to mention you are married is a scrape.'

'I guess that was a bad choice of words.' Scott smiles wryly. I'm annoyed with him, but he still looks devastatingly gorgeous. I wish he would hurry up and choose a shirt so I wouldn't be so distracted by his defined body.

'Look, we will get the legals sorted, and Dawn will be out of here. She always was a bimbo. She couldn't plan her way out of a paper bag. It doesn't surprise me that this has happened to her. She is only staying for tonight. I promise. I'll admit it's bad timing. I'm so sorry I didn't tell you about her.'

'I don't understand why you didn't mention her before now. It's okay if you are getting divorced. People do it all the time, so it wouldn't have made a difference to me either way. I just wanted you to be honest, that's all. I have had enough of duplicity.'

Even as I say these words, I realise how hypocritical they are. There is so much I haven't told Scott. There is no way I can tell him everything about me. What would he think if I did?

Scott sighs. 'Dawn is a part of my life that I would rather forget. She and I parted ways years ago. It's been so long since I've even seen her. I've been so busy with my business, I must have overlooked finalising the divorce. It probably boils down to a silly mistake, like a missed signature somewhere. I'm going to have to discuss it with Henry. I'm so sorry, babes.'

Henry is Scott's solicitor. He is often at the house for some reason or another. Usually, he disappears behind Scott's study door while they talk business.

Scott owns a luxury men's clothing company. I don't delve too much into it, but it must be doing well if our lifestyle and home are anything to go by. That's why he moved up here from his hometown of Harrogate: to be closer to a larger target market and the networking opportunities Manchester offers.

'You don't have to apologise. This is just unexpected, that's all.'

My fiancé buttons his shirt quickly and wraps his warm arms around me. The warmth is welcome after being damp and cool for so long. It would be nice to rewind to this embrace several hours ago and forget any of this happened.

'Thanks for being so understanding about this,' he mutters against my ear. 'I love you so much. What we have is amazing. It's nothing like my marriage to Dawn.'

'I love you too. It's all just a shock. I was so looking forward to getting married to you.'

'And you will. Look, the worst that will happen is we have a ceremony-only affair in Greece and get the legal formalities taken care of when we return home. It will not boil down to that though.'

'Are you sure?'

'I'm positive we can work this out. It's a good

thing Henry is coming to dinner. I'll see if I can pull him aside before dinner, see what he can do.'

That reminds me. 'Dinner!'

I forget about wriggling and zipping my way into the elegant cocktail dress I'd chosen for tonight's gathering. Instead, I pull on the jeans and long-sleeved t-shirt I was wearing earlier and dash downstairs. I hurry through the glass doors that lead to the open-plan kitchen and dining area.

The overlooked dinner has been all but ruined. It's the wrong side of overdone as I pull out the trays and slide them onto the kitchen island. The edges of the roast potatoes are black. The Yorkshire puddings are dark brown and rock solid when I tap them on the marble worktop. The roast chicken is salvageable if I serve it without the skin. Then again, it would be pretty dry. What am I going to do?

I wonder if I can make the Greek canapés from the fridge stretch.

Scott appears behind me.

'It's ruined,' I tell him. 'I can't serve this.'

My fiancé puts his chin on my shoulder, his hands on my hips. 'Time for plan B.'

I sigh. Scott is talking about the Greek restaurant he took me to to celebrate our engagement. He wanted us to do a complete country-specific feast for tonight's dinner. 'That was your plan A, if we are honest, wasn't it?'

He grins. 'Maybe. I swear I didn't distract

you on purpose.'

I roll my eyes. 'There isn't enough time to get there and back before people arrive.'

'Sure there is. We still have all the canapés and the wine. That will keep people busy. Booze and nibbles. It will be all right, Sam. No one will know any different. It will fit in with our theme perfectly.'

'I guess. How quick can you be?'

'I'll have the food back here before anyone has even got through their first glass of Agiorgitiko. I promise.'

He kisses me quickly on the cheek. I watch him through the tall glass doors that separate the kitchen-diner from the entrance hall. He quickly drops into one of the velvet chairs under the stairs and pulls his designer trainers on. He blows me a kiss before jogging outside to his electric Jaguar. I watch him through the exterior glass doors as he follows the curve of the driveway and drives out of sight through the tall hedges.

When I first saw this house, I joked that it had a goldfish bowl feel to it. It feels like people outside can see right through to the kitchen, where I am now. The thick wooden gates are locked at night when we have the lights on. I can only hope that there is never anyone out there watching.

Still, this place can make me feel rather exposed.

FOUR

I start throwing away the burned food, wondering what to tell Sara. She will expect the special dinner I promised her.

My text yesterday described the recipe I found online for extra-large Yorkshire puddings. It felt more important than ever to cook something from the heart for her, especially with what she is going through now with Patricia's worsening dementia. The sentiment has gone over Scott's head. Maybe I haven't done a great job of explaining.

I dread what Sara would make of Scott inadvertently getting his way over the choice of cuisine. She would say he did it on purpose. I will just have to avoid telling her.

'I hope that wasn't my fault.'

Dawn appears behind me. I jump as I scrape roast potatoes into the bin. The panic over the food makes me forget she's here. I'm so used to being alone in this big house when Scott isn't around.

'No, don't worry about it. I should have had a closer eye on things. I got distracted.'

Dawn smiles knowingly. 'Yeah, it looked like it. Scott was never one for meal prep. You probably know that already, don't you?'

She runs her hands over the white gloss kitchen doors and gold pull handles. 'You know, I don't remember ever cooking much in this house. Nothing more than eggs florentine for the weekend. You know, romantic breakfast in bed and all that.'

I nod and try to smile while pushing down thoughts of Scott in this house with another woman. It's hard to think of myself almost as the intruder in this situation, especially with the surprise of Dawn sprung on me. As Scott said, though, he hasn't seen his ex for years. He didn't specify how many.

I know I haven't done anything wrong. I just feel a little odd navigating my way around Dawn's old kitchen while she watches me. With her expensive long highlights, and glamorous clothing, she looks like she belongs here. She wears a short-sleeved purple satin top and an elegant floral skirt.

Her eyelashes are full and dark, and her brows, too. I'm more aware than ever of my lack of makeup and of my casual clothes. Dawn looks better dressed for a dinner party than I do, and it wasn't her intention to walk into one. It was a coincidence she arrived here at the same time we are having a dinner party.

I don't have time to attempt to coerce my

lank hair into any kind of desirable shape—not that mine would ever fall elegantly around my face in those subtle waves like Dawn's. Her beautiful hair looks effortless as if she woke up that way this morning.

My experience with hair styling extends to the occasional YouTube tutorial. They never work for me. I always get in a tangle, and the end result is sad and limp.

I'm just grateful if I have time to brush my dirty blonde hair before rushing out the door for work. There is no point in getting glammed up for my daily grind anyway—I'm a teaching assistant, not a model.

The kids won't notice what I look like. They don't care if, by some miracle, I grow my hair beyond shoulder length. I'm always exhausted and flattened by the end of the school day. I dread what state a coiffed hairstyle would end up in after all those hours, even if I did manage to pull something other than a quick ponytail off.

I look at the ornate clock on the wall. It's just gone half-six. Sara's train will be arriving at the station soon. I should have asked Scott to pick her up on his way. He doesn't answer his phone when I step out into the garden to call him, so I assume he is either driving or engrossed in ordering the food.

He was supposed to greet the guests while I popped out to get Sara. After all, they are all primarily his friends. At least one of us has to be here to welcome them.

I step back inside the kitchen. Dawn has settled herself at the breakfast bar.

She has helped herself to one of the glass bottles of Scottish spring water from the fridge. She raises it questioningly, even though she has twisted the lid off already. 'I hope you don't mind. It's a scorcher out there today. I've been sweating like a pig all day with all that heavy luggage.'

'Not at all. Help yourself to anything, please.'

'Thanks. I thought it would be okay. I know those are Scott's drinks. He was always particular about not drinking tap water.'

'Well, I have them too. We share them.'

'Of course. What's his is yours and all that. And he does have a lot to offer, doesn't he?'

I give a half-shrug. It must be tough for Dawn to see her almost ex-husband with someone else. I don't like her tone, but I don't expect her to be my friend. I feel the same vibe coming from Scott's friends whenever I've bumped into some here and there. They all think I'm after money. If only my life was that simple.

I glance at the clock again. Scott won't make it back before I have to pick up my best friend.

I try Scott's phone again. He isn't answering.

'Something wrong?'

'I'm supposed to pick up my friend from the station. Her train arrives any minute. But our other guests will be arriving soon. Scott was supposed to be here to let them in.'

'I can do that if you want to just pop out.'

'Really? That would be amazing. All you have to do is let them in and sit them down. Maybe open some wine, perhaps?'

'Let's not go nuts. I'm not a butler.'

I look at her uncertainly.

She leans forward and flashes her pristine teeth at me. 'Just kidding! Go and get your friend. What time is her train?'

'Six-forty.'

'Blimey! You better get going. I'll get the door and pop a cork or two. The station is a five-minute car ride. I've done that drive a thousand times. Don't worry about a thing, babes.'

I wonder who started that term of endearment. Maybe Scott got it from Dawn? It kind of taints it for me now when I think of him using it on me.

'Thanks so much.' I grab my keys and slip on my shoes. 'I'll be back before you know it.'

As Scott did, I jog out to the car and hurry to the station.

*

I park my little Aygo in the car park and look around for Sara. According to the board, her train arrived a few minutes ago. When I arrive on the platform, people are still milling around and dispersing.

I walk the length of the platform, but Sara isn't here. I pull out my phone to give her a call. Then I notice a text from her I'd overlooked in my stack of notifications. I must have been occupied when it came in earlier this afternoon.

Running a little late. Got the train that gets in at 19:02 instead. Only one change instead of four! xx

I glance up at the arrivals board. The train is due to arrive in fifteen or so minutes. There isn't much point driving home and then back again.

I don't have much choice but to wait. I want to tell Dawn I will be longer than I said, but I don't have her number, and we don't have a home phone either.

I feel bad leaving her to let everyone in by herself. We only invited a few people. Scott had six friends who said they would come, some with their partners. They might not turn up bang on seven, either. It will be okay, I tell myself.

I text Sara to say I'll be here when she arrives and then take a seat on the platform bench. It's a beautiful warm day. The sun is hot on my face. I'm sweating beneath the long sleeves of my t-shirt.

Summer is hard when you have parts you want to hide. I'd love to roll up my sleeves or, dare I say, wear something sleeveless. A halter neck might be nice. I used to have a nice floral one when I was little. Mum used to love dressing me up in pretty garments.

I have a few minutes to kill and no one to judge me, so I take a moment to imagine what it would be like to have a little girl to choose dresses for. I could pair her outfits with matching bows and hair accessories. We could even wear co-ords. The big house Scott and I share would be a wonderful place to raise kids.

A station announcement dispels the fantasy. Sara's train has been delayed by a few minutes. A short while later it is rumbling down the track.

The doors open, and streams of commuters hop off. After a few minutes, I spot Sara. Her warm brown eyes fix on me, and her smooth skin dimples neatly in a grin. Her dark, natural curls bounce as she waves at me ecstatically.

I grin back before the crowd allows us to join in a bear hug, in which we move our weight from foot to foot in sync.

I get a hit of the vanilla perfume she has used for years. It reminds me of her mother and the good times the three of us shared together. A wave of good memories washes over me. It's comfort and good times. I've really missed my friend.

Sara pulls back from me and grins. 'I can't believe my best friend is getting married before me! I thought you had gone off men?'

I laugh. 'Not completely! I still like to dabble in the species. I've chosen some corkers before, but this one is different.'

My best friend is dressed in a pretty cocktail dress quite similar to the one I had planned tonight. It is a deep plum and has long lace sleeves right down to the wrists. I appreciate the meaning behind her choice. She has chosen something that won't make me look or feel out of place if our other female guests have gone for strappy, revealing dresses. At least the two of us will be in our own little club.

Sara grabs her small wheelie case and we walk towards the car park. 'Urggh, it's what they all say, isn't it? I'll be the judge of that. You've only known the guy for months. It's all so sudden.'

'You'll understand when you meet Scott. You will love him, I promise.'

'I can't believe you are getting married so soon. Should you give it longer before you dive in?'

'You've said all this on the phone. I know what you mean. I wouldn't have believed you if you told me I would get hitched after knowing a guy for less than half a year, but Scott is special. We've really clicked.'

'Have you honestly not argued yet?'

I hesitate as I think about this afternoon. 'Not yet.'

Sara pauses as she pulls on her seatbelt. 'Uh oh.'

'It's not an argument exactly. It's just…I sort of found out Scott is married this afternoon.'

'No! That's the oldest one in the book. The polite, charming, handsome guy turns out to be married with three kids and a Labrador. Oh, Sam, I'm so sorry.'

'No, it's not like that. I meant I found out he isn't quite divorced. There has been some kind of technicality in the paperwork or something.'

'Oh. So they are definitely over?'

'Yes, for certain. Scott says he hasn't seen Dawn for years.'

'Are you sure? What forced him to confess in the end? Didn't find her underwear somewhere you shouldn't have, did you?'

I cringe inwardly as I consider what I'm about to tell my friend. 'Nothing like that. She got kicked out of her rented place. She didn't have anywhere else to go. So…'

As expected, Sara's eyebrows shoot upwards. 'You can't be for real. Your beloved hasn't moved her in with you, has he?'

I nod. 'Just for tonight.'

Sara presses her fingers to her neat lips as she processes this. My friend is one of the lucky ones who can walk about with the defined features other women take ages to paint on. She literally wakes up like that, except she seems to have dark circles on this occasion. 'Gosh, it's the kind of thing you hear on Jerry Springer.'

I laugh at this. 'Not quite.'

'I'm serious!'

'I don't think so, Sara. Also, I don't think

41

that show is a thing any more.'

'Yeah, they don't make 'em like they used to. But Scott has moved some other woman in just weeks before your wedding day. That's... unusual.'

'It's two weeks. There is still time. This all literally happened this afternoon. Dawn turned up on the doorstep with all her stuff this afternoon. Her landlady kicked her out. Scott couldn't just turn her away. I don't think he would have done that, even if Dawn didn't legally still have a right to the house. Scott is too good for that.'

'Mm. Mr Wonderful can do no wrong, eh?'

'Not exactly. But I'd like to think that if Scott and I ever parted ways, he wouldn't just turn me away if I had nowhere to go. I would be more worried, to be honest, if he had been cold towards her and told her to get lost. She really was desperate.'

'Would you turn up with your stuff on your ex's doorstep, though? I wouldn't. It takes some nerve to do that. His wife must be aware he is getting remarried.'

'She didn't seem surprised to see me.'

'I bet she didn't. Gosh, Sam. All this is happening so close to your wedding day. Hold on, how can he marry you if he isn't divorced yet? Does that mean the wedding is off?'

'No. Scott says the worst-case scenario is we have the ceremony in Greece as planned, but we only make it legal in the UK after everything is ironed out here.'

Sara lets out a low breath. 'That's not ideal, is it?'

'I'll admit it's not the best start. But it might not come to that. Scott is going to speak to his solicitor.'

Her dark eyes lock onto me as I navigate onto my leafy suburban street. 'I'm surprised you would stand for that after everything you went through with You-Know-Who.'

'I thought you might say that. Scott isn't anything like Adam. I've made sure of it.'

There is a pause. 'I don't know, Sam. You have seemed different since you have been with Scott. It's like you are determined to push on, no matter what. Are there any other red flags you are ignoring?'

I shake my head as I pull onto the driveway. 'Of course not. Everything is perfect.'

'There isn't any such thing,' Sara says as the engine dies. 'Everyone has flaws, something to hide. You know that better than anyone, *Sam*.'

I look at her sharply. We are encased within my car and far enough from the house, but both sets of windows are open in this warm weather.

I assume our guests are at the back of the property, spilling out into the garden through the bifold patio doors, immersed in conversation.

Let's hope the booze and nibbles are enough

to distract them.

FIVE

'Well, this place certainly looks the part,' Sara says as we swing our legs from my car.

She stares up at the property's angular glass facade in awe. 'Google Street View doesn't do it justice.'

'I know what you mean. I Googled it too before I came here.'

'Glad to hear it. I assume Scott isn't compensating for something?'

'No, and shhh!'

We both burst out laughing. I think I catch a flicker of movement in the upstairs window, but it can't be; that's the master bedroom, and Scott isn't here.

I have missed Sara since I moved up North. She understands why I felt I had to go. There were too many memories back in Bournemouth. Sara still loves living there. One day, I must pluck up the courage to visit her. Thank goodness for Skype, though. We can still stay connected as though the distance is nothing.

Scott's car isn't on the driveway. He still isn't back yet with the main courses.

I wonder how Dawn is doing with the guests. It's not the best first impression having Scott's ex greeting everyone as they arrive. I notice no one else has parked on the driveway.

The house is surprisingly still and quiet when we walk in.

Sara's heels echo around the entrance hall as she parks her wheelie case under the stairs. 'Wow. I think you could squeeze a small townhouse into this bit alone. Do you think Scott would go for that?' she asks sarcastically.

'I don't know,' I grin. 'It's a conversation starter for when he gets back with the food.'

The kitchen and dining area are also devoid of people. I expected to walk into a room full of people settling in, perhaps Dawn, nearby pouring wine into their waiting glasses.

There is no one here, however. 'Hello? Dawn?'

Sara steps out onto the patio through the open doors. 'Where is everyone?'

'I'm not sure.'

Dawn's bare-footed form descends the open riser staircase. She smiles brightly. 'Hiya. I was beginning to think I'd been abandoned!'

I smile politely. 'Has no one arrived for dinner yet?'

'Not yet. It turns out you had nothing to worry about. You've beaten everyone to it.' She picks up a glass of wine from the kitchen island and takes a sip. 'No one has arrived at all.'

'Oh.' I glance at the big metallic kitchen clock.

So does Dawn. 'It's only gone twenty past. It's a dinner party, not a day in court! You know, in some cultures, it's rude to be exactly on time.'

'Really?' Sara asks. 'Which ones?

'France, for one, and the Middle East.'

I know very little of Scott's friends. I just know he knows most of them through his business. One or more of them might be from these countries. I never thought to ask.

What does Dawn know that I don't?

'Are Scott's friends likely to arrive late?'

Dawn shrugs. 'It depends who he invited. Scott has connections all over the world through his business dealings. When I was the hostess, quite a few liked to leave a sort of buffer, if you will, of half an hour or more. It's custom in many countries to allow the host time to finish preparations and socialise with earlier arrivals.' She gestures to Sara.

Sara smiles. 'Sounds like my plumber. He likes to leave a good forty minutes to an hour-and-a-half buffer before he shows up to do any work.'

Dawn almost chokes on another sip of wine as she bursts out laughing. 'Oh my goodness, don't!'

She raises her glass to me questioningly. 'Would you like some?'

Dawn makes the offer as though I'm the

guest who has arrived at her house and she is playing the polite host.

For some reason, I follow suit and answer politely, 'No thanks. I don't drink.'

'I'll have a drop,' Sara says beside me as we settle at the breakfast bar. She shoots me an incredulous look as Dawn crosses the room to take a bottle of Greek wine from the bar.

Dawn fetches glasses and pours Sara some of the deep red liquid. She pours a J20 for me. She tops up her own glass whilst she is at it. 'Let's get this party started. It's a celebration, after all. I'm not sure where the groom is, though!'

I frown at the clock. 'I think he should be here by now.'

'Oh, that's gorgeous.' Sara winces in appreciation as she sips her drink. 'Where is Mr Wonderful, anyway?'

It's my turn to shoot my friend a look. 'Scott popped out to get the main course for dinner.'

'Are we not having our usual roast?'

'We were. I spent ages on it, but it got burned. I'm so sorry.'

Dawn holds up her palm. 'I think you have me to blame for that. I think my sudden arrival was a bit of a shock for the happy couple. Very sorry.'

'That's all right. I could smell it when I came in, that's all. I'm sure the alternative will be delicious.'

'Speaking of which...' Dawn, the host, trots

over to the fridge and places the plates of Greek canapés I prepared this morning out on the breakfast bar.

She peels back the clingfilm on a cool feta, cucumber and onion salad, herby-lemon shrimp, ramekins of creamy dips and marinated olives, just to name a few. 'We can't let our punctual guest go hungry now. Long train journeys are hell in this hot weather, aren't they?'

'You can say that again,' Sara says, helping herself to a mini kofta. 'This is delicious. Did you make these yourself, Sam?'

'Yes. Scott wanted to order in, but I thought it would add a more personal touch if I made the food myself. Especially since only some people coming tonight will be at the wedding. Hence, the Greek theme. They can still get a flavour of the celebrations.'

'Hmm.' Dawn tries a kofta, too. And another. Then another two.

No one else has arrived yet. I start wondering if I made enough of each food item. I've never catered for so many people before. There should be a dozen or so. I was guessing at quantities, and now the plate is quickly being demolished. Dawn moves to the other plates of food, too.

This doesn't go unnoticed by Sara. 'You look like you haven't eaten for days.'

'Not properly.' She piles some stuffed queen olives into her mouth. 'I've had a bit of trouble at home. I've been scrambling around trying to get some accommodation sorted. Self-care has gone out of the window. You could say cooking has been the last thing on my mind.'

'I bet. Have you narrowed down your list of properties?'

'I have a shortlist. The place I most wanted won't be available to view until tomorrow.'

My shoulders relax a little. Dawn has somewhere lined up. That's good news. 'What time is the viewing?'

'Six-thirty.'

Sara nods as she takes a canapé. 'You'll have a job to get your stuff together and out quickly if you take it. Unless you are travelling light?'

Dawn smiles. 'I am, actually. Possessions only weigh you down. I've learned to live more minimally these days.'

'Cool.'

I think of the suitcases Dawn turned up with. Was that all she owned in the world? I've always kept my things to a minimum in case I had to move again in a hurry. Dawn practically makes me look like a hoarder.

'Where is the new place?' I ask Dawn. 'Is it local?'

She nods. 'Yep. I'd kind of like to try somewhere new. But my life is in and around Manchester. It would be hard to say goodbye.'

I nod; I felt like that when I left my hometown. 'Where would you like to live?'

'Somewhere by the coast might be nice, although I'd miss the big city lights.' She turns to Sara. 'You live in Bournemouth, don't you?'

'Born and bred.'

Did I tell Dawn that Sara was coming here from Bournemouth? I don't recall.

Dawn nibbles at a crispy halloumi bite. 'What's that like? Is it upbeat enough, or is it lowkey, not much to do?'

Sara gives me a half-glance at this. 'Depends what you're after. It's not a tiny coastal community. If you've got a decent budget, there is something for everyone. I suppose you will have a decent bit left over once your divorce is finalised.'

My friend gestures around her with her wine glass. 'I'll pretend I didn't look it up on Zoopla earlier and say I'm guessing this place must be worth a fair bit. You could move to quite a few places with just half its value.'

'True.'

'That would take a while to be sorted, though. More than a day anyway.'

Dawn shrugs and peers at a plate of spinach and feta parcels, choosing which one to pounce on. 'I'm not going to end up with half this place. Scott and I don't have children. On paper, I didn't contribute anything towards the mortgage. And I'm not planning on being here until we have dotted all the I's and crossed the T's on the legal side. As you said, that might take a while.'

'Scott said he didn't think it would,' I pipe up. 'He thinks Henry might be able to sort things faster than that. Henry is Scott's solicitor,' I add for Sara's benefit.

Dawn seems to think this comment is for her. 'Yes, I know old Henry. He has known your fiancé since Scott was a little boy. I suppose he is a guest tonight.'

The doorbell chimes through the entrance hall.

Dawn gets up from her stool and heads towards the door. 'Speak of the devil. I wonder if that is him now?'

I get up quickly. 'I'll answer it.'

'Sorry, of course. Where's my head? It's your party!'

SIX

It isn't Henry at the door. It's Scott's best friend Richie and his partner. He looks the same age as Scott; I'm guessing they were friends at school, as Scott has mentioned him often. His young girlfriend, Lily, looks barely out of her teens.

Richie keeps his arm around his partner, almost like she might run away if he lets go. She is wearing a short pink satin cocktail dress that makes me self-conscious about my jeans and t-shirt combo. I want to go and change, but I can't leave everyone, especially without Scott here.

This couple is closely followed by another friend of Scott's work colleague, Nigel. He arrives alone and seems quiet and reserved. He hovers around the periphery of the growing group with a glass of wine. He doesn't seem overly interested in the food.

Then, shortly after, Helen and Max arrive, who remind me of myself and Scott. As soon as they walk in the door, I know I will relate to them the most. They are a similar age and seem down to earth like me. Max is dressed in a suit much like the ones Scott often wears. He might even be one of Scott's favourite customers, perhaps. Like everyone else, they don't introduce themselves much beyond their first names.

So far, I have gleaned that all these people know Scott only through his work. I don't know what I was expecting. Some more personal friends, I suppose. The only person who knows Scott on a more personal level is Henry, who has been a close friend to Scott for most of my fiancé's life.

Helen is wearing a neat pencil skirt with an emerald green satin blouse with long sleeves; it's similar to the dress I had selected for tonight. If only I had had the chance to change into it, maybe she would have been more warm to me.

Her eyes flick between Dawn and me often. So do everyone's, apart from Lily's, who seems oblivious to Dawn's role as Scott's ex.

Dawn made a big show of greeting each guest as they arrived in the dining room. She air-kissed them animatedly, her glass of wine in her hand. 'So good to see you! How have you been?'

They look surprised to see her. Their eyes widen slightly before they glance at me. A polite smile is forced upon their faces. They weren't expecting Scott's almost ex-wife to be here.

The atmosphere isn't what I hoped. I thought it would be more casual and relaxed. I envisaged being at Scott's side and being introduced to these people.

Instead, the conversation is stilted. It's sparse, and I have to work for it, making small talk with strangers. I'm so glad Sara is here. I've never been good in group situations. We are a few guests short. Perhaps the no-shows would be the missing ingredients to this gathering. Are they the social glue that would bind us all together?

That should be my fiancé, in all honesty, but he still isn't back yet.

The only thing we all have in common is Scott. And he isn't here with the food. The canapés have been demolished. I'm aware there weren't enough to go around, not after Dawn went for them with such gusto.

Now, everyone seems on edge, waiting for the main course to arrive.

I excuse myself to use the bathroom. Scott still isn't answering his phone. I feel like leaving an angry voicemail, but I don't. We have yet to argue. I don't want the night of our pre-wedding dinner to be the point where that changes.

Besides, he must be very nearly home by now. I've added some generous time estimates to his journey in my head. My calculations tell me he must be about to walk in the door any minute.

When I return downstairs, red-cheeked and flustered, Sara suggests we move the gathering outside to the dining table on the patio. I'm grateful to her.

The gentle breeze is warm and humid, but

it's slightly less claustrophobic out here.

Somehow, Dawn seems to have settled herself in a seat at the head of the table, as though she is the host. 'So, Sam. Why don't you tell us all how you met Scott?'

'Oh, well. It's a funny story, actually. We met by accident in a coffee shop. I turned to take my latte from the counter and bumped right into Scott. Unfortunately, he got covered. So did I.'

Everyone laughs and nods as they picture the scene.

'How embarrassing!' Dawn presses a palm to her smooth forehead. 'I bet Scott didn't like that one bit. He is so particular about his clothes being perfect. How on earth did you get him to go out with you after that?'

'Well, he asked for my number. I wasn't entirely sure he wasn't going to send me the dry cleaning bill.'

Helen laughs at this and nods knowingly. 'Yes, I wouldn't have put that past Scott.'

Next to her, her husband Max chimes in. 'True. Did he at least offer to buy you another latte?'

'He did. Scott was very nice about it all. I was mortified. The ground would have been welcome to swallow me up.'

'Luckily, it didn't,' Dawn smiles, raising her wine glass to me. It's not her first, and it's almost empty. 'So what happened next in the great Sam and Scott love story? Did you manage to dodge the dry cleaning bill? Or has Scott found a way for you to work off your debt?'

Sara wades in with a laugh to lighten the awkward undercurrent. 'I'd wager he has let it go by now!'

Helen asks, 'So, how long have you two been together now, Sam?'

'We had our coffee shop meeting back in January. So almost six months now.'

Lily's eyes light up at this. 'Wow! That's so fast! That's almost how long Richie and I have been together. We just had our five-month anniversary last week.'

She looks enthusiastically at Richie beside her but he seems keen on swishing his wine around his glass all of a sudden, as though nothing is more important.

Nigel nods. 'When you know, you just know, I suppose,' he says flatly.

Dawn looks dreamily towards the hedge. I can't tell what she thinks of this revelation. How long was it before Scott popped the question to her? More or less time? Was it a drunken Vegas wedding? Did they date for years whilst she dropped hints all over the place? Did she push Scott into it before he was ready? Who called time on their relationship in the end? I'm guessing it was Scott, but he didn't say.

Helen smiles. 'So how did Scott propose?'

I smile at the memory. 'It was on a weekend away in Formby last month. Scott arranged an evening picnic on the beach as a surprise. I thought we were just going for a walk. He set up a cosy blanket in a private dune for the sunset. We had glasses of sparkling grape juice and these cute tiramisu desserts. There were so many candles. Scott arranged hundreds of them in a heart-shape surrounding us. It was really beautiful.'

'Sounds like a fire hazard.' Dawn has recovered herself and laughs at her own joke.

I blink at her. That's precisely what I had thought as I sat with the sea of tiny little flames surrounding me, flickering in the cool evening breeze.

Any one of those lights could have caught onto the oversized hoodie I had thrown on for what I thought was going to be a casual stroll along the beach, hand-in-hand with Scott; Fire could have caught the tartan picnic rug or gingham lining of the picnic basket.

Even the plastic cutlery could have ignited. The base ingredient of plastic is petroleum. It's highly flammable. Most people don't realise.

Sara clears her throat loudly beside me, bringing me back to the here and now. 'Whose for a top-up?'

My friend stands and fetches more wine from the bar, moving to each of the outstretched glasses in turn.

'To the happy couple,' she says brightly. 'The half that turned up anyway!'

There is an appreciative murmur at this. Dawn laughs particularly hard.

Where is Scott?

'So what is it you do for a living, Sam?' Max asks after a large gulp of wine.

'I'm a teaching assistant. At Ridgewood Primary.'

'Oh, that's nice. I've heard it's a decent school. I'm always reading about some project or other going on there in the local rag.'

I nod. 'It's a wonderful school. I love working there. The kids are amazing.'

Dawn smiles. 'The teachers always say that about the school they work at, don't they? The real test is if they would send their own children there. So would you?'

'Well, I suppose so.'

Dawn tilts her head slightly. 'Hmm. See?'

There are titters from the other guests.

'No, really, the school is great. I just haven't thought about choosing a school yet.'

Yet? Why did I just say that? Kids are certainly not on my radar. I'm not sure how that would go down with these people; do any of them have or want children? I don't know. Now it looks like I don't believe in my workplace.

Helen reels off the names of the nearest private schools. She tells me which one she has already selected for her one-year-old who is currently at home with their babysitter.

So she does have a child. She nods pointedly

as she makes the recommendations, as though I need to mentally bookmark this for later. I don't know if I want kids after the childhood I had.

'I'm not sure Sam wants children,' Dawn says abruptly, watching me closely. 'That's not why you are here, is it? You didn't check in to Casa de Scott so you could change nappies and wait on hand and foot for some little brat.'

'Well, I wouldn't say that.' My face reddens. 'I love Scott.'

Dawn looks flushed, too, even beneath her pristine foundation. She must be tipsy after the amount of wine she has downed. We have gone through so many bottles already.

'Why not? It's true. A teaching assistant could never afford to live in a house like this. You have to admit there are perks to getting married to a guy as loaded as Scott. It's just a bonus that he is hot. I bet you couldn't believe your luck.'

'Sam doesn't care about money,' Sara says faithfully, rushing to my aid.

'Of course not. Silly Dawn.' She slaps her wrist. 'It's just a coincidence Scott has a stack of cash and a nice house. I suppose Sam might be a secret millionaire. It's unfair of me to judge her without knowing her.'

Scott's ex blinks at me politely, her perfect eyebrows raised. 'So, are you secretly loaded?'

All eyes are on me. The atmosphere is tense. 'No. I'm not.'

'It doesn't look like it. Millionaires don't

usually go about the place wearing supermarket brands.'

More heat rushes to my face. Beside me, Sara bristles. 'And you were loaded when you married Scott, were you?'

Dawn sets down her wine glass with a grin. 'As a matter of fact, I was. I inherited my father's estate young. Scott was down on his luck when I met him. I gave him over half-a million in capital to finance his clothing business.'

There is some uncomfortable shuffling around the room. Most of the others are politely half-smiling as they examine their drinks glasses or the colourful modern art Scott has on the walls. Only Lily pays attention to the exchange as though she is watching television.

I swallow and shrug, pulling down the sleeves of my basic George t-shirt. It feels like I repeat this action a hundred times a day. 'As you said, people in my profession don't get paid much. I could have chosen to be something else if money motivated me. But I love my work, so I'm happy. For me, it's about making a difference in the lives of the children I see daily. I wouldn't change it for the world.'

Nigel nods. 'Quite right. Money can't buy you happiness. Good for you, Sam, for doing something you love.'

It's a classic line from someone who has never had to worry about money. I think Nigel is the friend of Scott's who owns a coastal marina somewhere. I'm not quite sure. He doesn't look poor anyway. It's evident from his accent and attitude.

'Yes, money isn't everything,' Sara nods. 'It's having interests and good friends and health that matters at the end of the day. Spending time with my mum recently has made me realise this. She has dementia.'

My friend goes on to describe how living with Patricia is on a day-to-day basis. Sara is usually very reserved, especially when it comes to delicate subjects. The fact that she talks in detail with these strangers now shows how much she cares for me. She is throwing herself under a bus to move the topic on.

The details she shares now are sure to push thoughts of me being a money-grabbing cow from everyone's minds.

Sara is the best friend I could ask for.

As she talks, I realise it's worse than I thought. Patricia's care routine seems highly challenging. She has a carer to help Sara so she can still go out to work as an administrator for a builder's merchant. I make a mental note to chat to her about this later.

Part of me is disappointed she didn't confide in me over the phone about how bad things have become. She is putting on a cheery face for the occasion. She looks tired now that I look at her closely.

The conversation moves on to the wedding.

Helen asks me about plans for the big day, whether I have everything organised, whether the dress meets my expectations and more. It turns out she and Max own a store near Scott's on King Street; that is their connection to my fiancé. The three have become pally over the years, sharing the ups and downs of being a luxury retailer in the city.

Dawn looks sulky now as Helen asks about the fabric and cut of my dress, but thankfully, she doesn't pipe up again.

Scott finally arrives with several large bags of food and Henry, his faithful solicitor, at his side. The old man's eyes flick towards Dawn as he steps out onto the patio. He gives her a curt nod.

I have the feeling Scott has filled him in already on what has happened. Is that what took him so long to get back here?

My fiancé seems to note the empty seats around the table but doesn't say anything.

'So, what have I missed?' he says as he serves plates of warm Greek food.

Dawn shoots me a look but buries her face in her wine glass and says nothing.

SEVEN

At least others are looking overdressed with the new arrivals. Scott still wears his shirt and jeans from earlier, although they are less casual than mine.

Henry is wearing the same stiff suit he always seems to have on. He hasn't made any adjustments for the warm weather either. This makes me feel better.

The main courses Scott has brought over are delicious. Everyone chooses portions of what they fancy.

We feast on moussaka and kofta. I try some pastitsio—the Greek equivalent of lasagne, layered with plenty of creamy sauce and flavoured with cinnamon. There are also dolmades—vine leaves stuffed with meat and rice. The restaurant Scott ordered from certainly makes great food and deserves all its good reviews.

By the time we have finished eating, it is getting late. Richie raises a toast to Scott and me, the happy couple. He has been tasked with running the business for Scott while we are away in Greece. Richie shares his disappointment that he won't be able to attend the wedding.

Although his girlfriend looks more genuinely disappointed than he does, I think. It seems to have only just occurred to her that she won't be treated to a stay in the sun.

Out of the guests here tonight, only Sara and Henry will be attending the wedding.

Scott's parents, Marty and Katherine, perpetually travel the world, which is why I haven't met them yet. They are away in Egypt at the moment but will fly to Greece when it's time to see their son tie the knot.

Helen and Max have childcare commitments, and the others seem to be more casual acquaintances of Scott's. They are close enough to be pally, but not enough to make the flights.

One of the no-show couples, Libby and Dave, was supposed to attend our special day, but I'm not quite sure what happened to them tonight. Does that mean they are still on for the wedding?

The other couple that was absent tonight didn't RSVP. I suppose I will meet them in time.

Either way, the ceremony would always be a small affair, which suits me fine.

Scott seems eager to move the evening along. We thank our guests for coming as everyone gathers their coats and bags. Helen seems to have warmed to me, which I feel positive about. I feel like the two of us could be good friends.

She hugs me goodbye before stepping out onto the driveway.

'Good luck,' she says.

'Thanks.' Am I imagining it, or did her eyes linger on Dawn, still at the patio table as she said this?

Once everyone has left, Scott shuts the front door and takes a deep breath.

'Where did you get to?' I ask him. The initial embarrassment of having to lead a dinner party with strangers and no go-between has worn off. Our guests were at least a little familiar by the time they left. I've maybe even made some friends. I still feel abandoned, and I'm annoyed that Dawn made a scene. I explain this to my fiancé.

'I'm so sorry, babes.' Scott wraps his arms around me. We are still in the grand hallway, but I know that Dawn can see us from the back garden, where she still sips wine, even if she can't hear what we say. 'I ran into Henry, and we got caught up in talking. Then we went over to his office. He pulled up all the paperwork to see where my divorce went wrong. He has found the problem. It's a minor thing.'

'A minor thing which means you and Dawn are still legally married?'

'Yes. Unfortunately, so. I was granted a piece of paper by the judge that said the divorce was permitted—the decree nisi. But I never got the final document that meant the divorce was complete.'

'Why not?'

Scott shakes his head. 'It was supposed to arrive in the post, but I've been so busy with other things that I overlooked it and didn't notice when it didn't arrive.'

'How could you not notice?'

'I told you, I was busy. I get a lot of post on all sorts of matters. You know how busy my business keeps me. It slipped my mind. I didn't realise I was in such a hurry for the divorce when I applied for the final bit of paperwork. Then I met you.'

I smile. I can't stay mad at Scott. 'Why did Dawn leave you?'

He sighs. 'It's complicated. Dawn left abruptly. She said she'd had enough and went abroad to find herself. She wanted to do some soul-searching or something. Her brother died suddenly, you see. Suicide.'

'Oh, how horrible. That's why she left you?'

He nods. 'That was a large part of it. We were over by then anyway. She went off the rails at that point. She hadn't bothered much with her family. Her father had passed away years prior and Warren was all she had left. I think she felt guilty. So she took off, and this is the first time I have seen her since. I promise I haven't seen Dawn for years. I've completely moved on.'

I let this sink in for a few moments. I hadn't realised there was so much going on behind Dawn's bolshie exterior. 'Can you get the final document before the wedding?'

Scott nods. 'Of course. It can be finalised in two weeks or so.'

I search my partner's beautiful eyes. 'It can be, or it will be? We only have two weeks.'

'Henry is positive we can still go ahead with our original plan. The decree absolute takes two, maybe three weeks max to come through.'

'Three? That won't make it in time.'

'Don't be negative. Henry will push it through first thing on Monday morning. He guarantees it will arrive in time. Dawn said she is only staying for the night until she gets herself sorted. So none of it shall be an issue.'

'She said she has an appointment to see a new place tomorrow.'

Scott perks up at this. 'That's great news. See? This whole thing will be sorted. Don't worry.'

I look at the used plates, cutlery, glasses, and napkins strewn all over the kitchen and the table outside. Takeaway packages are everywhere, too. The white tablecloth outside is covered with bits of food and red wine. It looks permanently stained.

Scott reads my mind. 'Leave them. I'll call someone to come in and clean up tomorrow.'

'I can do it.'

'But you don't have to. You should get used to that.'

'It's hard after clearing up myself my whole adult life. I'm used to not having servants, you know.'

'I know that. Get used to being treated like a queen. That's how it will be from now on. Isn't there something else you would rather do this evening, other than cleaning?'

I smile as my fiancé's hands snake around my waist. I glance over to Dawn through the patio doors, but luckily, she is facing the other way, staring at the hedge with slumped shoulders. 'You go up to bed. I'll lock up.'

Scott glances outside at Dawn. 'I think we should leave her be.'

'What about security? We always lock all the doors and windows before bed.'

'Dawn's the most dangerous thing in the area. No one is getting past her.'

I look up at Scott in surprise. 'What do you mean by that?'

He smiles. 'I don't know. I wouldn't like to get on the wrong side of her, that's all.'

'Aren't you already on her bad side if you are getting divorced?'

He shrugs. 'Not really. She left me, remember? Not the other way around. She has no reason to be angry with me. I just meant I wouldn't want to face her in a fight or confrontation or something like that...I don't know what I meant, actually. I've had a lot of wine. I've no idea what I'm saying. Aren't you tired too? Let's go to bed.'

Scott does look drained. I kiss him on the cheek.

'I'll join you in a minute. I want to say goodnight to Sara and make sure she is settled into the guest room for the night.'

Upstairs, I separate from Scott, who has tried to entice me into the bedroom the whole way up the staircase.

I fend off his wandering hands and head to the second-best guest room across the landing.

Dawn's unexpected arrival earlier saw her swoop in on the main guest room I had prepared for Sara.

I'd filled a vase with pretty yellow roses, freshly laundered the bedding and put some KitKat bars on her bedside cabinet; they are her favourite type of chocolate. That room also has a balcony overlooking the back garden and an ensuite bathroom.

But she didn't get to see that as Dawn had already moved her things in there earlier this afternoon. It's been hectic since her arrival.

Sara is now in the smaller guest room. I knock on the door.

EIGHT

'Come in!'

The smaller guest room is pleasant. I just hadn't made the little preparations I wanted for my best friend. This bedroom overlooks the garden, too. On the other hand, it's pretty plain —all grey and white and nothing else. It has a comfy double bed and a wall-mounted TV.

The flowers would have brightened it up, no doubt. I can't exactly confiscate the bunch from Dawn's room. I don't want to invade her privacy if all her stuff is in there either.

'You got everything you need?' I ask Sara as she pulls some paisley pyjamas from her suitcase.

'Yeah, all set. I'm pretty exhausted now. What an evening.'

I wince. 'It could have been worse. At least Dawn didn't throw her wine at me or anything.'

'At one point, it looked like it was going that way. If looks could kill!'

I frown. 'Scott says Dawn left him, not the other way around, so she shouldn't be too upset.'

Sara looks sceptical as she sits on the bed

and crosses her legs. I join her, flopping down on my back and staring at the smooth white ceiling. I'm drained after this evening.

'I don't know, Sam. No wife wants to see her ex move on with another woman. It's just awkward. It must knock your confidence, whoever you are. Especially when the woman is younger.'

'I'm not younger.'

'You are. Dawn's hiding a lot under all that slap. She must be at least five years older than Scott, maybe more.'

I think about this for a second. 'She isn't that much older than me then. Ten years max. I don't think it means much.'

Sara shrugs. 'Maybe not. You have to watch your back until she leaves tomorrow. She really laid into you at dinner, in front of everyone, too.'

I groan. 'That wasn't nice, was it? I think she may have been a bit drunk by that point. She was trying to score some points for her bruised ego. As you said, finding her husband has moved on can't be easy. She didn't mean anything by it, I don't think.'

'That's not the point. She made you look like a money-grabber in front of Scott's friends. Don't forget, they knew Scott and Dawn long before you appeared. Apart from Lily, who was probably still in school.'

I snort. 'I know. But Helen seemed nice. Max, too.'

'First impressions stick. Don't forget that. What Dawn accused you of will be forever in the back of their minds.'

'I'll just have to work extra hard to change their opinion. I don't want anyone thinking I'm just some desperate greedy-grabber.'

'Sam,' Sara warns. Don't do anything reckless. You don't want to regret it later.'

A moment of silence passes. Sara lowers her voice. 'So how much does Scott know?'

'He accepts me as I am.'

'A thirty-four-year-old teaching assistant with no baggage and a penchant for chocolate? That's it?'

'That's what I am, isn't it? Scott doesn't care what I do for a living. He says I could give up my job if I wanted. We don't talk about work much. He doesn't talk about his business that often, either. He can tell men's fashion isn't my area. I mention it sometimes if one of the children has done something sweet or funny. But not much beyond that. We are just our true selves if you know what I mean. He doesn't ask questions. We just enjoy each other's company.'

'So basically, you just have sex?'

I roll my eyes. 'No. We care for each other. Deeply. We really do enjoy being with each other.'

'Just as long as you are enjoying it.'

'Of course. I'm happy. I'm in love. I wouldn't give Scott up for anything.'

Sara and I chat for a little while longer. I

tell her about the local botanical gardens we will visit tomorrow with Scott.

'Sounds great,' she says. I know she isn't crazy about gardens in general. The place was Scott's suggestion. He loves that sort of thing, having been raised in the large country estate he is used to that sort of thing I guess. But I know Sara is keen on getting to know him better.

After midnight, I wish her goodnight.

I'm tempted to go downstairs and ensure the doors are locked, but I haven't heard Dawn come upstairs. I have no desire to be alone with her, so I decide to leave it. Scott wasn't worried about the security aspect. He has lived in this house longer than I have.

The master bedroom is at the front of the house. It doesn't have a balcony, but it does have the beautiful ensuite bathroom Scott and I were enjoying earlier. Along with the walk-in wardrobe I've been needing for years.

Scott's heavy breathing and prone form tell me he is well and truly asleep by the time I slip inside the room.

The sliding door of the walk-in wardrobe is still ajar. My chosen dress for tonight is slumped in a circle on the carpet. I close the door and flick on the light as I pull on an oversized short-sleeve t-shirt for sleeping in.

At least in the darkness, I feel comfortable enough to expose my skin to the air. It feels good, especially in this heat.

I pick up my cocktail dress and slide it onto a hanger. I tug the zip up to stop the smooth satin sliding off again, but it seems jammed. I wrangle with it for a few seconds before I realise the zip is broken.

This is the most expensive garment I own. Other than trying it on in the shop, I haven't worn it yet. Scott took me to a boutique retailer in Manchester and told me to choose anything I wanted for tonight's dinner party. This number had got the seal of approval from my fiancé.

More importantly, I felt comfortable in it. The dark green lacy sleeves adequately covered me, and the short cut in the leg compensated for the lack of skin on show up top. For once, I felt good in something. It reminds me of the wedding dress I have chosen.

Now, it's broken beyond repair. The teeth are bent and buckled. I know instantly that the garment can't be fixed.

Did I do that while hurrying to squeeze it on before dinner?

I wonder if I can return it. I don't like wasting money, not when I've lived with hardly any for so long. Before I trained to be a teaching assistant, I drifted from job to job. I spent a long time without employment, scraping by selling my possessions and relying on the support of others, Sara included. I'll never forget that.

I can't remember ruining the zip of this dress like this. It was such a rush earlier. Maybe I did impart enough force to bend and destroy the zip teeth?

I remove the dress from the hanger and fold it up, replacing it on an empty shelf. I'll deal with that another day.

I get some air from the window overlooking the hedge-lined driveway. My little Toyota is parked beneath me.

After a few minutes, I slide under the covers next to Scott and realise how exhausted I am after a draining evening.

NINE

I sleep longer than I intended. I'd planned on rising early and tackling the mess in the kitchen before anyone else got up. I want our guests to see the house at its best. But it is past ten before I even become conscious.

Scott is already gone, leaving me alone in the bedroom.

Usually, when this happens, I might find a rose with a note attached to what Scott has left me for breakfast. But there isn't one this morning, I realise as I reach across to his side of the bed.

It's looking like another glorious day again. It certainly is warm when I get dressed. I shower, pull on a purple long-sleeved wrap dress and head downstairs.

Scott and Sara are already at the breakfast bar, each with a glass of orange juice and empty plates awaiting breakfast.

The patio doors are open, letting in the smell of summer. Sunlight illuminates the white marble surfaces and gleaming floor.

The place is immaculate. I sigh. I wanted the

satisfaction of cleaning it myself. Has Scott seen off paid help already?

My fiancé and my best friend turn as I enter the room.

'Morning,' they both say.

I smile and return the greeting. 'Did I oversleep? You should have woken me.'

Sara shakes her head. 'No, you're fine. I think you were tired after yesterday's frivolities. We thought you needed the sleep.'

The kitchen is warm, not just from the summer air wafting in from outside. There is a delicious scent of food in the air.

Just then, Dawn emerges from the garden. She steps through the concertina doors wearing bright pink rubber gloves and carrying a bucket and sponge.

'Morning, Sam!' she says brightly. 'I think everything is ship-shape again outside. The house is restored to its former glory!'

'She was up before us,' Sara explains. 'Cleaning from top to bottom.'

'Oh,' I say in surprise. 'You didn't have to do that. I was going to take care of it.'

'Don't be silly. It's the least I could do. You and Scott didn't have to put me up, but you did. I want to say thank you. And sorry. I think I got a little drunk last night. I might have said some things I'm cringing over today. I couldn't sleep after how I behaved.'

'It's already forgotten,' I say, as though

Dawn's words don't sting every time I think of them, not to mention the damage to my future relationship with Scott's closest friends.

Dawn shrugs. 'Anyway, I wanted to do something nice before I leave later.'

'Thanks. The place looks amazing.'

Dawn is pinning her hopes on the property she is viewing this evening. I hope it meets her expectations.

The oven pings. It turns out Dawn has made breakfast, too.

She removes a batch of fresh lemon and blueberry muffins from the oven. She has baked them alongside her personal recipe for granola. There are other plates and dishes of little treats, too. She certainly has been busy.

Dawn serves us all this alongside some cold yoghurt from the fridge. I wonder where she got all the ingredients. Perhaps she cleared the contents of her kitchen when she left her flat. She has also managed to clean up after herself as she has gone along. There isn't the trail of dishes and spilt ingredients as when I make anything.

'I thought you didn't cook,' I say as I help myself to a muffin. It's delicious and still warm from the oven.

'I didn't when I lived here. Too busy living the life of luxury. All we ate was takeaway food or out at restaurants. Scott is the only one who can't cook now. I've educated myself in recent years in all sorts. Not just cooking. I'm much older and wiser these days.'

I glance up and see that Scott and Dawn have been looking at each other for a moment too long. Then, the exchange is gone. Scott helps himself to coffee, but he doesn't look happy.

Is he having second thoughts about Dawn? Does he think he has made a mistake by moving on when the pair hadn't talked it through?

I clear my throat and address him. 'I think we need to get going soon if we want to see the gardens. Sara's return train is quite early this afternoon. She has to get back tonight for Patricia.'

He looks distracted. 'Hmm?'

'We were heading out today, remember? The three of us?'

Scott nods. 'I'm going to have to pass on that one. So sorry. Henry has been in touch. There is some business I need to take care of at his office.'

My mouth opens. 'What business? It's Sunday. I thought we were going out.'

'I know, babes. I'm so sorry. I wouldn't miss it for the world. You know that. It's unavoidable.'

Scott is keeping tight-lipped. I suspect the abrupt change has to do with Dawn, so I don't push it further. Not with her so close by.

'That's a shame,' Sara nudges me in the ribs. 'I guess it's just you and me then, just like old times.'

'Sounds fun,' Dawn smiles, taking a sip of coffee.

Scott turns to her. 'Why don't you join them?'

'What?' I stammer in surprise.

Dawn shakes her head. 'I'm sure Sam doesn't want me hanging around. She wants to have some quality time with her bestie. I'll stay here in the house, reminisce. Maybe I can find some more odd jobs that need my attention.'

Scott sets down his coffee and looks at me almost beseechingly. 'Sam doesn't mind. Do you?'

'Well…no, of course not. But I don't think Dawn would like it. It's only some botanical gardens—nothing exciting.'

Is Scott uncomfortable leaving Dawn alone in our house? I can't imagine why.

Dawn shrugs. 'Are you talking about Fletcher Moss? Scott and I used to go there all the time. I wouldn't mind taking a walk down memory lane. But I don't want to cramp your style.'

Great. Another thing Scott and Dawn christened together first. Scott neglected to mention this.

He certainly speaks up now. 'You won't be cramping anything, Dawn. Don't worry. It will allow you and Sam to get to know each other.'

I feel like punching Scott for the first time ever. Why is he so determined for me to babysit his soon-to-be ex-wife? He is going to get grilled later.

For now, I can only smile politely and wait

for Dawn to get ready to go out. I thought she was already dressed for the day.

It takes her longer than I expect to get herself together. She changes out of her "housework" jeans and t-shirt into a pretty strappy floral dress—the kind I would love to wear.

An hour later, the three of us walk around the local gardens.

The surroundings are stunning. The sky is the most perfect shade of blue. We might very well be abroad with the various palms and exotic red foliage set against it. It is nice to be immersed in a tranquil environment surrounded by trees and plants. It feels like anywhere other than the busy outskirts of Manchester.

The only thing that would improve this outing is if my friend and I were with Scott, not his ex. I wanted Sara to get to know my fiancé. They haven't had a chance to talk properly yet, apart from before I joined them for breakfast this morning. Sara still hasn't seen what I see in Scott. It's a shame.

At the very least, chatting freely with Sara would have been nice. But with Dawn trailing beside us, I need to watch what I say. I don't feel like I can approach the sensitive subject of Patricia and her declining condition. Sara has dark circles under her eyes. She looks exhausted. I want to ask her how she is really coping, but I don't want to in front of Dawn. I don't feel I would get an honest answer. I don't want her to feel uncomfortable, either.

Instead, Sara and I both make polite small talk for Dawn's sake. At least Scott's ex is friendly today. She is like a different person. Perhaps she has got over the shock of seeing her husband moving on with someone else, someone younger.

Sara was right. Close up, Dawn looks to be in her mid-forties—ten years or so my senior. Scott is in the middle, bridging the gap between our ages. I guess the small difference seemed even smaller when Scott and Dawn first got together, whenever that was.

Scott and I haven't had the chance to discuss things either. We will have to sit down and chat when Dawn leaves tonight.

The afternoon comes sooner than I had hoped. We have a late lunch in the charming café, and then it is time to see Sara off at the train station.

I lift Sara's case from the car and walk her into the station. Dawn opts to stay in the vehicle, thankfully.

I try and cram everything I want to say to Sara into the walk to her platform.

'Are you coping with looking after your mum? Really?'

She nods. 'Yeah, yeah. That's all fine. This weekend has been nice. I can't get my neighbour to babysit Mum very often. I don't want to take the piss.'

'What about hiring more help?' I ask as we reach the platform.

Sara shrugs. 'I have Mum's carer, Jill, who takes care of Mum while I am at work. I don't really want to get Mum full-time care.'

'Why not? I think you might need the support. You look tired. It sounds like you go to your job and then come home and keep working.'

'That's exactly what it is. I'm so glad someone understands that. I should have known you would.'

'Then why not look into hiring more help? Have you considered full-time care?'

'Of course.'

'Then why not do it?'

'I don't know.' She shrugs, then catches my eye. 'It's not a money thing,' Sara says quickly.

'Are you sure?'

'Positive.'

'I don't believe you. If you need money for care, help, or anything else, I could talk with Scott. Maybe he could give me a loan or something. I could explain the situation.'

'No way—don't do that because of me! I'm fine, honestly. I want to take care of Mum.'

'You're running yourself ragged. I don't want my best friend burned out.'

'I'm not. Things have just got on top of me, that's all. Everyone has those moments where it all seems too much, don't they? Then it passes.

I'm not going to quit.'

A station announcement comes over the speakers. Sara's train is on its way.

I'm not ready for her to leave yet. 'Is that what you think I've done by moving up North?'

'No, you had your reasons for leaving. I admire that. You've made a fresh start. And it appears you have landed on your feet here.'

I raise my eyebrows. 'Appears?'

She shrugs. 'You have only known your fella for six-months. How well can you possibly know him?'

'I know people keep throwing around the number of months we have had together, but it's not the same. Remember, I researched Scott before our first date. I didn't just stumble into the situation. We have spent a lot of time together, too. I've hardly come up for air.'

'That doesn't sound that good to me. Isn't that exactly what Adam did? He love bombed you into not being able to think for yourself.'

'I know what Adam did. He was a nightmare. If I'm honest, he slipped up really early on. I just didn't want to admit it. It had been so long since I'd been with someone, and I just wanted it to work.'

'Exactly. Now it feels like you are doing the same thing again.'

I sigh. Why is Sara being so difficult? Why can't she see what I can see? She hasn't been a fly on the wall during the most memorable moments I've enjoyed with Scott. Not that I would want her to be. 'Scott is special. He is the one for me, even if I can't explain it.'

'Try me.'

'I already have. Scott and I have so much in common. He is smart and funny. He knows all my favourite things and makes sure I always have them. He's so sweet. Adam only ever wanted to do what Adam wanted to do. He didn't care what I wanted. It was always his choice of restaurant, his movie night. He would never let me choose anything for the house, either. Remember the fiasco when I tried to paint the kitchen sage green?'

'You did paint the kitchen. It was gorgeous.'

'I know. But Adam went on and on about it so much that I painted it white again the next weekend. It was unbelievable. He wouldn't even let me choose the type of mop I wanted for cleaning, for goodness sake. Come on now, Sara. You can't compare that control freak to Scott.'

Sara nods and takes a deep breath. 'Okay. You seem pretty sure. It's nice to see you so assertive. You've made up your mind, haven't you? In that case, I'm happy for you.'

She moves in and wraps her arms around me, patting me on the back. 'I've always got a spare room if you decide things aren't going as you expected. Especially with this thing with Dawn. You need to watch out for that one. I'd be a lot happier if she were gone already. Are you sure you will be all right?'

'Yes, thanks. Dawn should be gone later this evening. Tomorrow morning, max. I'll bear your offer in mind, though—I'm overdue a visit. Next time, I will have to come down and see you.'

'You should. Mum would love to see you too.'

'Do you think she would recognise me? I've changed a lot. She won't call me Sam for one thing, so Scott can't come with me.'

'She might get a shock when she first sees you. Mum flits between times. She might expect you to be a little girl in pigtails.'

I roll my eyes. 'When did I ever wear my hair like that?'

'I'm sure you did once. I remember you definitely did one day when you knocked on my door to go butterfly catching. You had a cute pink matching t-shirt and shorts combo.'

I grimace. 'I have no recollection of that.'

'It was a long time ago. I can still see it in my mind's eye.' She nods. 'Definitely happened.'

'I'll have to take your word for it.'

'You should. You know what else, too? You should wear short sleeves again.'

I fiddle with my engagement ring. 'You know I can't do that.'

Sara tuts. 'It's a scorching summer we're having. The papers say it's only going to get worse. What are you going to do when you get to Greece? If you think it's hot here, you are in for a shock! People are a lot more open-minded than they used to be. Anything goes. Others are supposed to be more tolerant these days.'

'*Supposed to be*. That has yet to trickle down to everyone, though.'

'You can't live your life based on what random strangers might think of you. Good people won't mind. Just be comfortable in yourself.'

'What is it with people and their cliché phrases this weekend? "Money won't buy you happiness". "Be yourself".'

'Maybe we have a point. What does Scott think of your arms?'

I shrug. 'He has never mentioned them.'

Sara looks at me thoughtfully for a few moments. She looks troubled.

'What is it?' I ask her. 'The fact Scott hasn't said anything is a good thing. Adam gave me the third degree over it. Early on, too. I wondered at one point if he was from the newspaper or something.'

'You're too paranoid. Six months, though, and your beloved hasn't brought up the subject? Do you think he will ask before the wedding?'

'No,' I say with confidence. 'I don't think he will. He has barely even looked at my arms. He seems more interested in my other bits for some reason.'

Sara shares my smile at this. 'I can see how he might be. Doesn't it strike you as odd he hasn't said a single word about your scars, though? Has he not prompted you at all over the subject?'

'No, I told you. It doesn't matter to him. He has accepted me as I am. That's a good thing.'

My friend still doesn't look convinced, but she nods and gives me another quick squeeze as her train rolls in. 'As long as you're happy, I'm happy. And if you're not, then call me straight away. I'm always just a call or text away.'

I nod. 'I know. Likewise. If you need to talk or need some help with your mum, just let me know, and I will get you sorted.'

'I can't ask you to do that. Just enjoy yourself and don't worry about me. This is a special time. Appreciate your last days of freedom! I'll see you for your Santorini hen night before the wedding. I promise not to get you too disoriented before your big day!'

She waves and disappears through the train doors. I lose sight of her, so I wave broadly towards the darkened windows as the train pulls away. If she can see me, I hope she appreciates the sentiment.

When the train has rolled out of sight, I turn with a heavy heart at the thought of entertaining Dawn until Scott gets home and almost walk right into her.

I gasp in surprise—I thought she was waiting in the car.

'Sorry,' she says. 'I didn't mean to make you jump.'

'How long were you standing there?'

She shrugs. 'Not long.'

I have the feeling she isn't being truthful. How much did she overhear?

Dawn nods towards the railway track Sara's train departed on. 'It looks like you wanted to go with her.'

'Oh. Sara is my best friend. I miss her sometimes.'

'Why did you leave her behind?'

I shrug as we walk back to the car. 'I'd spent my whole life in Bournemouth. I just wanted a change, that was all.'

'You're not running away from anything?'

'Of course not.'

'Do you want to pack your bags and hop on the next train?'

'Of course not. I'm getting married in less than two weeks.'

Dawn sighs. 'I don't know, *Sam*. A lot can happen in two weeks.'

I look at Dawn sharply. What does she mean by that? She didn't just emphasise my name, did she? Does she suspect it is not my real one?

I push these thoughts down. There is no way Scott's ex could know that I am lying about who I really am. Could she?

TEN

The car journey home with Dawn leaves me feeling like I'm going crazy. Dawn is completely sweet again. It's almost like I imagined the brief exchange before we got in the car at the railway station.

Scott still isn't back when we get home. I send out a feeler text to try and prompt him along and let him know that I am back with Dawn. I don't get a response, however, which is unusual. Scott is usually so quick with his replies. I suppose he is busy trying to sort something important out.

It's another hot day, much more humid than earlier. Dawn fetches herself a bottle of chilled mineral water from the fridge. 'Would you like one?'

'No, thank you.' It's such a strange feeling to be treated like a guest in your own house. Luckily, it's only until tonight.

I ask Dawn more about the property she will view this evening.

'It's gorgeous. You should see it.'

She pulls her phone out and shows me the

Rightmove listing. She is right. The property is lovely, but the price tag isn't. I wonder how Dawn is planning to finance this flat. It is a trendy place located in a smart new development in Manchester city centre. It has all the mod cons and doesn't come cheap.

'What kind of work do you usually do?' I ask as Dawn takes her phone back.

'All sorts. Little bits here and there. You know how it is.'

I do. In my younger years, I drifted from job to job, trying to find a way to fund my lifestyle.

Looking at Dawn, it's not difficult to picture her perhaps as a rich kid left to her own devices as an adult. She may have had an inheritance but was clueless about how to make it work for her.

I bet she and Scott were well-suited to each other for this reason. She provided the funding for his business, and he provided a consistent lifestyle. But then something went wrong. Dawn pulled away for her own reasons after her brother's death.

And now, here we all are. I have the feeling Dawn wants Scott back. Is that really why she is here?

Scott's ex fans herself with her hand to no avail. It is hot today. I'm sweating underneath my wrap dress. Usually, at home, I would wear something cooler, especially with Scott gone. I'm nowhere near confident enough to do it with a guest in the house.

'You look hot,' she says. 'Why don't you put something more comfortable on in this heat?'

'I'm fine.'

I subconsciously pull my sleeves down over my wrists. Dawn notices this and watches me curiously. I sense she is about to open her mouth to ask me about this motion.

Luckily, I am saved by Scott's return. 'How are you two getting along?'

'Great,' Dawn smiles.

'That's nice to hear.' He fetches himself a bottle of his favourite water and sits at the kitchen island a few seats from Dawn.

They look like the perfect power couple. Dawn is glossy and beautiful. Scott is handsome and well-dressed. In their designer kitchen, they look like they are in an advert for their particular water brand.

She turns to Scott as she makes lines in the condensation of her bottle. 'Are Marty and Katherine flying in for the wedding? I noticed they weren't here for dinner last night.'

Scott nods as he twists the lid from his bottle. 'Yes, they will be. They are away in Egypt at the moment, but they will be in Greece for the big day.'

'That's nice. You'll have to give them my love. It's been a while since we have caught up.'

'Yes, Mum is often asking after you. I think she misses you.' This last bit comes across as an afterthought.

'Oh really?' Dawn seems genuinely cheered by this. 'I'll have to give her a call sometime.'

'Sure.' He nods again but doesn't seem enthused.

'You know, I have misplaced your mum's number. Can you give it to me?'

'I'll probably do it later.'

'Why not now?'

'I can't remember her current number. Mum has been through a few phones. She lost one in Jamaica and had another stolen in Rome.'

'Oh, how unfortunate. You'll get it for me later, though?'

'When I get the chance.'

She turns to me thoughtfully. 'You don't mind, do you, Sam? I hope you don't feel like I'm treading on your toes by speaking to Scott's parents. They are still my in-laws, technically.'

I shrug. 'I don't mind.'

'Are you sure? I feel like a bit of a third wheel around here at the moment.'

'Don't worry about it. It's nice to meet someone else from Scott's life.'

'I can imagine. Have you met Scott's Mum and Dad yet?'

'Not yet. I'll meet them for the first time at the wedding.'

'Yes, it was the same when Scott and I got married. That was the only time I've ever met them. They were always jetting off here, there, and everywhere.'

'They're retired,' Scott interjects. 'They can enjoy themselves.'

'I suppose so,' Dawn concedes. 'What about you, Sam? You only had one guest at dinner. Do you have family coming to the wedding, as well as Sara?'

I nod as I get up to fetch myself a drink, too. 'Maybe. I've sent out invites.'

Dawn raises her eyebrows. 'Did no one RSVP yet?'

'No.'

'That's shocking. Have you had a falling out?'

I shrug. 'Nothing like that. We just aren't a close family. We've drifted apart.'

'Your family should respond to a wedding invitation, for goodness sake. What about your parents? Don't they want to see their little girl have the fairytale wedding in Greece?'

'I'm the youngest of several siblings,' I repeat for Dawn's sake. I've already told Scott all this. He sits quietly and sips his water as I recount it. 'My older siblings have already done the wedding thing and divorce thing a few times. It's no big deal for my parents. They don't travel like they used to these days either.'

Scott believed my story with no question as we wrote out invitations to our nearest and dearest. His pile was significantly larger. I was left to take my scant handful of invitations to the post box. Scott wasn't there to see that Sara's was the only one I posted. The others were hastily ripped to shreds in my car and dropped in a public bin. There is no way my parents will come to my wedding.

Scott's ex looks at me so thoughtfully that I panic momentarily. Does she spot a trace of deceit?

'I see,' she says finally. 'You are from a poor family. Is that why you are the way you are?'

I brace myself. 'What way is that?'

'Oh, you know. I just mean that you haven't had the ambition to do more with your life. You come across as a little, I don't know. Downtrodden?'

I don't know what to say as Dawn looks at my limp hair and chewed fingernails. I had applied some eyeliner around my dark green eyes to boost my confidence today, but now it seems futile.

Scott rushes to my aid. He stands up and places his hands on my shoulders, reassuringly brushing his thumbs against them. 'Come on now, Dawn. I don't think that's very nice to say. I think Sam is wonderful. Obviously. She's beautiful, warm and intelligent.'

I feel a rush of warmth inside me. Scott does love me. I feel the same way. I'm so lucky to have found him.

Dawn raises her palms quickly. 'Oh, I didn't mean anything by it. I just meant I can see where you're coming from, Sam. Things haven't been easy for you, have they?'

Scott sighs behind me. 'Look, Dawn. Let's keep things friendly. Maybe you should make sure you aren't late for your property viewing.'

Dawn looks at the large ornate clock on the wall in surprise. 'I still have a good few hours yet.'

'You don't want to miss it,' he says pointedly. 'Don't you think you should get going?'

'I would, but I told you I don't have a car.'

'So? Get the train. The station isn't far.'

'The train? With all my luggage?'

'You made it here with all your belongings, did you not? Besides, you won't take everything you own to the viewing, will you? You need to see the place first.'

'No, but I want to get in there fast. The flat is a gem, I can tell already. It will get snapped up, and I'm the one planning on doing said snapping. It's going to be mine. I will need to start moving ASAP, so I'll need you to give me a ride.'

'You managed to get all your things here without any help.'

'Hardly. It was a real struggle. I just assumed you would drive me this evening.'

'You didn't mention it. I have dinner reservations with Sam tonight.'

'It won't take long. The viewing is at half-six. Since when do you eat dinner so early? Anyway, I would have thought you would be enthusiastic about me not staying here another night, Scotty?'

'No can do, Dawn. I can only advise you to get the train to the viewing. The best I can do is hire a driver to move your things across if you decide to take the flat. I'm not driving into Manchester tonight anyway. I want to have a few drinks. We are hiring a driver tonight ourselves. You can't expect me to change my plans with my *fiancé* at the drop of a hat.'

Scott seems to add extra stress to this word as though trying to prove something to Dawn, who purses her lips in defeat. It looks almost like she is trying not to cry.

I feel a pang for her. Especially after all the hurt Adam dealt me. I don't like being used as a pawn in a battle of wills between these two. On the other hand, I like to think Scott is making his stance clear when his ex is being so awkward.

Scott has chosen me. Dawn needs to accept that. I'm not too fond of it when marriages fail. Things can get pretty toxic. It's best to move on before anyone does anything they later regret.

At least Dawn seems enthusiastic about this flat she is going to see. Hopefully, we will have seen the last of her by this evening.

ELEVEN

'Don't worry about Dawn,' Scott says as he cuts into his steak.

'I'm not,' I lie.

We are seated in the gorgeous restaurant my fiancé chose for dinner. Tonight was the official start of the run-up to our wedding, and this meal was like a celebratory toast to the beginning of this exciting phase of our lives.

After all, we only get to go through this process together once. I had believed it was Scott's first time, too, but I've accepted that it isn't. I can certainly see why Scott wanted to keep the memory of Dawn compartmentalised. She can be quite high-maintenance.

This place has stunning views across the city. Lights twinkle from all angles as dusk falls across Manchester. It's really quite beautiful.

The food is incredible, too. My risotto is deliciously creamy and melts in the mouth.

My thoughts stray to Scott's ex, however. She didn't look happy as we left for dinner. The slinky dress I've slipped into for dinner was met with a jealous raking over as we stepped out of the door.

Scott called his trusted vehicle hire firm before we left and gave Dawn a free pass to have her possessions moved for her. There aren't many, so it shouldn't take long. One trip should do it.

There's no reason she shouldn't be gone by the time we get back.

'Is everything all right, babes?' Scott looks across the table at me, a look of curiosity on his handsome face.

I take a sip of sparkling apple juice. 'I don't know. I guess I'm still hurt by what Dawn said at the dinner party. About my career. She tried to make it look like I'm only dating you for your money.'

Scott laughs at this. 'That's ridiculous.'

'That's basically what everyone was thinking at dinner yesterday. Dawn made sure of it.'

'Maybe she is a little jealous that I've moved on so quickly. It's nothing to worry about. I know you're not after my money.'

I feel relieved that Scott laughs the matter off so readily. I still feel uneasy.

'I know you believe that. But I don't want our friends thinking I'm marrying you to make a quick profit or something.'

'They won't, honestly.'

'You weren't there when Dawn was setting me up. She made me feel like a peasant while she revelled in the fact that she was a rich kid who financed your business.'

'Oh, she loves that old chestnut. She used to wheel it out in arguments all the time.'

'I can imagine.'

'Don't go thinking Dawn is cleverer or superior to you just because she had all that money. She inherited that nest egg. She didn't earn it. She was quite frivolous when I met her. She would have squandered the lot had she not used it to help me launch my menswear brand. Think nothing more of it. Let's enjoy tonight.'

'Okay.'

We certainly do enjoy it.

Scott orders more drinks, and we choose some delicious little treats from the dessert menu. I don't know if it's the striking sunset across the city, or the wonderful company, but the trio of cheesecake, panna cotta, and lemon mousse are the best I have ever tasted.

After a late-night movie screening, we decide to call it a night. Scott whispers all the things we could be doing in our privacy at home before the credits roll, so he calls his hired driver to come and pick us up.

Scott is all over me as we are driven home. I find myself fending him off, worried about what the driver will be able to see in the rearview mirror.

My fiancé keeps whispering to me not to worry about it, but I feel self-conscious. I guess

I've always been a private person, even before the event that ruined my life. It's my natural personality. I'm not my gregarious father or vain mother.

When the car pulls up on our driveway, my insides relax. The windows of the house are dark. We are truly alone again, I realise as we let ourselves into a silent home. Dawn must be settling into her new place.

I smile. Twelve days of bliss until the wedding. There is nothing to enjoy but each other.

My heart flutters with excitement as I consider all the things Scott said he would do to me when we got home. He turns the under-cabinet lights on in the kitchen for some ambience. Despite the amount of glass in this house, the back garden isn't overlooked. It's just as well, really.

My fiancé seats me at the grand piano beside the concertina patio doors and moves to the fridge.

I burst into girlish giggles; I can't remember the last time I did such a thing. 'Are you really going to do that? I thought you were joking!'

Scott smiles at me devilishly. At certain angles, he reminds me of Henry Cavill, just not as bulky. Scott doesn't overdo the gym. He has a naturally toned physique he doesn't have to work for. Nature has blessed him in so many ways.

I've only seen a couple of photos of his

parents. High-quality shots clearly taken by a professional. They are both gorgeous, too. They make a stunning couple, but I can't quite decide which one he looks like. Hopefully, it will become more evident at the wedding when I meet them in person.

Scott kicks the fridge shut and turns back to me with something in his hand. 'We can't get married until we have eaten whipped cream off each other at least once,' he says.

I lean back against the piano, laughing with my face in my hands. Beneath my spine, keys play a discordant rhythm. It's been a while since I have been this giddy.

Scott's fingers fumble behind my back for the zip of my dress. My back arches to accommodate him. Black satin slips over my shoulders, from my arms and down my front. I'm left in the matching strapless bra and knickers I chose for this occasion.

Scott looks at the burgundy set approvingly. His face seems frozen in this position for too many moments.

He is suddenly illuminated as I blink in confusion. The full glare of the kitchen comes into view now, too. My reactions aren't very quick, but it doesn't take long to realise what has happened.

Someone has flicked the overhead light on.

I tilt my head back at a sound on the other side of the piano. More keys tinkle as I twist and see a figure approaching from the lounge area, which is around a corner but open-plan.

The figure is upside down. But instantly recognisable.

It's Dawn. She is still here. My fiancé and I weren't alone, after all.

TWELVE

Scott scrambles up first. I'm quick to retrieve the dress slipping down over my thighs and hastily pull my arms back inside, protecting my scars from the sudden harsh lighting. Scott had to zip me into this number earlier after I had squeezed myself beneath the satin.

He doesn't offer to do so again now. It seems he is too busy staring across the kitchen at his wife. His stance is clumsy. He has enjoyed a few glasses of champagne, expecting a quiet night at home.

He blinks in the harsh kitchen light. 'I thought you had gone?'

Dawn grimaces. 'No. Still here.'

'Why?' Scott asks stupidly. His usual posh accent is slipping. He sounds more down to earth when he is drunk, but this evening, he is almost abrupt.

'The flat didn't work out. I'm going to have to find somewhere else.'

It occurs to me that Dawn would have heard everything from the moment we stepped inside the house. The lights are off in the lounge area.

Was she sitting in the dark for hours awaiting our return?

'What happened?' I ask. I pull together the two sides of my dress. It's just my fist keeping me one step away from a wardrobe malfunction.

Dawn doesn't look at me. She is red in the face and seems to be barely holding in her emotions. I can't tell if she is angry because something went wrong at the property viewing or upset about the way we arrived home.

I suspect the nature of our arrival didn't help. Either way, I'm mortified. I want to apologise, then realise this is my home, and I shouldn't have to.

'I'm going to be staying for a little longer, I'm afraid,' Dawn says stiffly.

Scott groans. 'Why can't you find somewhere else? Why do you have to be here? I'm marrying someone else, babes. I've moved on. You should, too.'

Dawn's face remains unchanged. She wears the same unnerving smile. 'I can't move on Scott. If only you had stolen eleven good years of my life, it wouldn't have been so bad. But you stole my inheritance too. I don't have a steady income. My savings are running low. I can't just splash out on another place. I need to find somewhere on a budget.'

I think of the luxury apartment Dawn was so enthusiastic about earlier. 'The flat you were going to see wasn't cheap.'

'You're a clever one, aren't you? I'm surprised. Scott usually likes a good old bimbo—like me, or how I used to be, anyway.'

She flicks her hair back off her face with tight lips and a raised chin. 'A friend owns the place I went to see tonight. I recognised the inside of their home from the online listing. I thought they were going to let me have it at a discount. You know, mates rates.'

'Oh-ho.' A look of drawing comprehension spreads across Scott's face. 'Your ex, Pete. He owned a place in that area. That was his flat you went to see. You thought he was going to let you have it cheap. Or for free.'

Dawn's naivety surprises me. 'You thought the boyfriend from over a decade ago would give you a free place to live? On a gem of a flat in Manchester's city centre?'

'No, Sam,' Scott says. 'Dawn met Pete when we were together. I'll leave the rest to your imagination. That about sums up our marriage.'

'I won't stand here and be judged by you!' Dawn snaps. 'Do you want me to go through everything you did to me over the years? I bet you don't, Scotty. It might scare your bride-to-be away. I'm sure you don't want that. If you want your wedding to go ahead, you must be nicer to me.'

Scott stares. He is usually so astute, but alcohol has compromised his brain. 'What does that mean?'

'It means you had better do what you are told if you want to walk down the aisle in thirteen days.' She winces. 'Gosh. Thirteen days. I hope that's not an omen.'

'You can't stop the wedding. Henry has applied for the final bit of paperwork. He is doing everything he can to push it through fast. Our divorce will be official soon enough.'

Dawn tilts her head at him. 'Only if I allow it. I could make it so you have to wait five years if I don't approve of the divorce. Or I can apply to the court for a financial order. All the monetary details you have been trying to gloss over can be picked over at great length in the next few months before you get that precious bit of paper. And that paperwork is your golden ticket that means you can skip off into the sunset with another woman.'

Scott swallows. 'You can't do that.'

'You know full well I can. Henry will have advised you on what can and can't happen. He was always thorough. He knows his trade, and so do you. You know I can put the brakes on your wedding in the sun if I want to.'

'But why would you? You will get your cut from me eventually. Henry says you will get decent maintenance payments. Why ruin things for Sam and me? What's the point?'

'You know those payments are a pittance of what I am owed. You and Henry will not let me see even a fraction of this house. I gave you the money you so desperately needed. You wouldn't have a successful business without me. Scott Worthington-Hart would have been broke or worse if he hadn't taken my money.'

Scott looks angry now. 'I have a successful business because of me—my hard work, my dedication, and all the hours I have put in—blood, sweat, and tears, Dawn. You would never understand that.'

'I want my inheritance back,' she says quietly.

Scott laughs, but his face quickly falls. He drops his voice. 'I can't do that. I don't have that kind of capital lying around—you must know that. Besides, that was marital money. It was in our joint account and became commingled. You can't have it back. It legally became ours.'

Dawn wears an ugly smile now. 'You've done your research, haven't you? I can just picture Henry whispering in your ear, filling your head with all the jargon. Typical you. You've soaked it all up like a sponge, haven't you, Scotty?'

'I have. You don't seem surprised to hear it, either. I'm sure you understand you aren't entitled to that money back. You won't be left with nothing from the divorce, however. I advise you to cut your losses, Dawn. Leave with your dignity intact.'

She laughs bitterly. 'I doubt you would accept my advice to "cut your losses" if you can't have your dream wedding on the eighth of June!'

'Do you dare to try and stop me?' Scott steps forward. In the glare of the kitchen light, his features look more tense than I have ever seen them.

'I might.' Dawn shrugs, seemingly delighted to get such a reaction from Scott. 'Unless you can change my mind.'

'And how might one do that?' Scott says aggressively.

'First of all, you are going to allow me to stay here in this house without question. When the divorce is finalised, I suspect I won't be allowed to set foot inside this place again. It's such a beautiful house, and I currently have the right to stay. I've missed being here since I walked out, so I'm going to enjoy my stay as long as I can.'

Scott purses his lips. 'And if I don't allow it?'

'Then I'll contact the court first thing in the morning. I'll put a stop to your happy ever after.'

I look between them. Their eyes are locked, and they stare at each other as though daring the other one to look away first.

My fiancé doesn't want to be beaten.

'Fine,' he says through gritted teeth. He seems to keep his head still as he speaks, as though trying not to nod or back down physically.

He doesn't want to let Dawn win. Although, he may not have a choice.

THIRTEEN

'Are we still getting married?'

'Of course, babes. There isn't a force on this earth that could stop me from putting a ring on your finger in twelve days.'

Scott and I didn't get much sleep after our date night in Manchester—not for the reasons we were hoping for. We lie in bed this morning, pondering what has happened.

This latest turn of events has left me anxious about our wedding day. Is it going to happen at all? Even if we are forced to choose the ceremony-only backup option, Dawn has put a dampener on the whole experience.

What if the divorce doesn't come through by the time we jet off to Greece? Does that mean Scott's ex-wife will be here when we return from our two-week honeymoon? How far will she take this? Why is she so determined to live with us?

I turn my head to face my fiancé. 'What if the decree absolute doesn't come through in time?'

'It will. Henry assured me.'

'How do we know Dawn won't make an

application to the court without telling us?'

'I don't think she will. We just have to keep her sweet until we receive that decree.'

'What makes you so sure?'

'That's her bargaining chip. She won't throw it away, not now that she has laid down her demand.'

This troubles me more, the fact that Dawn is so determined to stay in our home. I haven't been here long but am quite fond of this place. I adore the beautiful light that floods through the glass and the quiet neighbourhood. It's a far cry from my flat in a converted building.

I voice my concerns. 'Why does she want to live here with us? Does she still feel like this is her home?'

My fiancé frowns. 'It hasn't been for years. I don't know why she has turned up now. She was always so...high-maintenance, if you will. She lived off her father's finances all her life until he passed away. She has probably realised since her abrupt departure that property doesn't come cheap in the real world. You have to pay a certain fee for quality.'

I look at the clock. It's still early. Usually, Scott and I would start the day with much more pleasant business. This is the first time we haven't made love after opening our eyes in the morning.

Now, we lie side by side as we remember the night before. My hands run subconsciously over my forearms. The scars are deepest here. The craters become less noticeable the higher you go; by my shoulders, they are nonexistent.

If I had left earlier that fateful day and gone out as I considered, I wouldn't have to walk around with this constant reminder. It's like a badge; a label indelibly stuck to my skin. I can never remove it.

It says: *Yes, I'm her—the unfortunate girl who was in the wrong place at the wrong time. You might have read my name in the papers. I have a different one now, of course. I'm pretending to be someone else, but these marks say otherwise.*

Every morning of my life, I have awoken, reflecting on the day I got these injuries. Every day, I try to rewrite history in my head. If only I could make the safe path a reality. But I can't. These marks will haunt me forever. As will my parent's absence. That was the day I lost them forever. So there is no way they will be at my wedding.

'Sam?'

Scott's handsome face comes into focus. 'You okay?'

'Sure.' I realise I was lost in the past. I've spent so long in a particular part of it. 'Sorry. I was just daydreaming.'

He smiles, exposing perfect white teeth. 'Glad to have you back. You had zoned out there for a minute.'

I remember what Sara said about Scott not

mentioning my arms. Is now a good time? I test the water, watching him closely for a reaction. 'Do you think Dawn noticed my arms last night?'

Scott isn't expecting the question. It's there for a split second—a rabbit caught in the headlights.

He shakes his head slightly, before breaking into another smile, this one is more mischievous. 'I think Dawn saw a lot of things, from both of us. A lot more than we bargained for, I'll admit. That's an image she won't forget.'

I share his smile as he kisses me on the lips and gets up.

'I'm going for a quick shower,' he says over his shoulder as his naked form disappears into the ensuite.

As the water splashes noisily over him, I think of his reaction. I'm not sure what to take from it. That moment seemed a casual way for me to bring up the subject of my scars.

Is it wrong that he glossed over it? Maybe my appearance bothers him, after all. Then again, there are plenty of women ready to throw themselves at Scott; I see them all the time as their stare roves over his expensive clothes and defined features.

Then their gaze slides across me, as though mentally comparing themselves. Scott has chosen to be with me, not anyone else. No matter how perfectly smooth and even their skin.

I pick up my phone to text Sara and get her opinion, but I can't think of a way to word what just happened in a way that isn't biased against Scott. Sara still hasn't gotten to know him the way I had planned. She won't judge it right; I just know it.

Instead, I wrap my dressing gown around myself and head downstairs to make some coffee, maybe some breakfast. I'm starving. Scott and I have been awake for a while, not daring to leave the room.

Someone else must have had the same idea, I realise as I descend the stairs.

The engine whirs on the expensive blender Scott got me for our three month anniversary. I've used it everyday for a breakfast smoothie since I received it.

This morning, however, Dawn has got to it first. A vibrant green concoction is whizzing around the glass jug. She has been very busy in the kitchen.

The room is in a mess when I walk in through the glass doors—mixing bowls and floury batter are all over the kitchen island. Used chopping boards, and knives are in every direction. Discarded fruit and vegetables litter every surface. Sunlight streams in on bowls and cups piled high in the sink.

Sara was right. It does take some nerve to set up camp in your ex's house when he has moved on with someone else.

'Morning!' Dawn says brightly as she ends the racket and pours a pea-green smoothie into one of my favourite drinking glasses. She takes a slip and smiles cheerfully, her perfectly made-up face dimpled at the cheeks. 'Sleep well?'

My eyes are puffy. I've burned the candle at both ends and I'm wearing the comfortable old dressing gown Scott has failed to prise from my possession.

I've had it for years, and it's worn just right. I'm not letting it go, not even for the designer one my partner got me. I'm set in my ways on many things; this is one of them. It may be comforting, but I don't feel confident in it across from perfect Dawn.

'Not really,' I answer as I sit at the kitchen island and pour myself some orange juice. After the brazen demand Dawn made last night, does she expect me to be friendly? She is practically holding my wedding day to ransom in return for accommodation. How am I supposed to respond to this?

'That's a shame. Some breakfast will cheer you up.'

'What have you made?'

Everything, by the look of it. I eye the mess of used dishes, blueberries, squeezed lemons and sliced peppers. The onion skins are too much for me first thing in the morning. It doesn't immediately occur to me what one single dish these ingredients could amount to.

'I didn't know what you liked, so I did a bit of everything.'

Bingo.

'Great,' I say flatly as Dawn removes a tray of cheesy bacon frittata from the oven. She uses the comical bear paw oven gloves I now remember came from Adam. He knew I loved bears. These gloves were the only nice present he got for me.

In another way, they were a sign that he wanted me to be his kitchen slave, cooking for him whatever he ordered. There is only one reason I've kept the things: to remind myself never to allow anyone to take advantage of me again.

'How much would you like, Sam?' Dawn hovers with the hot tray by my side. In her other hand, she holds a large, sharp knife waiting to slice into the frittata.

'I don't really want any.'

'Don't be silly,' she says in a sing-song voice. 'Guests in this house should be more polite.'

'I'm not a guest. I live here.'

'For now,' she smiles, gripping the knife. 'Just let me know where I should cut.'

The heat of the tray warms my face. It must be over two hundred degrees straight from the oven. All I can think about is how the tray would stick to my skin if she pushed it at me, and how much it would hurt.

I'm not sure how serious Dawn is, but I don't want to play some silly game with her.

I stand up. 'I'm not that hungry. I usually just have a smoothie.'

Dawn nods knowingly. 'Same. I'm afraid you'll have to clean the blender if you want to use it, though. I've already had mine for the day. You're out of spinach, by the way. And bananas. I didn't pick any up this morning from the shops when I went out for everything else.'

'Right.'

Dawn places the hot tray of baked eggs and knife on a board, and I let out a breath I didn't know I was holding.

Dawn removes her splattered apron and drops it on the bar stool next to me.

'Where are you going?' I ask her.

'For a run. I trust you will have this cleaned up by the time I get back?'

My mouth opens in surprise. 'Not right now. I have to be somewhere soon. I have my final dress fitting.'

'Oh, how lovely. It gets exciting at this point, doesn't it? What time?'

'Ten.'

'Is that at the bridal place in the village?'

'Yes,' I say slowly, wondering what is coming next.

'That's nice. They have the most amazing dresses, don't they? I got mine from there. I'll come with you.'

I blink. 'What?'

'I think you heard me. Silly Sam. I'll come

with you to your fitting.'

'There is no need,' I say quickly. 'I'm happy to go on my own. It's basically just to pick the dress up. I'm confident it will fit.'

'Don't be silly. It will be fun. Besides, I can't wait to see you in your dress.'

FOURTEEN

Scott nods along with Dawn's suggestion that she accompany me to my dress fitting when he joins us. He is clearly annoyed but bites his tongue. I have a good mind to sneak off while Dawn is out for her jog or while she extensively showers and dresses afterwards.

But I've already told her where and when it is. She knows exactly where the shop is as she knows the village even better than I do. There is no way around it. I could kick myself that it didn't occur to me to lie sooner. I should have said I was going for a walk. Or would she have wanted to accompany me on that, too?

So, at ten, I walk through the door of the village bridal shop with Dawn at my side. It's either this or take the risk that Dawn will make a court application. There is no way I want to jeopardise the wedding. I plant a smile on my face and try not to make this look too awkward.

The shop owner, Ellen, welcomes me warmly as she has done every time I come here.

Then her gaze moves to Scott's ex and does a double take. I swear I see a spark of recognition, but she smiles and leads me to the back room where my dress hangs up, waiting.

Excitement flutters in my stomach. I've been waiting for this day for ages. The day I finally get to take the dress home. I've dreamed of wearing it alone in the master bedroom, just to try it out in private and enjoy it before I have to put it on for real.

It's all starting to look pretty real now, especially when I slip into the gown now that the alterations have been made. I've gone for a white trumpet-silhouette dress with a small train that trails behind me as I walk.

Obviously, I had to opt for long sleeves. Still, they are delicate and made with decorative white lace that covers my arms enough that I will have the confidence to walk down the aisle. The back is open and runs down in a deep v-shape. I fell in love with the design as soon as I saw it. It's the perfect dress for someone with body hang-ups like mine.

Ellen gasps and clasps her hands together with a grin as I emerge from the dressing room. Dawn's face has gone very stiff. She seems unable to say anything as she eyes me in my dress.

'Wow,' Ellen says. 'You look absolutely stunning. The most beautiful bride.'

Dawn chuckles. 'Ellen, you say that to all your brides. Do you remember my fitting when I was here choosing a dress to marry Scott?'

'Mm,' Ellen says noncommittally,

deliberately focussing her attention on the dress and nothing else.

She gets me to walk, sit, and bend; she checks the hems and seams as I do so. 'It fits like a glove, doesn't it? Are you happy, Sam?'

'Delighted!' I beam. 'You've done the most amazing job. It's so beautiful. This dress is the most gorgeous thing I've ever owned. It's perfect.'

I've never had anything altered before, always wearing clothes as they have come off the rack. Scott gets his business wear made to measure just for him. He even gets his ties custom-made to perfectly complement his height and build.

I wouldn't consider doing anything similar —not that I need it with my job as a teaching assistant. I've spent my career in George cardigans, floral blouses, and Primark leggings. That dress sense has followed me into my personal life, as Dawn so helpfully pointed out at our dinner party on Saturday.

When Scott lays out an expensive garment as a surprise gift for a date, it feels like I'm stepping into the shoes of a Disney princess.

It seems like it now. Of course, Scott hasn't seen this dress. Isn't it bad luck before the wedding day?

Ellen slips a finger beneath the lace on my shoulder. 'Tight enough?'

'Yes, it's perfect.' I'm ecstatic and can't wait

to take my new dress home.

Dawn tilts her head at me. 'Are you sure you like the dress, Sam?'

'Positive.'

'You seem like you are holding back. What's wrong?'

Ellen raises her eyebrows at me. She looks slightly offended.

'Nothing,' I say slightly too firmly, taken aback by Dawn's strange comment. 'I love it.'

'Don't be shy,' Dawn says. 'Ellen told me that when I had my dress fitting here. Do you remember my dress, Ellen?'

She nods curtly. 'Ball-gown silhouette. Pearl and embroidery. Very beautiful.'

'Aww, you remembered after all these years. You're so sweet. I wish I still had it. I guess it's no good without the husband to go with it! Scott's hoping the second time's a charm with this one.' She nods her head at me and laughs.

Ellen smiles politely. 'I'm sure Mr and Mrs Worthington-Hart will make a wonderful couple.'

'That's the hope, isn't it? Sam had better not go away for any length of time. She might come home to find Scott has found bride number three! Ha ha.'

'That's not what happened,' I say quietly, cringing inside.

Ellen gestures to the dressing room. 'If you're happy, Sam, I'll wrap your dress up, and you'll be good to go.'

'Thanks so much.'

In the changing room, I slip out of my dress as efficiently as I can, mindful not to damage anything. I'm eager to leave the shop. Dawn is chatting some more to Ellen and I dread to think what she is saying.

Is one piece of paper worth all this stress? I sincerely hope Scott is working hard with Henry while I am here. Maybe they can find a way to stop Dawn from interfering with proceedings. Henry might have a legal trick up his sleeve that Scott and I don't know about yet.

Something. Anything. The thought of Dawn staying with us until the wedding is unimaginable.

She is still talking as I pull back the curtain and approach Ellen with my dress. 'I'm still Mrs Worthington-Hart, you know. Technically, the divorce isn't finalised yet. I'm not sure how Sam expects to get married to my husband before everything is legally signed off.'

Ellen takes the dress from me and carefully wraps it in a protective garment bag as though it costs a million dollars. It is far too expensive for something I would wear, in my opinion, but Scott says I am worth it.

Ellen holds the door open for the three of us: Dawn, me, and the wedding dress. Yes, three, that's how much I love this dress.

'Thanks so much for everything,' I say to her

on the way out.

She nods and smiles. But this time, the warmth doesn't seem to reach her eyes. 'Best wishes for a beautiful wedding day. Congratulations.'

Dawn snorts as we set off down the street. 'That's exactly what she said to me when I picked my dress up. I bet she says that to everyone. The same lines. Seriously, it's like she is reading from a script.'

I ignore her and march on ahead. Ellen was a lot more friendly before Dawn showed up. Today was supposed to be special. A key part of the wedding experience. Dawn has done her best to ruin it. I feel I'm well within my rights to hurry ahead to the car and leave her behind to walk home. But I don't dare. I don't want to do anything to trigger her into contacting the court. In twelve days time this won't be an issue either way.

At the car, I carefully lay out my precious cargo upon the back seats as though it is a puppy I just picked up from a breeder.

At home, Dawn watches me from the hall as I disappear upstairs with my dress. I find a safe home for it in the walk-in wardrobe. My gaze falls upon the ruined cocktail dress on the shelf. I remember how Dawn appeared from upstairs when I returned home on Saturday. There had been a flicker of movement at the window, too. Had she been in here, sabotaging my outfit for the evening?

Or am I being too paranoid? She may be bitter, but she only wants free accommodation in this house, right? Until she gets herself sorted.

Either way, there is no way I am letting her near this dress.

FIFTEEN

The next day, Scott has some business to attend to at his shop. I'm faced with the prospect of being alone in the house with Dawn. We beat her to the kitchen this morning. Perhaps she is having a lie in? One can only hope.

'Can't it wait? I ask him as he finishes his granola. We are both seated at the breakfast bar. 'I thought we agreed to take time off work to be with each other. What's wrong with the person you hired to cover for you?'

'They require my assistance with something.'

'Is it that important?'

'It is when my business is at stake.'

'Can't you just instruct them over the phone?'

'I'm afraid not. Everything has to be just so. You know how I am.'

'Yes, I do.' I groan. 'You need to learn how to delegate.'

'You are right.' He kisses me on the forehead. 'You need to teach me how to do that.'

I laugh. 'I'm a teaching assistant, not a drill

sergeant.'

'Same principle,' he grins as he turns to put his shoes on. He calls out a farewell, and I hear his Jaguar whirr away.

It isn't long before Dawn emerges. Was she waiting for him to leave?

'Morning,' She says brightly. 'Has Scotty gone?'

'Yes, he won't be long,' I lie. In reality, I know that Scott might take a while. He has a tendency to show someone how to do something and then end up doing it himself. He is quite particular about things, too. Things have to be done a certain way for him to be satisfied.

Dawn seems to understand this. 'Huh. If he has gone to show someone how something should be done, he will be there for a while. Let's be honest.'

She gets the ingredients for a smoothie out but then stops when she sees my used blender jug in the sink. I beat her to it today.

I lift my glass of banana smoothie as though to explain. A picture paints a thousand words.

She sighs. 'I would greatly appreciate it, Sam, if you could wash that for me.'

'I'm sure you would.'

She turns her head slowly to me. The look on her face suddenly seems quite scary, even with the generous amount of makeup she is already wearing.

Reluctantly, I get up from my barstool and

wash the blender jug and blade attachment.

Dawn watches over my shoulder. 'Make sure you do a good job there. I like equipment to be clean.'

I grit my teeth as I shake out the excess water and dry it hurriedly with a towel.

She starts dropping frozen ingredients inside. 'Thanks very much for that. It's a shame I had to ask,' she says.

I shake my head. I don't trust myself to say anything.

'Oh dear.'

'What is it now?'

'I seem to have run out of matcha powder.'

'So?'

'I can't have a green smoothie without it.' She places her palms out at her sides. Her body language says, What can you do?

I suppose I will be asked to get some for her at some point. 'Fine. I'm going to the shops later anyway. Just write it on the shopping list. It's right next to you on the worktop.'

Dawn smiles in a way that I've grown accustomed to fearing. The skin on my shoulders prickles a little.

'I said I can't have my smoothie until I get it. What part of that don't you understand?'

Now I just prickle at her rudeness. 'What do you expect me to do about it right now?'

'Do you have other plans?'

'No.'

'Then you won't mind running out and getting me some of my powder, will you?'

I want to tell her no, to flatly refuse her request when she has posed it so aggressively. But I can tell by the way she looks at me that I have no choice—not if I don't want my wedding interfered with.

'Good,' she says as she watches me set aside my glass and go to put on my shoes. 'You're a fast learner. I'm sure Scott appreciates that.'

'Where do I find the stuff you want?'

'I get mine from a cute little tea shop in the city.' She takes the shopping list pad and scribbles down the details.

'I'm not going into the city centre for one silly ingredient.'

She shrugs. 'Well, why don't you pick something up for yourself while you are there? They have all sorts of good-quality tea powders. You might be able to find something to fix your complexion. I've heard green tea is good for the skin, you know, for spots and scars and so on. I've never tried it myself, of course. I haven't had the need.'

I stare at her. How personal is her remark? It's hard to tell if she is being generally rude or if she knows about my scars. Her eyes give nothing away as I take the scrap of paper from her with the address of the tea shop.

There is no way I'm driving into the city on a petty errand. An hour round trip for one fussy ingredient? She can forget it.

I drive into the village and spot a Holland and Barrett instead. I manage to bag a flukey parking spot nearby and dash inside. The assistant pounces on me as soon as I walk in the door and is happy to direct me to the matcha section. I cringe when I see the prices of the various brands, but I resign myself to tapping my card on the reader for a tiny bag of whatever this stuff is anyway.

I'm grateful Scott set us up with a joint bank account. He keeps it topped up with a decent amount of funds. He told me I can buy whatever I want with this card. I've never met anyone so generous in my life. I haven't taken too many liberties with this, only treating myself to a few overdue shopping sprees. Maybe I splashed out in a couple of shops I shouldn't have. My splurge purchases were mainly lingerie, something I haven't really bought before.

I guess I felt kind of guilty spending someone else's money and bought something that Scott could appreciate in the end. I only wore the items once, as I felt a little owned and conflicted for thinking this way.

Needless to say, the garments have been left in the back of the walk-in wardrobe. And I use the term *garments* loosely.

I'm obviously back sooner than Dawn expects. She descends the stairs with a look of surprise as I walk in through the door. I toss her the pouch and head upstairs myself. I have the sudden urge to check on my wedding dress.

She pulls a face. 'What is this?'

'It's what you asked for.'

'No, it isn't. This isn't from the shop I told you to visit.'

'I know, but it's the same stuff. It certainly wasn't cheap.'

She turns over the pouch. 'This one is vanilla flavoured. It has sweeteners and all sorts of rubbish in it. I wanted pure powder. I'm not putting this into my body.'

She throws it back at me.

My reflexes stop the thing hitting me in the face. 'Look, I'm sorry, but I tried! You'll just have to do without it.'

'It's not good enough.'

'Dawn, please. You can't have me running errands for you like this. I know you're upset that Scott is getting remarried, but please be reasonable. This isn't personal. Scott and I just... clicked. I didn't expect that I would ever find someone like him. Neither of us mean you any harm. We just want to be married. Please don't ruin our wedding because your marriage didn't work out the way you expected. Anyway, you were the one who left Scott, weren't you? It wasn't his fault. Or mine. What do you say?'

Dawn has gone very still. Her face is fixed on mine. The silence runs on for a few long moments. 'Are you finished?' she says finally.

I sigh. It was worth a try. 'I suppose I am.'

'Good. Let me tell you where I am, just in case it wasn't clear before. Scott only remains a success because of me. He gets to keep this house because of me and my inheritance, even if I legally have no claim to it after the divorce. He would have lost it all if I hadn't stepped in and saved his sorry behind. So he owes me. There is no way that I am going to allow another woman to come in and profit from my money.'

'I'm not trying to get anything from Scott other than his love.'

She responds with an ugly smirk. 'You are fooling no one with this virtuous peasant routine.'

I fold my arms across my chest. 'Am I not?'

'No. So, let me set things straight. My inheritance paid for half this house and its contents. That blender you used this morning? Mine. The warm water you used to shower in this morning? Mine. The clothes you are hiding goodness-knows-what under? Mine.' She eyes the leggings and hoodie I put on this morning. 'Apart from the supermarket specials, of course. Get the idea?'

I shake my head with an open mouth. I don't know what to say.

She must be joking, right?

SIXTEEN

It turns out Dawn isn't joking. I'm back in the car again, fuming about having to find the very particular ingredient she requested. But this time, I'm shaking all over with repressed fury.

I'd have liked to have set Dawn straight. I wanted to shout the truth at her just now. But that would ruin everything I've built here. I've landed on my feet with Scott. It wouldn't do to forget that.

Instead, I do some deep breathing to the best of my ability and send Sara a text before I set off.

Call me when you get the chance. Things have gone a bit wild here. I could do with a chat xx

I've barely left the driveway when my phone lights up with a call from my best friend.

'Hey, how are things with you?' I say. Even I can tell my voice sounds strange.

Sara can tell, too. 'Is everything all right?'

'Not really. Have you got a few minutes?'

'Sure. I'm on my break. What's up, hun? Has something happened with Scott?'

'No. Things are fine between us. It's his wife

who is the problem.'

I explain to Sara what has happened; about Dawn's failure to leave on Sunday and her behaviour since, including what happened in the dress shop and this wild goose chase she has me on this morning.

Sara swears when she hears what Dawn said to me just now. 'She's a total nutter. I thought she was good to go when I left?'

'So did I. I'm not sure what happened with the flat. She made it sound like she was expecting the guy to give it to her for free.'

'Prime property in the middle of a city? She is either having a laugh or is seriously messed up in the head if she thinks someone will hand her the keys for nothing. I'm not sure what would be worse if she has set up camp in your house. What are you going to do?'

'I don't know. I guess we have to do what she says. Or else she will stop the wedding.'

Sara is quiet for a moment. 'What does Scott have to say about all this?'

'He is working with his solicitor to find a solution. I don't think there is one, though. He wants us to cooperate with Dawn. Scott seems a little afraid of her, if I'm honest.'

'I'm not surprised.' She is quiet for a moment. 'Do you think she really was kicked out of her last place? Maybe the landlady wasn't selling after all? It sounds like she could have invented that to get into your house.'

'I think that part was real. She has fallen on hard times. I think she genuinely needs a place to stay while she gets herself together.'

'Are you sure? What if she doesn't? She could be with you longer than you expect. I've heard all sorts of stories about people not being able to evict tenants and that's with a formal tenancy agreement. There are loads of laws preventing people from being thrown into the street and made homeless. Maybe that is her game? She might be making herself at home for the long haul.'

I groan. 'That doesn't make me feel better. Why would Dawn move in with us if she didn't have to?'

'Good question. You need to check with her landlady. That is if she isn't buried beneath a patio.'

'That isn't funny.' I wouldn't put it past Dawn after the look on her face earlier. 'I've no idea where she lived before she arrived on the doorstep.'

'Have you Googled her?'

'No,' I say, feeling foolish. I probably should have done it. It's just been so intense, having her presence constantly in the house.

'Hold on a sec. I'll do it.' Sara is quiet for a few minutes. She is still on the other end of the line. I can hear her muttering now and then. A few moments later, she comes back with a noise of triumph.

'Voila. Dawn Worthington-Hart. Thanks, Scott, for the unusual name. It makes his wife easy to find.'

Ex-wife, I want to correct her, but I can't. Not yet. Not until that decree absolute comes through. 'So what did you find?'

'I have her phone number and her address.'

'How did you do that?' I marvel.

'Easy. One thing leads to another online. I found her Instagram profile, and her number was on one of the image posts. It seems she offers an Airbnb co-host service. Did you know that?'

'No. Dawn made it sound like she did odd jobs here and there. She wouldn't tell me any more than that.'

'She hasn't done much to hide her online activities. She is an open book. I searched for her phone number. It looks like she sold some furniture earlier in the year. Her address is attached. I'm texting it to you now. Maybe you can find something out from that?'

'Thanks.'

'Do you want me to try and find the landlady's info?'

'No, that's okay. I'll do it. It's in Crumpsall. I know the area, don't I? That's where my flat was. I can drop by on the way back from the city once I've got her ladyship's speciality tea.'

'Sam?'

'Yes?'

'Be careful. I don't like the sound of the

situation over there. Keep your eyes open. Remember, you can come to me any time.'

'Thanks, hun. I appreciate that.' Even as I say the words, I know I won't put upon Sara. There is also no way I will let go of Scott now that I have him. He is the best thing that has ever happened to me. I'm so close to my dream wedding, too. This time is the start of the rest of my life. I'm not going to let it slip through my fingers.

No matter what.

SEVENTEEN

I fork out for Dawn's requested ingredient and then head over to the area I left behind when I met Scott. The address Sara texted me is just a few streets away from the flat I lived in before I moved into Scott's house.

I wonder if Dawn and I even crossed paths on the streets of Crumpsall? Did she spot Scott or his car driving past when he came to stay over those few times?

I pull up outside a small, purpose-built block of four flats. The lawn is overgrown and separated from the road by a mossy low fence. I look at the windows of both the ground floor flats. Dawn apparently lived at number one.

There are blinds up at both the windows. Something the landlady does for all their tenants? Or has someone on a short let been moved in whilst the purchase goes through? There isn't a for-sale board up. Either it hasn't gone up yet, or the sale has gone through already. The latter is unlikely. Don't those things take ages? I wouldn't know. I've never been in a position to buy a property. Once Scott and I are married, I will probably never have to.

I step out of the car and take a glance around. The street is deserted. I head up the uneven path and peer through the window of one of the flats. It's the living room.

A woman on the sofa glances up at the sight of me.

I duck away. Shit.

Before I can reach the car, the front door opens, and she collars me. 'Can I help you?'

I turn back to her. 'Hi, sorry. I didn't mean to startle you. I was looking for a friend of mine. Dawn. Dawn Worthington-Hart. Does she still live here?'

The woman shakes her head. 'I'm the owner. Dawn lives in the other flat.' She points. 'She handed her notice in at the weekend, so she won't be here for long. Come to think of it, I haven't seen her for a few days.'

'She gave her notice? Are you sure?'

'Yes, on Saturday.'

'So the flat isn't for sale?'

'No, it's not,' the woman says slowly. She looks at me suspiciously. 'Who are you, sorry?'

'I'm a friend of hers.'

'What's your name? I'll tell her you were asking after her. I have her number.' She raises her phone to illustrate.

'No, don't do that.' I've said it too quickly. 'I mean, it's fine. I'll catch up with her another time. We do pilates together, so I'll see her soon enough. I was in the area and thought I would drop by. No big deal.'

The last thing I need is this woman alerting Dawn to the fact I turned up here asking about her.

I'm back in my car and pulling away before the woman closes the front door. I pick up the jar of Dawn's speciality tea from the passenger seat and let myself in through the front door. As I step into the entrance hall, I realise I've stepped onto an envelope.

The postman often visits the house at this time, but this item wasn't delivered with the regular mail. There is no stamp or name on the front. I rip it open. Inside is a piece of white card with a single line of neatly printed words.

You had better watch yourself

EIGHTEEN

I stare at the message for a few moments in shock. Is this Dawn's idea of a joke? She can't be serious. Leaving me threatening notes is another level. Where is she anyway? She had better not be anywhere near my wedding dress.

'Dawn?' I call out from the bottom of the stairs. 'Are you up there?'

She isn't in the kitchen or back garden. I jog upstairs. After I'm satisfied no one has been in the master bedroom, I knock on the guest room door.

No answer.

There is no one inside when I push the door open. I'm shocked by the mess; the room is in disarray.

Dawn's clothes are spread out everywhere, even on the floor. You can hardly see the silver carpet beneath the colourful collection of garments atop it. It's like Dawn has unzipped her suitcase and thrown the contents out, not caring where they land.

The roses I bought for Sara have been removed from the vase, and the yellow petals are plucked and scattered all around the room. The KitKat wrappers are in the mess all over the floor, too. Chocolate and crumbs are squashed into the carpet in more than one place. What condition might the ensuite bathroom be in?

'What are you doing in here?'

I spin around to see Dawn. I hadn't heard her come in.

She is flushed in the face and in her workout attire: matching leggings and a cropped sports top. She has the toned stomach I have always dreamed of.

'I asked you what you were doing in here,' she says aggressively. 'You aren't allowed in my room while I'm out—or when I am in here, for that matter. What's your game?'

'*My game*? I wanted to talk to you about this.' I shove the piece of card at her with the threatening message.

She feigns bewilderment as she takes it from me, but her expression quickly changes as she looks at the text. She even has the audacity to stifle a smirk. 'So?'

'Is that all you have to say?'

She shrugs. 'I don't know what you want from me.'

'Why did you leave me a threatening note?'

'I didn't.' She folds the card neatly and slides it into the top drawer of the bedside cabinet.

'I want to show that to Scott. Give it back.'

'Give what back? I don't know what you are

talking about, *Sam*.'

'Why do you keep saying my name like that?'

'It's not your real name, is it?'

'Yes, it is.' She's doing that staring contest thing again, as she did with her ex the other night. I try not to blink but fail and look down at what little carpet I can see. 'I don't know what would make you think otherwise.'

'You don't, do you? I reckon you're hiding something. What is it?'

The muggy heat of the day suddenly seems unbearable. I respond to her question with another to deflect the attention from me. 'You are the only one hiding something, Dawn. Why did you pretend you had been kicked out of your flat? I spoke to your landlady. She isn't selling.'

Dawn stares at me for a few moments. It's impossible to tell what she is thinking. 'That's not what she told me,' she says finally. 'I was told I had to leave. Maybe she wanted the place clear for a friend or family member to move in? I don't know. She just wanted me gone, that's all I know.'

'She told me you handed your notice in—on Saturday.'

'Whatever.' She turns towards the ensuite door. 'It's a hot day. I need to shower after my run. So if you don't mind.'

I'm forced to leave the bedroom.

I want to stay and protest that Dawn can't have jogged very far while I was out. But I guess

I was gone for well over an hour. She would have had plenty of time to print that note, leave it on the doorstep and still have time for a workout in today's heat. The hair around the edges of her face is wet with sweat, so she has obviously been up to something.

I'm not sure where she printed the message exactly, as Scott's downstairs study is always locked. He carries the key about his person. I head downstairs and check the door handle. It still seems locked. Does Dawn have a spare key she could have used to access the printer?

Ideally, I would like to confront her over it. Scott wouldn't like it if he found she was sneaking inside his study. He locks his office to keep work separate from his personal life. Even I'm not invited in there when he has to work. It's his way of compartmentalising it, he says. He regrets having to bring work home, but sometimes it's unavoidable.

I look back upstairs uncertainly. Outside the guest room door, I listen hard, my ear close to the wooden panel. There is the definite sound of water splashing. Dawn is in the shower.

It's not like I'm going to start going through her stuff, but there is no way I'm not going to collect that threatening message as evidence to show Scott later.

I'm virtually holding my breath as I push down the door handle and tread carefully across the floor to the bedside cabinet. When I pull open the top drawer, I'm shocked.

The card with the message is gone.

Dawn must have taken it into the bathroom with her after I left the room.

She certainly is devious. Sara was right. Ironically, my friend delivered a very similar message to the card at the railway station that day.

Maybe I do need to watch my back.

NINETEEN

When Scott gets home later that evening, I waste no time in telling him what Dawn has done over a home-cooked bolognese. We dine out in the garden—alone, thankfully. The warm sun is becoming low in the sky, casting a bright red glow over our food.

Scott frowns as he forks his pasta. 'Living with Dawn was never easy. She made my life very difficult sometimes. Try not to antagonise her.'

My mouth drops open. 'I didn't!'

'Did you not?' Scott looks at me with his beautiful eyes. They have dark circles today. He looks more weary than I have ever seen him. 'You two had a perfectly peaceful morning, did you? Something must have set her off. Are you sure you had no disagreements at all?'

As I remember the matcha powder incident, I purse my lips. 'Well, there was something. She wanted this fussy ingredient for breakfast and sent me right across the city for it.'

'I see. That was likely what triggered Dawn. Might it have been easier to have simply purchased what she wanted?'

'Are you for real?' I cross my arms. 'She was having me on! It was ridiculous. I'm not her slave.'

He nods quickly and sets down his cutlery to wrap his arm around me. 'I know. I hate this, too—more than you, in fact. I thought Dawn was a part of my past—not the future I'm looking forward to with you.'

He kisses the top of my head and mutters against my ear, in case Dawn can hear through her open bedroom window. 'Just remember it's not for much longer. This is only a temporary arrangement. Eleven days. Then her ransom over the wedding is nullified.'

'Is she even going to let us have the wedding?'

'I told you, babes. Wild horses couldn't stop me from putting a ring on your finger and making my love for you official. I won't allow Dawn to jeopardise it. I love you, Sam.'

'I love you too. I just wish we didn't have to be around her for the next eleven days.'

'I tell you what. Why don't we have a few nights away somewhere?'

'Really? But we are jetting off soon for the wedding.'

He leans back from the table and pulls out his phone. 'So? I'm not talking about abroad. Perhaps a nice hotel in the countryside. You just said you can't enjoy domestic repose with Dawn around.'

'I can't.'

'Then why don't we go and do something about it? Things have got on top of you here. Some perspective will do you good.'

'I thought you didn't want to leave her unattended in the house?'

'Ideally not. But the most valuable thing here is you. I can't have my precious being upset. Besides, we don't have to go far. There are many fine hotels in the area.' He lifts my hand and kisses it as he scrolls through short-stay options. He finds a luxury spa hotel. We will check in tomorrow. It's half an hour's drive away in Macclesfield and looks wonderful.

Scott starts booking us in for five nights.

'Better make it four,' I tell him as I see the dates on his screen.

'Why?'

I shake my head. 'I have somewhere to be on the second.'

'Somewhere secret, eh?' he asks with a flash of mischief. He is obviously curious, but I don't give anything away.

'Just something I need to do before the wedding,' I shrug. 'No big deal.'

It is a big deal, of course—the biggest of my life—but I don't say anything more.

My fiancé looks at me thoughtfully for a moment but then blinks it away. He books us in for four nights instead. That leaves us a day to go home and pack for the wedding as well as run my errand.

'It doesn't add much to my journey time if I need to drop into my boutique,' he says. 'We can also pop home if we need anything, but it keeps us away from Dawn. We will return for a day or two to pack and leave refreshed and ready for Greece. The three of us should be happy with that arrangement.'

I wrap my arms around his neck and kiss him deeply. I want to make up for keeping secrets from him. I love that he hasn't questioned me. Adam would have started the third degree by now. 'Thank you.'

He kisses me back in kind. 'You're more than welcome.'

Dawn still hasn't emerged from her room, but that's not something to complain about. We retire to the lounge and make the most of her absence. It's quite a cosy room compared to the vastness of the others in the house.

The bar is in one corner near the patio doors, and opposite it is a rather modest corner sofa, much more like an ordinary house. This is one of my favourite places to relax.

I make some popcorn on the stove whilst Scott loads up Netflix on the TV.

With my fiancé by my side, relaxation isn't the only thing on my mind. The movie he puts on is merely a pretence. Soon, we have both lost the thread of what is going on. Our hands and mouths are all over each other.

The bowl of fresh popcorn is largely untouched. His hands push my skirt higher around my waist.

I hear the rustle of the kernels as my knee nudges the coffee table. Heat rises in my neck as Scott's attention moves lower.

'So,' comes a loud voice I know all too well. 'What are we watching?'

I open my eyes in time to see Dawn quickly reaching toward me. I flinch, expecting her to yank a fistful of hair. Then I realise she is grabbing the remote from the sofa beside me.

Scott scrambles up. I push myself into an upright position, slipping my knickers up and my skirt back down over my thighs. Surreptitiously, I check the buttons on my cotton shirt are still fastened.

'Budge up,' she says, jerking the remote. I do as I am told as she drops herself down on the sofa between Scott and me.

We share a glance behind her back, but Scott shakes his head. He punches some cushions into place and stands up after a few moments to pour a shot of something from the bar. He knocks it back stiffly.

Dawn leans her head back, not taking her eyes off the television. 'I'll have a cosmo whilst you're up, babes.'

He turns to look at her as though he wants to say something snarky back, but he doesn't. He simply goes about making his wife the drink she requested.

I watch him work at the bar with a new urge. There was a time when I could have enjoyed that bottle of Cointreau in his hand on its own. On my own. That craving comes upon me again. The amber liquid looks inviting. Citrus is the perfect partner for a balmy summer's evening, isn't it?

Dawn nudges me with her elbow. 'I fancy a bowl of popcorn, too.'

I gesture to the bowl on the coffee table. 'This is fresh. Help yourself.'

'It was fresh when you made it twenty minutes ago. But you and Scotty have had your sticky fingers in it, and I know all too well where they have been. So I'll have a fresh batch if you don't mind.'

My eyes sting with tears. Whether from frustration or embarrassment, I don't know. 'I do mind, actually.'

'Then I won't have a problem visiting the courts tomorrow.'

Scott returns from the freezer with a bottle of vodka in his hand. He gives me a warning look. 'Sam, this is only temporary, remember?'

Dawn probably thinks he is talking about the time until the wedding, not the trip Scott booked for tomorrow.

'Fine,' I say through gritted teeth. 'Sweet or salty?'

TWENTY

The look on Dawn's face as we head out the next morning with our suitcases is worth the upheaval of leaving our home for a few days.

It's priceless. She wasn't expecting it at all. Scott's ex had obviously been looking forward to spending the next week or so torturing us. She is most disappointed to find we are taking a four-day break.

'You can't leave,' she says on the driveway as Scott loads our cases into his Jaguar.

Scott closes the car boot. 'I'm sorry, Dawn. I think some space is what we all need. Things have gotten a little out of hand here, don't you think? You can have some time alone in the house. You said you wanted to enjoy it before you leave, so here's your chance.'

She crosses her arms in defeat and watches us as we drive away. Her expression of repressed fury is unsettling in the rearview mirror. The only thing I can do is mentally shake it off.

I'm so glad I convinced Scott I needed to bring my wedding dress. He thought I was being paranoid, but I don't trust Dawn alone in the

153

house with it.

Scott double-checked his office door was firmly secured. It's a shame he couldn't have installed a lock on the master bedroom before we left. I've been forced to take my folder of documents with me, too. I don't want Dawn prying through it whilst I am gone. I just have to pray she hasn't done so already. Goodness knows what she could have gleaned. It seemed untouched when I collected it from its hiding place under a pile of clothes in the walk-in wardrobe.

'Does Dawn have a key for your office?' I ask Scott as we drive through the countryside.

He frowns at this. 'No. I have the only copy safe in my pocket. Why?'

I shrug. 'I just wondered how she printed that note.'

He ponders this for a few moments. 'She could have done it in too many ways to mention. Printing services are available in every store and online. She might have her own printer in one of her suitcases. I wouldn't know. Some of the devices are pretty compact these days.'

True, there could have been any number of things in the mess that is Dawn's room especially if her whole life was in those suitcases. A printer could well be in one of them.

Scott reaches for my hand and grasps it as we speed towards our getaway. He keeps an eye on the road. 'Anyway, forget about it all now. Let's enjoy the next few days.'

The hotel is wonderful. It's a gem set in acres of unspoiled Macclesfield countryside. The trees and gardens are in full bloom. There is an amazing view of the vista from the outdoor pool. Luckily, it's warm enough to enjoy at this time of year. The sun is glorious. It beats down hot and makes the water look like crystal.

Others swim nearby, so I'm mindful to keep my arms below the surface when they are too close.

My fiancé has some business calls to make while I swim. I see him on the phone in the distance, strolling around the lush grounds.

On the afternoon of the second day, he makes up for his absence by treating me to afternoon tea with scones and fancy cakes. Then we both go for a relaxing massage. The stress of the last few days is worked from my muscles.

Scott's phone starts buzzing with a call from his ex. He mutes his phone and apologises when he gets a disapproving look from his masseuse.

It's not the first time since we left she has tried to get in touch. Dawn keeps calling and hanging up. It's like she wants to remind us that she still exists. As though she is saying: I'm still waiting for you at home. Don't forget that.

Afterwards, I feel like I'm floating on a cloud as my fiancé and I sit on loungers beside the outdoor pool. We have a mocktail each and enjoy the post-massage glow, the sun beating down on us.

Scott's phone rings again. This time, he checks the screen and turns the device off without comment.

We have a wonderful rest of the evening together. We chill out and go to our room for some quality time.

Even though it's only been a few days since we thoroughly enjoyed each other, it feels like forever. Our bodies press into each other hungrily. Afterwards, we go down and have a wonderful dinner. The food is amazing. Everything is perfect.

Even Dawn has gone quiet now. Scott switched his phone back on, but her calls have not recommenced.

The next day, I wake up more content than I have recently. Sunlight pours into the room. It's another beautiful day.

I'm tangled in the crisp white sheets. When I open my eyes, I realise the damage to my arms looks too stark against the immaculate crisp sheets. I slide them underneath the duvet and pull it over myself as I look around for Scott.

He is sitting atop the bed, fully clothed, leaning down to pull on his socks.

'Going somewhere?' I ask him lazily as I shuffle closer. I wonder if he is popping into his boutique again. He works so hard.

'We have to go,' he says quietly.

His tone has me on edge, snapping me unpleasantly from my dreamy state. There is none of his usual charm in his voice. 'What? Why?'

A muscle in his cheek twitches. 'We've had a break-in.'

I blink. 'What?'

'Someone broke into our home last night. Dawn says there is quite a bit of damage. We need to make an assessment and tell the police what is missing.'

'I don't believe this.' I sit up. 'What about Dawn? What was she doing whilst burglars were running around the place?'

'She says she stayed with a friend last night. She returned in the morning to find the aftermath.'

Aftermath? 'How bad is it?'

'I can't be sure until I see it. Dawn tends to make things sound more dramatic than they are.'

My heart sinks. Somehow, I think it might be every bit as bad as Dawn says. Is it too much of a coincidence that there is a break-in the moment we leave her unattended in our home?

TWENTY-ONE

It's a shock when we get home and walk in through the front door. Our beautiful home has been violated.

There is broken glass and tipped over furniture. Each one of the dining chairs is in a different position.

Drawers are pulled out, and the contents are thrown everywhere. The pots of the statement plants are smashed, and soil and leaves are all over the tiled floor.

Later in the morning, I find the kitchen clock with bent and broken hands stuffed into a large drawer in the kitchen island. It's bizarre what the burglars have done.

The Jo Malone reed diffuser just last week has been launched at the concertina patio doors. The aroma of English pear and freesia is overpowering. Luckily, the doors themselves remain unbroken; they are made from toughened glass. Scott made sure of that when he chose them.

Wherever I look, there is something askew. There is mess everywhere, as though the apparent burglars tipped everything over they could see. Nothing much is missing, just minor things here and there of no real value. The whole house is reminiscent of the guest room Dawn is staying in.

Ironically, her room doesn't seem so untidy now, even though this space seems to have been hit the hardest by the intruders. Not one single drawer remains inside the units.

The empty vase of flowers has been smashed right against the wall, as has a compact printer.

'That's not mine,' she says quickly when my gaze falls upon it.

I ignore her and jot this item down on the ever-growing list of damaged and missing things.

Many of her garments are missing, her most expensive and beloved pieces, apparently. The remaining ones are ripped and torn in various places, rendering them useless.

She can't find one item that isn't ruined, apart from the clothes on her back. Even her underwear is destroyed. She fishes a lacy Agent Provocateur set out of the toilet and looks at it with disdain.

'An anniversary present from Scotty. Nice.' She drops into a bin bag along with many other things. If she had been travelling light before, I don't know what you would call this. She has been left with hardly anything.

When we finished putting the room back together, it looks much tidier than before the burglars arrived. That's something, I guess.

The fact that Dawn has taken a hit, too, surprises me. The master bedroom isn't too bad. My clothes, shoes, handbags and accessories are strewn everywhere, of course. On the other hand, nothing appears to be broken or ruined permanently.

You have to appreciate the small things in these situations, I guess. I'm so glad I had the presence of mind to take my wedding dress with me. It's still locked safely in the boot of the car.

Part of me was prepared to find the master bedroom in total disarray whilst Dawn's guest room was untouched.

If anything, it's the other way around. It's odd. I guess Dawn is smart. She obviously didn't want suspicion to fall on her as soon as Scott and I walked through the door. Maybe this is all a way to get Scott to buy her a new wardrobe while she is here.

Sure enough, she soon has her hand out for Scott's credit card once the initial clean up is finished upstairs.

He isn't keen on handing it over as he kicks some broken glass aside. 'I don't think so.'

'Don't get cheap on me, Scotty. I have nothing left to wear! What do you expect me to do?'

'I don't care,' he says coldly.

'Oh really? You won't mind if I take a little trip into the city then?'

'I think you've done enough, to be honest.'

She takes on a look of indignation and gestures around her. 'Do you think I did all this?'

We say nothing.

'I wasn't even here when this happened! I was at a friend's house.' Her fingers wander over the red mini-dress she wore last night. She still has it on, supposedly because of the chaos she hasn't had time to change. 'I came back in the morning to find the house like this. I couldn't make this much mess on my own.'

I look up at her. 'So you had help?'

'It wasn't me, you stupid cow!'

'Who was it, then?'

'Search me. I've no clue. Maybe Scotty does.' She rounds on her husband instead. 'He's always liked to splash the cash. What's the point of being rich if you don't rub it in everyone's face? If you ask me, he has brought this on himself. I've been an innocent victim.'

Scott and I both scoff.

'I have!' she insists. 'It would be a mistake if you blame me.'

I look around for the vacuum cleaner.

'Leave it,' Scott says. 'I'll get someone in. They can take care of this mess. I don't want you to have to deal with it.'

Dawn chuckles. 'No, we can't have Miss Perfect tarnishing her nails, can we? Not that it would matter,' she adds, looking at my natural, unpainted tips. They are a stark contrast to her highly manicured set.

'Come on, Sam,' Scott says, putting a hand on my back. 'We can hand the list to the police. I'll call in a cleaning team. We'll go back to the hotel whilst they work.'

I nod and follow him.

'I don't think so.'

We both turn back to look at Dawn.

'What now?' Scott asks.

'You two aren't going to leave me here. Not again. It gets awfully lonely in this house when you are alone, you know. That's why I had to seek company last night somewhere else.'

'You want us to stay?' I ask incredulously. It occurs to me that all this was a punishment for our abrupt departure. It worked. It brought us home. Now, it seems Dawn doesn't want us to leave.

She nods. 'Of course. I don't feel safe in this big house all alone. Look what happened when you did. You can't leave me again. I mean it.'

Dawn's eyes are manic as she says this, and I don't doubt her.

'Fine,' Scott eventually concedes with a sigh.

Dawn's smile widens, victorious. 'Thank you, Scotty. I knew you would come through for me. You did promise me in your vows all those years ago, after all. For better, for worse. Till death do us part.'

Scott turns his back on his wife and pulls out his phone.

It's hard to shake my unease as Scott contacts his trusty cleaning company and makes arrangements. I'd been looking forward to several days of freedom away from Dawn and her scheming.

As we wait for the cleaners, I can't help shaking the feeling that there is much more to this break-in than meets the eye.

TWENTY-TWO

The cleaning company is fast and efficient, so I can see why Scott uses them. They have our house put together and looking neat again by early evening. However, it will take a long time for the smell of the broken reed diffuser to fade.

The living room is one of the first areas to be finished. I pour myself a stiff drink and sit on the sofa with the television on.

The TV is wall-mounted, so it is supposedly rendered safe from burglars, had there been any genuine ones. Would thieves have taken the television? Are TVs valuable these days?

I'm tired. I don't know what to believe. Dawn is pretty convincing, but she is also pretty erratic. So, who knows?

My phone buzzes with a message from Sara.

How are things going up there? Are you two enjoying your stay at the spa hotel? So jealous, btw! I'm assuming you didn't unzip your suitcase to find a stowaway inside? Three's a crowd! xx

I smile grimly and text back an update on the latest happenings and the fact that they have cut our getaway short. Her reply comes back fast.

Oh my god! Do you think Dawn set the whole thing up?

I don't know, I text back. It looks that way. She had a printer too, which explains how she could produce that note.

Another message comes through.

Was anything of yours missing? xx

No. Just some cheap Primark jewellery and a few items of clothing. Nothing important xx

Sara asks, *What about documents? xx*

I realise what she is getting at.

No, nothing like that. I took all my paperwork with me on the trip. I worried Dawn might go snooping! It's all safe in a folder.

That's my girl! xx

I smile, then see another text from my friend.

The big day is coming up soon, isn't it? You said it was happening before you set off for the wedding. I know you have to have it sorted before you leave the country. Are you ready to face it again? xx

I make my phone screen black. Sara isn't talking about the wedding. She is talking about the person I must meet a few days before our trip to Greece. I'm not sure how to answer that one.

I take another sip of Coke, wishing it had something more substantial added. I glance over to the unattended bar in the far corner. I could slip in some vodka. No one would see it in the cola. I just need a little something to get me through this challenging day.

I grip the glass as temptation washes over me. It's intense. I haven't had a craving like that for years. Scott knows I don't drink. When I first told him, he seemed to instinctively understand why not. I've got over my addiction now after several years of being sober.

There was a slip after the Adam fallout, but I've recovered again. Gone are the days when I would start the day with a beer.

I got fired from one of my first teaching jobs when it was discovered I kept a bottle of whiskey in my handbag. My pathetic, inebriated self thought carrying one of those miniature bottles was genius. No one would notice if I took a tiny sip in a toilet cubicle at break and lunch times.

It turned out later my colleagues could smell it.

But that was ages ago. I'm recovered now and working at a whole new school. Alcohol isn't a problem for me these days. I'm so grateful to Scott for understanding without me having to tell him. It helps that he doesn't offer me a drink when the situation arises. He even tries to curb his own consumption around me most of the time.

The dinner party was different; we had guests. That was the first time I've seen Scott tipsy since we've been together.

Adam always gave me a hard time about the no-alcohol thing, nagging me about being "unsociable" and leaving him to drink alone. He drank himself silly often. It was hard to be around him and not be tempted. He had a bottle of vintage wine in the back of the cupboard; he told me he was saving it for a special occasion.

When I left him, I stashed it in my holdall. I only intended to deprive him of it, to punish him for his cheating and awful treatment of me. I wanted to throw it in a bin or tip it away somewhere.

I ended up downing the lot. That set me up for a colossal bingeing session. I was soon staggering to the supermarket every day for a while. It took me months to get myself back together after that.

Now, I stare at some property show without seeing it. I just put it on for the company. Scott is directing cleaners around the house, and Dawn has been wandering from room to room. She is now seated at the patio table with a chamomile tea.

I look back at Sara's message. *Are you ready to face it again?*

Am I ready? I don't know. I'd hoped that I'd never have to go and meet that person again. Once should have been enough. It would have been. But I was foolish. I've brought this upcoming meeting on myself.

Movement in the corner of my eye makes me think Dawn is coming to join me on the sofa as she did the other night. I quickly put my phone out of sight. Then I realise it's one of the cleaners.

'I found this upstairs. It's for you, I think.' She hands me an envelope and exits the room again.

'Oh, thanks.' I take the envelope from her and stare at it. It looks just like the one that Dawn left for me on the doormat the other day.

'Wait!' I catch up with the cleaner in the dining room. 'Where exactly did you find this?'

She gestures with one palm flat over the other. She doesn't seem to speak English very well. 'Under your pillow.'

She nods. I thank her again as she heads back upstairs.

I tear the envelope open and stare at the card. It bears another neatly printed message.

You were warned. Don't try to hide from me.

When I glance up through the patio doors, I realise Dawn has turned from her drink to watch me open the envelope closely. Our eyes meet. A smirk plays at the corner of her full lips.

I make a big show of animatedly tearing up the note and throwing it in the bin.

This was a well-planned chain of events. She had the note printed before she smashed her printer. Clever. Does she think that absolves her from suspicion? It certainly doesn't in my eyes.

How many more of these delightful little messages has she got prepared? Perhaps she even has different options based on what she thinks Scott and I might do next.

The thought is chilling. It makes me wonder what she is planning to do to us.

I shiver. All I wanted was to be married and live happily ever after.

Is that so much to ask?

TWENTY-THREE

'I need your car.'

Nothing can prepare me for the fact that Dawn is standing over me as I wake in bed a few days later. I'm barely conscious as I open my eyes. 'Excuse me?'

'Your car. I need to borrow it. Where do you keep your keys? I can't find them.'

I blink and plunge my arms under the duvet when I realise this isn't a nightmare. Not in the true sense anyway, just a waking one I can't seem to shake.

The light is quite dim in here as the curtains are still drawn. Brilliant sunlight beams against them. How much did Dawn see?

Has she seen my scars? They are on display in the short-sleeved t-shirt I sleep in. Crushing embarrassment grips my insides at the thought.

'Get out!' I shout at Dawn.

'That's not polite, now is it, Sam?'

I look at my fiancé's half of the bed, but it is empty. 'Where is Scott?'

Dawn shrugs. 'He left. Had some business to take care of, apparently. He said he would be back this afternoon.'

'You shouldn't be in here,' I say as I scramble into a seated position against the headboard, pulling the duvet up with me.

'I don't want to be, trust me.' She crosses her arms across her chest. 'I have some errands to run, and I need your car for the day. Scott has taken his to work, unfortunately. Trust me, I'd prefer cruising around in a Jaguar than what you have parked on the driveway.'

I feel a stab of annoyance over this. Scott offered me a more luxurious vehicle, but I turned him down, even when he took me around various showrooms. I'm quite attached to my little car. It is trusty and just the right size for me. And then there's the fuel economy.

There is no way I'm letting Dawn in it alone. What state would it be in when she got back? Would it come back at all?

Now I notice what Dawn is wearing—one of my favourite tops; a navy long-sleeved one. The first thing she has done is pull the sleeves up. Is that because she is hot? Or is she trying to prove a point to me that she is free to wear what she wants without fear? If only I could do the same.

She has paired this with some denim shorts. They have a rough hem cut above mid-thigh. I don't remember seeing these in the tiny pile of clothes she managed to salvage yesterday. The button bears the words "Next Jeans".

That's unusual for Dawn. She would never

touch a high street label. Did Scott get cheap on her after all? I've no recollection of him handing his credit card over in the end.

I get a spark of recognition as I stare at her unusual garment choice. The shade of denim and the fixings look familiar, just like my favourite pair of jeans—exactly like my favourite pair of jeans.

Dawn has turned them into shorts, I realise. When did she even take them? Has she made her mods this morning while I was sleeping?

I groan in fury. 'You've ruined my favourite jeans! I needed those today.'

I have to go and meet the figure I've been hating most of my adult life. I could have done with the confidence boost today. They are my lucky pair.

Is this an omen? I'm going to fail when I meet them later. Again.

Dawn moves over to the curtains and pulls them open, flooding the room with light, and looks down at her outfit nonchalantly.

She seems no more harassed than if she was in a fitting room somewhere, pulling back the curtain to show her friend what she is planning to buy from a trendy boutique.

'Not ruined,' she says. 'I've improved them. Not that I had much to work with. Honestly, I don't know how you can walk around the place wearing the things you do. It's like Scott has lost his head when it comes to you. He knows about fashion too, so I can't imagine why. Has he not said anything to you about your atrocious wardrobe choices?'

I grimace. 'The only thing unpleasant is your attitude! You can't treat people like this. Please leave my bedroom.'

'It's not your bedroom. And I can, and will treat you how I like. Now tell me where you keep your car keys, and I will leave you in peace for the day—well, most of it, anyway.'

'You can't have my car. I told you, I have somewhere to be.'

My insides squirm at the thought of my secret meeting today. I would have been happy to carry on sleeping. I could have spent this extra time in slumber, not dreading what I have to do later. I feel queasy.

'We can have a girl's outing, then' Dawn retorts. 'What fun! We can carpool. You tell me where you want to be dropped off. I can't promise I will be able to give you a ride home, though, so you will likely have to make your own way home.'

'No.' I push myself up higher against the statement headboard. It's one of those tall, fixed-to-the-wall kinds. 'I have somewhere important to go. I'm sorry, but you can't have my car.'

Dawn looks sulky. 'Then I'm sorry, Sam. You can't have your wedding. What's so important anyway? Is it worth costing you your dream ceremony in the sun?'

As a matter of fact, it is, but I don't tell Dawn this. I don't tell her I've been anticipating this day for so many years. It's been a long wait. Nor have I mentioned it to Scott or any of my exes, not even Adam. So I can't let anything slip. Only Sara knows my secret. It's safe with her.

Maybe I should have told Scott? Can I make such a revelation, when I am so deep in lies? If I told him the truth, would he turn his back on me for lying all this time?

I don't give Dawn any nuggets. Instead, I throw caution to the wind. 'You'll have to make your own way to wherever you want to go. You can use Scott's driver. I'll leave you the number once I've got showered and dressed. Wait downstairs.'

Dawn looks as though I've just hit her. 'I'm the one calling the shots, remember? Do you think you are going to order me around?'

'Not at all,' I say calmly, even though I'm anything but. I'm hoping Dawn will cooperate. 'I'm asking you nicely. You can't use my car, so please wait downstairs.'

She stays rooted to the plush carpet at the foot of the king-sized bed, crossing her arms in defiance.

My heart pounds with the thought of what I am about to do. I might be sick.

'Fine,' I say.

I yank back the duvet cover and swing my legs out of bed. I'm well aware of Dawn's look of shock as she stares at my arms, which are laid bare in the morning light. I storm past her to select my second favourite pair of jeans and the second smartest top I own from the walk-in wardrobe. Instead of what I had in mind, it's going to have to be a floral blouse and black denim.

No big deal, I tell myself.

Dawn says nothing. It's evident from her silence that her thoughts are racing as she stares at my scars with a kind of horrified relish. I breeze past her and shut the ensuite bathroom door on her horrorstruck expression.

On the other side, I pull the lock across firmly and almost collapse, shaking on the floor.

Today is the day I've been waiting for for so long.

It's my day of judgement—the one where I meet a person who will decide the fate of the rest of my life. For everyone's sake, I hope I don't fail again.

TWENTY-FOUR

The effect of revealing my arms to Dawn has the outcome I hoped for.

She was stunned into silence. I had braced myself for an insult, a scathing remark, or, at the very least, questions like the kind Adam fired at me.

None came, however. She is gone by the time I step out of the shower and back into the bedroom. She isn't downstairs when I head down for breakfast, either. For a panicked second, I think she has perhaps discovered my hiding place for my keys and taken my car anyway. It's still out on the driveway when I take a peek, so that's not it.

I presume she is up in her room. Not that I want to find out. I've got bigger fish to fry today.

As per my routine, I start making something for breakfast. I find myself flitting from preparing toast, then a smoothie. In the end, I leave it. My squirming stomach surely can't tolerate food anyway.

I jog back upstairs. The reflection in the walk-in wardrobe mirror doesn't look too bad.

I look like a reasonably-together woman. That's what they are looking for, right?

I've been imagining this day for so long. Every time I have, I've been wearing the outfit that Dawn has snatched for herself. There is no way she could have known this, but it doesn't help my self-confidence.

I find my folder of documents under a pile of clothes, just where I left it. Hopefully, Dawn didn't rummage too far when looking for things to take this morning. I shiver at the thought of her in my bedroom while I was asleep.

Inside the folder is evidence of the sensible woman I'm playing the part of—except that I've been immersed in the role for so long that I've become her.

I sit on the bed and do a last check of the paperwork before I leave. There is a stack of employment references from the various schools I have worked at. My start and end dates are included, along with glowing written references.

There isn't an end date at my current school, Ridgewood Primary. It's my longest post, and I can't imagine leaving it. The kids are wonderful, and the staff friendly. I don't care what Dawn said; I would send my children there, if I had any. She caught me off-guard at the dinner party, that was all.

I flip through more pages. There is a doctor's note specifying they have no concerns about my drinking. This is backed up by evidence of rehabilitation from the addiction program I completed. It's been years since I've had a problem with alcohol, I'm proud to say. I had a minor blip after the debacle with Adam, but it was only very brief. I've come such a long way in the last ten years.

My bank statements back this up. No visits to off-licences. One hundred per cent wholesome, stable spending. Evidence of being a sensible human being. That's what I am being assessed for, to prove myself worthy of receiving what should have been mine years ago.

Sara provides a glowing character reference. I've included my address in my cover letter. Moving into a house worth well over a million with Scott has surely helped my case for stability immensely. One look at Street View speaks volumes to anyone who looks.

It's all here. I take a deep breath. There is nothing more to do than to head off for my meeting.

I'm so nervous. The last time I did this, I was twenty-five and far worse off than I was when I was evaluated at twenty-one.

I was a party animal as a teenager, reckless. Seven years later, I was just a wreck.

I was an alcoholic, couldn't keep a job down and had no direction in my life. Sara tried to help me. However, there was only so much she could do when I was avoiding her. I knew she was the only good thing in my life, so I pushed her away.

It took me years to get back on track once I finally accepted her help.

I'll never take my best friend for granted. If all goes well today, she is at the top of my list of people to help. She deserves it. Aside from being my best friend, I feel I owe her, after all her hard work, for dragging me back onto the rails and keeping me there long enough to realise she was right.

I stand up. I'm ready.

TWENTY-FIVE

By the time I get to the office in Manchester, I am a nervous wreck. I haven't been like this for years. In the waiting room, I do some deep breathing. Just the way my therapist in Bournemouth showed me. It's been years since Sara talked me into seeing one, but I still remember the techniques.

It works a little. Or maybe it just distracts me from my butterflies and sweating palms as I clutch my folder.

Finally, the receptionist tells me I can see Mr Silverman now. It's a man dealing with my case, just like in Bournemouth.

When my last remaining relative, Uncle Derek, died, my case was passed onto a new company in Manchester.

Is that a good thing? I wouldn't say I liked the man Uncle Derek had instructed at the Bournemouth trust. His name was Richard. In fact, I spent years hating him for his decision to defer this day. At twenty-one he turned me down. The second time I saw Richard was when I was twenty-five, still in a state and convinced

I couldn't be denied what was rightfully mine again.

I was wrong. After assessing the state of my life that time around, he added ten extra years of waiting. That sentence seemed like forever when I was twenty-five.

I'd also directed my resentment towards Uncle Derek, by not talking to him. Not that we were ever close in the first place. He refused to take me in after my parents died, didn't want his bachelor lifestyle ruined, probably. I regret not making more effort to bond now that he is gone. Everyone does, don't they? He died just before Christmas last year.

I'm sure Derek would have loved to have met Scott and seen how happy he has made me. But it wasn't to be. The timing was off by a month or so.

'There will be a new assessment, ready for your thirty-fifth birthday,' Richard had said years ago as I'd sat in his office fuming, my eyes boring holes into his. It didn't help that I'd been on a massive bender the night before. I was still drunk in the morning. The thought makes me cringe.

I'll officially make the turn into my mid-thirties shortly. As long as Dawn doesn't derail everything, I'll be on my honeymoon.

What will Scott say when he learns the truth? He will eventually, of course. Most people would be happy, but I'm not sure how my husband-to-be might react. I have the impression he likes to think he is a white knight rescuing me from my life of near poverty.

How will he react when he realises I'm far wealthier than he is?

Will he be annoyed with me for keeping this part of myself hidden? Maybe I won't tell him at all. It's not like Scott needs the money. I've lived as an adult without much. I'm pretty used to it.

Sara could benefit the most from the windfall. She could get Patricia the best help money could buy. Or she could convert her house with a granny wing or something to make life easier.

The last thing I need to do is start spending this money in my head. I've made that mistake before, and it just makes the disappointment all the more crushing if I were to get another 'No'.

I've got a good feeling about today, however. How can I be turned down again? My life is in order and has been for a while. My father's money has to be mine today. My inheritance, which I've waited for all these years, surely can't be deferred any longer.

When would the next assessment be set for if it was? When I'm fifty? Again that seems an unimaginable milestone at my age. Even forty sounds scary.

As I enter the room and shut the door behind me, the man dealing with my case introduces himself as Jonathan. I'm initially shocked by how young he is. I'm not used to being in this seat opposite someone my junior. Richard was a grey-haired almost fatherly figure. I hated him and eventually came to realise he was right—just like with real parents.

This man stands up from his desk as I walk in. 'Miss Samantha Thorpe?'

'Yes, but please just call me Sam.'

'Okay, Sam. I'm Jonathan,' he smiles stiffly as he shakes my hand. 'It's nice to meet you. I'm the trust administrator for the late Mr Stephen Golding's estate.'

The greeting is cursory. Said a hundred times or more over in this room, I imagine.

Jonathan wears a grey suit and checkered shirt. His tie is a plain, smooth, satin one, similar to the ones Scott wears.

Richard was old school, with patterned ties and shoulder pads. In a funny way, I miss that. It's a shame I'm not visiting him today. Before Uncle Derek died, he passed on the responsibility to a new trust firm, one more local, as he knew I had moved my life to another part of the country years ago.

Perhaps he thought Richard had seen too much of me. He had seen me at my very worst, after all. But I've genuinely turned my life around. I'd have liked Richard to have seen that.

Jonathan takes his seat at his desk again and looks through my folder. He nods and mutters as he reads each page, shuffling through the paperwork like an ASMR video.

He checks my passport and driving licence against my change of name deed. My name is Samantha Thorpe these days. Not Holly Golding.

He makes notes here and there on the extensive form he has to fill in. My mind drifts to home, wondering what Dawn might be doing now. Did she call the chauffeur company? Or has she taken the opportunity to enjoy the house while everyone else is away?

I've taken my wedding dress with me on this outing. It's locked safely in the boot of my car. I hope all this travelling around doesn't crease it up too much. I must remember to pack a garment steamer for Greece.

'Well, Sam,' Jonathan says at last, interrupting my thoughts. 'Everything looks to be in order here. Your employment verification is great. I'm happy with your bank statements and satisfied you are over your drinking problem. Your references are glowing. It all paints a picture of a well-established individual. I have no qualms about signing this off today.'

'That's it?' I blurt out more bluntly than I had hoped. 'I can have the money now?'

He smiles. 'Indeed, as stipulated in the trust document, the balance of just over one-point-one million pounds will be transferred to your nominated bank account on your thirty-fifth birthday.' He checks my passport. 'That falls on the fifteenth of June, so you should receive those funds either on that date, or within several working days. It should be quite a birthday present.'

'Yes.' I blink, letting myself process the news. 'I'll be on my honeymoon.'

'Oh, how wonderful. A double celebration. Your fiancé will be happy.'

I nod politely, not wanting to admit that he is oblivious. Scott thinks I'm a teaching assistant with hardly anything to my name. He has been happy to accept me as I am, scars and all. I'm not sure how to go about altering this image. We are happy as we are.

Maybe I shouldn't tell him at all? The thought seems appealing right now. Everything needs to be perfect on my wedding day. I won't allow anything to jeopardise it.

TWENTY-SIX

As I drive home, the weight of everything gets to me. My face screws up against my will a few times on the journey.

I had thought today was just a matter of money. Form filling and assessments. But it's more than that, isn't it? That money symbolises everything that happened all those years ago. I was just sixteen when my parents died in the horrific manner they did.

Should I have told Scott that? Probably. Instead, he thinks my parents were neglectful. Drug users, probably. He believes this is the reason I spent my teens in foster homes and why I am so cool about inviting them to the wedding. My fiancé hasn't pried. He is so respectful, letting me reveal parts of myself to him gradually when I feel ready.

I'm not sure when I will be able to tell him the truth—that my name isn't really Samantha; it's Holly. No one has called me that for years. I'm much more used to Sam.

Holly has bad connotations.

What happened when I was sixteen made

me hate my name, my own identity. Seeing that name again on the paperwork forced me to admit I was the girl it all happened to. It's almost too much to bear.

So I'm more than happy to be Sam, the teaching assistant. Not Holly, the girl splashed all over the national papers for months, even years. The press loved my story. They were fascinated by it.

I'm a grown woman, and I've left all that behind. My hair is short, cropped around my shoulders, and does not flow down my back as it did then. I keep my head down, away from the public eye. You won't find me on social media.

Most importantly, I keep my scars hidden. The proof of what happened that day was marked on my body forever.

Pulling the car up the driveway, I check my reflection in the mirror. I grab a tissue and clean up the smudged mascara.

When I enter the house, I find Scott and Dawn in the living room together. They are on opposite ends of the corner sofa. The atmosphere is palpable. Something I can't identify hangs in it. Scott is nursing a tumbler of whiskey.

Has Dawn dispensed punishments for my refusal to let her use my vehicle?

'Hey you,' Scott says as he reaches out for my hand. I join him on the sofa. He kisses me on the cheek and slides his arm around me. It's comforting after the day I've had. It would be wonderful to lean into him and forget all about today, but I'm too aware that Dawn keeps an eye on us, a muscle in her cheek twitching.

Her gaze keeps moving down to the long sleeves of my floral blouse. She hasn't forgotten about my scars. Is she about to fire questions at me? Has she interrogated Scott about them whilst I was out?

Even though I anticipate her bringing up the subject now, she doesn't.

The TV is on in the background, and A Place in the Sun is wittering on. I can't concentrate on it.

'Did you have a nice day?' Scott asks me when Dawn gets up to make herself a cup of tea.

I shrug. 'It was okay.'

'You said something about having an errand to run.'

'Yes, I did.' Versions of the truth come to me in various forms. I am bursting to tell Scott, but I'm not sure how to approach it. With Dawn in the other room is not the right moment, even though this would be perfect timing.

He strokes my upper arm. 'Anything interesting?'

I shrug. 'No. Just last-minute stuff before we leave the country. Boring.'

'Wedding stuff?'

'Yes, that kind of thing.'

He gives me a playful nudge. 'That's not boring!'

I smile and bite my lip. Scott deserves to know the truth. Maybe I can tell him once we jet off and are truly alone. How about on the plane?

Dawn returns and hovers a cup of tea in front of my face. My muscles tense, thinking she is about to launch the scalding drink at me. Then I realise she is proffering it politely.

Okay, not politely. But she is handing it to me. 'Do you want it or not?'

'Oh, thanks,' I say as I take the hot cup. I look down at the amber liquid suspiciously, wondering what it is laced with.

The kitchen is on the other side of the living room wall. Dawn could have slipped all sorts into it without me knowing. I wonder what she plumped for. Laxatives, maybe? That's a classic. Or something more exotic?

Scott's ex notices I haven't taken a sip after a while. Hers is almost finished. She nods at the cup in my hands. 'I haven't poisoned yours, you know.'

'That's reassuring,' I say sarcastically, wondering why on earth Dawn took it upon herself to make me a drink.

Scott's phone buzzes in his pocket, right next to my hip. I lean forward so he can pull it out.

I catch sight of a handsome older couple on the screen. It's an incoming video call.

'Aren't those your parents?' I ask him, recognising them from the photos he has shown me.

He looks at the screen in surprise. 'Yes,' he says slowly. 'I wasn't expecting them to get in touch until the wedding...'

'Oh,' Dawn says. 'I may have given them a little call yesterday, Scotty. Sorry,' she adds quickly.

'Sorry for what?' Scott asks, baffled as his wife hastily leaves the room. 'How did you get their number?'

Dawn disappears into the kitchen with her tea, gazing over her shoulder as she goes.

I turn to Scott. 'How strange. She did look genuinely mortified. What is she sorry for?'

He shrugs, staring at the screen in confusion.

'Aren't you going to answer it?' I ask him with a nudge. 'You can't ignore your parents.'

'Er...I guess so.' Scott withdraws his hand from my shoulders and sits stiffly in his seat as he answers the video call. 'Hi, Mum. Hi, Dad.' He smiles with an air of slight trepidation. 'How're things?'

He seems a little formal, I think. I've never seen him interact with a family member before. He is an only child. His parents are his only relations, and they are always exploring exotic climes. This is the first time I've seen them in something other than a static image.

They are just as gorgeous as in their glossy snaps. As stunning as their photos are, it would have been nice to have some of them from their younger years perhaps. Most shots seem to be from the last decade or so.

I've moved along the sofa to be out of shot and place my tea down on the coffee table, not sure I can trust it. I suppose Scott will introduce me to his mum and dad in a moment instead of at the wedding as planned; I mentally prepare myself.

It looks gloriously sunny where they are in Egypt. I wonder which part they are in. From the backdrop of beige stone and bright blue sky, it's not obvious. I'm assuming the pyramids, but it could be any region from the limited backdrop.

His mother is well-spoken. She has the same accent as her son.

'Hello, Darling,' Katherine drawls. 'We're quite well, thank you. Oh, how your father and I have missed you!'

'I've missed you too, Mum. And you, Dad. To what do I owe this surprise call so soon before the wedding?'

Marty nods beside his wife, squinting in the bright sunlight. 'That's what we want to talk to you about, my boy. We won't be able to attend the wedding, after all.'

Scott's shoulders visibly slump. 'Oh.' He sounds devastated. 'Why not?'

'We are getting divorced.'

Scott blinks. 'What?'

'I think you heard us, dear,' Scott's mother

continues. 'We are separating. It's been in the pipeline for a while. It wouldn't be appropriate for us to attend the wedding and pretend everything is hunky-dory. We need time to work things out between us now that we have admitted our marriage is over.'

Scott shakes his head as he processes this fact. He looks knocked for six. I want to comfort him. I reach out and squeeze his knee gently, out of shot.

'Marriages don't always work out,' his mother drawls while her husband nods beside her. 'That's something to bear in mind, dear.'

Scott raises his eyebrows at the screen incredulously. 'That's your advice, is it?' he says shortly. 'Five days until my wedding, and that is what you are telling me?'

'It's not your first wedding, though, is it? You must know things don't always pan out as planned.'

'Thanks for that wonderful nugget, Mother. I'll think of you when I'm standing at the altar.'

She laughs nervously, raising a hand to shield her eyes from the sun. It looks like late afternoon there. They also enjoy the glorious sunshine that has beamed down on the UK all day. It's a wonderful summer weather-wise if you like the heat.

'I'm just preparing you, Scott dear. You have done the whole marriage thing before, and yet you are rushing through a divorce. I'm sad to hear it, too. I liked Dawn. She was always my favourite of all your partners. I can't judge whether you will be happier with this...um.'

'Sam,' Scott prompts her impatiently. He shakes his head angrily.

'Sam, that's right. She sounds like a nice lady, but don't you think you have been a bit hasty, giving Dawn the old heave-ho? I'm not sure you have given your marriage a chance. Eleven years, Scott. That's not something to be sniffed at. Maybe you should try couples therapy?'

I withdraw my hand from Scott's knee. His parents want him to give Dawn another chance. What on earth did Dawn say to them when she called them? Also, how could she get their number if Scott didn't provide it?

'That's enough, Mother,' Scott says quickly. 'You and Father have been married for much more than eleven years, and you are bringing things to an end, apparently. Maybe when you know something is right then it is. I won't be reconsidering Dawn, that's for sure. You haven't seen her behaviour this past week or so. Did she happen to tell you she has moved in with my fiancé and me?'

Scott's mother looks uncertain now. 'Let me think...I don't believe she mentioned it.'

I bet she didn't, I think bitterly. I wonder if it was Dawn's idea for the couple to call us this afternoon and share their news. Did they take the advice of their favourite of Scott's partners and decide they wouldn't attend the wedding together?

It's too much of a coincidence that Dawn called them yesterday, and they won't be there for the big day. This is her doing.

Scott seems devastated. Another score for Dawn.

Even she looked ashamed of what she had done as she scurried from the room just now. I hope she doesn't have any other tricks up her sleeve.

TWENTY-SEVEN

In bed later that night, I move closer to Scott. There is a heavy energy coming from him. It's palpable in his breathing and the air between us. His body remains tense as I wrap my arms around his neck and kiss him.

I've never seen him sad before. He is always looking to the future, upbeat and enthusiastic.

Now, he stares at the ceiling, lacking his usual energy. He looks troubled, even. His parents' bombshell has evidently hit him hard.

'Are you okay?' I ask him as I trace circles on his chest.

He nods stiffly. 'Fine.'

'It's probably a bit of a shock that your parents are splitting up. How long have they been married?'

Scott looks blank as he slides his hand beneath his head. 'I don't know. They've always been together as far as I can remember. It's just one of those things you take for granted.'

'I know what you mean,' I say quietly. 'It shatters your world when the foundations move, doesn't it?'

He tears himself from his trance-like stare at the ceiling. 'Are you ready to tell me what happened with your parents? I'm guessing there is a good reason why they didn't RSVP the wedding?'

My heart hammers. Is this the moment I tell Scott the truth about my mum and dad when he is reeling from his own personal devastation?

I nod. I'm still not sure where to start. Maybe at the beginning, I suppose. 'My father cheated on my mother quite a bit. He used to take these work trips all the time. Dad attracted a lot of attention wherever he went. He would pick up women along the way. A different one each time, by the sound of their rows.'

'That's terrible. No child should have to hear that.' Scott pulls me closer to his chest.

'I know. Their rows got bad sometimes.'

He pauses. 'Were they violent?'

'Sometimes.' I swallow. 'The worst one was when Dad found out my mother had met someone else. He didn't like the taste of his own medicine.'

'What happened?'

I clear my throat but can't seem to find the words. I shake my head and my fiancé seems to understand.

'Is that why they aren't coming to the wedding?' Scott asks softly after a few moments. His voice is so gentle. 'Are they not together any longer?'

They're dead. The wedding invites you saw me write out? I shredded and binned them. I don't have the siblings I invented either.

No, I can't say that. Not at this moment. Scott is too open and understanding. He has been knocked down this evening. He doesn't want to hear that I have lied to him about something important. Why did I decide to invent siblings, too? I just wanted to sound like someone else. I'm so used to playing the role of someone normal. I liked it so much. It was easier than admitting the truth.

When I ran into Scott in that coffee shop on that fateful day, I never imagined that our relationship would be a whirlwind romance that would lead to marriage. I'd have done it all differently if I had known this wasn't just a passing fling. Now I'm up to my neck in lies, and I don't see a way out—not without tainting our perfect synergy.

So I simply nod. 'Yes. That's right. They aren't together.'

I'll find another time to tell Scott the truth about my past. A time when he isn't reeling from his parent's revelation might be a good opportunity. It doesn't seem right tonight.

Another time. A better moment.

Yeah, right. I'm such a coward.

TWENTY-EIGHT

I can't explain it, but there seems to be something of a wedge between Scott and me after last night. After our cuddle, my fiance kissed me briefly goodnight and rolled over to sleep.

I'm sure it was long after midnight when I heard his breathing signify he had slipped into the oblivion of slumber. I stayed awake a little longer, pondering what Dawn had done and what it meant for our wedding day.

This morning I wake tired and not in a good way. Today was supposed to be the day we were leaving for Greece, hand-in-hand and excited about our impending wedding. The decree absolute still hasn't come through. Scott has said we should leave as late as possible to give the thing a chance to arrive so we know whether to go ahead with the legal side or just the ceremony.

He stirs now as I get out of bed. I want to do something special for him. Breakfast in bed would be nice. It would also keep us out of Dawn's way. She can have the run of the kitchen while Scott and I enjoy our food in peace.

As I head downstairs, I see the postman has been. I bundle up the various envelopes and plan to take them up with me once I've prepared Scott a tray of bagels, fruit, eggs, and coffee.

As I'm poaching eggs, I glance over at the pile of post. One envelope looks all too familiar.

I take it out and stare at it. It looks like the other notes, but this one has a stamp on it and our address. This one was mailed, not hand delivered. There is no addressee again.

I tear it open and reveal another card, just like the others.

The type on this one reads: *You were warned.*

I shake my head, tear the thing up, and drop it in the bin. This is the last thing Scott needs. Dawn has worn us both down with her antics. I will keep this one a secret, as I did the last one. Just a few more days. Then, we will know where we stand.

The wording of the message doesn't leave me, however. *You were warned.* Is that what the tense atmosphere was about yesterday when I came home and found Dawn and Scott in the lounge? Had she delivered that same warning to her ex in person?

I try and brighten my face as I carry a tray of food up to the master bedroom. There is no sign of Dawn on the way, which can only be a good thing.

Scott looks sleepy before he turns over and spots me.

'This looks amazing,' he says, cheering and sitting up in anticipation. 'I don't deserve you.'

His eyes look sombre for a moment as this sentiment hangs in the air.

'Yes, you do.' I smile as he goes straight for the fresh coffee. Black, no sugar.

I open the curtains with a mouthful of bagel as Scott starts tearing open letters. The sun has risen and is blazing in a cloudless sky. It's another hot day. I wonder what the weather would have been like in Greece had we flown there today.

I stare at the sun-drenched car park. Someone should water the flowers in the neat border.

'Scott,' I say tentatively. It's hard to say this, so I continue to stare out of the window. 'Do you think we should think about postponing the wedding?'

'What?'

'After what happened yesterday with your parents, it made me think. Maybe we should postpone it. That way, your mum and dad can get on with their split. Maybe we can all meet before the wedding if we set a later date? It might change their opinion of me if I'm not a stranger to them. They seem to favour Dawn...'

Scott has gone quiet. I chance a glance in his direction and see that he is smiling. He has the widest grin I have seen on his handsome face for a while.

'What is it?'

'We won't be postponing anything, Sam. Look!'

He shakes the piece of paper in his hand in triumph. It's important-looking with an official logo in the corner.

My heart flutters excitedly. 'Is that what I think it is?'

'Yes!' he grins. 'The decree absolute. Henry came through for us. The divorce is finalised. We can have our wedding just as we planned.'

I rush over and hug him. His body is still warm from sleep. 'That's it? It's over?'

'Absolutely.'

'So Dawn can't stop the wedding?'

'No. There's nothing she can do. Even if she physically grabs hold of your dress and stops you going down the aisle, she legally hasn't got a leg to stand on.'

This image troubles me. I'm quite protective over my dress. 'I wouldn't put it past Dawn.'

'I was joking!' he beams. It couldn't be more obvious that a massive weight has been lifted from him. 'Don't worry about Dawn anymore. She is officially in my past, I'm pleased to say.'

Dawn is not too happy to be told words to this effect later on. She looks blank as Scott tells her he received the final piece of paper that rids him of her. He seems to relish delivering this news. I don't blame him after his ex-wife's behaviour this past week or so. I personally wouldn't have made my glee so obvious.

She may be a nightmare, but she still has feelings. I think so anyway—somewhere deep down. Maybe.

I'm busy moving around the house and gathering up my things to pack for Greece. At one point, though, when I spot Dawn looking uncharacteristically pale, I make a cup of sweet tea and leave it on the coffee table in front of her.

I hope she isn't reacting badly to this news. I have sudden visions of her doing something stupid.

Afterwards, she hurries upstairs and shuts herself in her room. Her tea is untouched. At least there wasn't shouting. All is quiet. Perhaps too much so. Had I imagined the look on her face? Did it look like she was almost in tears?

When I'm satisfied I've finished packing, Dawn still has not emerged from her room. I hate to admit it, but I'm getting worried about her.

'Do you think she is all right?' I ask Scott as he packs socks and underwear into his own case.

'What, Dawn? I'm sure she's fine. I thought she took it quite well. Her little game is over. You should be pleased.'

'I am. Of course, I am. Dawn has just gone a bit quiet for my liking.'

Scott shrugs. 'Quiet is good. Much better than before when she was walking all over us, don't you think? I would enjoy it if I were you.'

'I guess.'

Scott is trying to decide which shirts to bring when I slip along the landing to the guest room.

I knock on the door. 'Dawn?'

There is no response. I know she is in there, however, so I try again.

Still nothing. I push the door open tentatively.

I'm surprised when I see what Dawn is doing. Her suitcase is on the bed as she finishes zipping it up.

The room is in order. The bed is neatly made. Other than a single suitcase, there is no other trace of her in the room. It's just how it was before she arrived.

'Going somewhere?' I ask her as she straightens up and turns to me in surprise.

Her eyes are watery. She shrugs. 'No point hanging around here. Scott says Henry will be in touch about the money from the divorce. Don't worry, it will be hardly anything. Scott won't have to sell the house. This will be your love nest for as long as you want, I suppose.'

'Where will you go?'

'I'm going back to my flat. The landlady hasn't found anyone else yet. The place was never ideal, being on the outskirts and all, but it's cheap.'

'The area isn't bad. I lived a few streets away from your flat for years before I moved in with Scott.'

Dawn continues to look gloomy. Her usual energy and drive is gone. She seems defeated on so many levels. I don't know what to say to comfort her. It's hard to feel sorry for her after everything she has done, but I would like to see some of her usual sparkle before we say goodbye forever.

'You don't need to say anything else, Sam. You've won. Scott is yours til death do you part. You don't have to gloat.'

'I'm not gloating,' I say quickly. 'Of course I'm not. Look, I'm a nice person. I didn't want a battle on my hands this whole time. Scott told me he was single. How was I to know otherwise? You didn't have to make this so hard for everyone.'

'I know. I'm sorry.'

I stare at her. There does seem to be genuine remorse playing around her neat features, just as there had been last night before the video call from Scott's parents. But why? Why didn't she have this thought sooner? The run-up to my wedding day would have been less of a nightmare.

'Are you going to be okay?' I find myself asking.

She groans. 'Is there anything more patronising than the other woman taking pity on the usurped wife?'

'I'm not trying to patronise you, I promise. And I'm certainly not the other woman. I just want to check to see if you are going to be fine once you've left here. That's all.'

She nods, although I think I can see tears forming in her eyes again. 'Don't worry about me, Sam. It's almost time for your wedding. I hope you have a wonderful day. You deserve to enjoy it.'

She moves closer to me suddenly. For a split second, I think this has all been a ruse that allowed her to get close enough to strangle me. Then I realise she is pulling me into a hug.

She gives me a squeeze that is almost comforting. 'All the best for Greece, babes. I hope your marriage to Scott makes you happier than mine did. I really do.'

TWENTY-NINE

Dawn leaves the house before our hired driver loads our suitcases into his car. My last encounter with her left me baffled as I watch her get into an Uber.

She didn't say goodbye to Scott at all. I suppose they will interact in the future, even if it is just through their solicitors to sort out the final financial settlement. By all accounts, it won't be much.

Scott assured me he wouldn't have to sell the house, which is just as well, really, as I've become quite attached to it.

This place is big and modern, not like the house my father had chosen to raise his family in. That was a traditional country estate by the sea, much larger and so far from the nearest neighbour that we rarely saw them.

My parent's house, in real terms, would easily be worth four times as much as Scott's abode. The trust fund money hasn't exactly enjoyed the same amount of inflation as other properties all these years. Still, my long-awaited inheritance is nothing to be sniffed at. It had my father's life insurance, personal assets and the value of the insurance covering the house.

I miss my childhood home sometimes. It had acres of wooded land I explored as a child and overlooked the sea. The views were stunning.

My bedroom windows let in the salty sea air as I played on the plush carpet with my Barbie dolls. I would spend hours staring out at the rolling waves, imagining what creatures were lurking beneath the surface.

My home now is much different. It's modern, white, and grey, far removed from the nineties pastels my mother decorated my childhood home with. It's a relief. If the two buildings were too similar, I might not be able to stand living with Scott in his luxury home.

*

On the plane now, Scott grips my hand. I'm nervous about flying. It's hard for my mind not to picture a million ways this metallic beast could turn into a fireball.

Death by fire is a horrible way to go. I know how awful it felt when flames reached out that day and scarred me for life. I have Dad to thank for that. He was the one who started the blaze that engulfed our happy home. Not before he shot and killed my mother and baby brother, of course.

I'll never forget how he turned into a deadly consuming monster that day. All because he had discovered that Mum had pulled a stunt like his and slept with someone else. Dad was beside himself that day. He was possessed.

'You okay?' Scott asks me now as the engines roar to life.

I nod. 'Absolutely. Never better.'

He grins. 'It's happening, Sam. We're going to be married. Can you believe it?'

'I can't wait.'

THIRTY

We don't die, after all. The plane touches down at Santorini International Airport, and we are fine.

The island is beautiful. We check into our hotel in Imerovigli, the most picturesque village I've ever seen. With its winding staircases and blue ornate doors, I might as well have slipped down the rabbit hole and wandered through Wonderland.

Scott tells me it's the prettiest part of Greece. He has been many times. This is my first time, and I stare around in wonderment.

It feels like our hotel is on top of the world. It looks down upon the sea and the various rocky outcrops of the Santorini caldera.

This is the view we will have as we say our vows. The sun beams down from a bright blue sky, hot and unrelenting. At least it's pretty windy; I hadn't expected that. It keeps me cool enough in my long-sleeved top.

Our room includes a private balcony and a swimming pool. Low walls separate us from the guests on either side of us. Scott has already booked and paid for the room to the left. It's for Sara when she arrives in a couple of days.

At eighteen hundred miles from home, it seems as though all of the things I was worrying about have dissolved in the vapour trail the plane left behind us. This is another world. Scott and I can be ourselves here. Maybe it won't be so bad to have fewer guests at our wedding. It might be more intimate.

Scott and I slip into our swimming things and enjoy the pool. The hotel has gone overboard with health and safety, it seems. Scott and I giggle about it. There is a life vest placed on each sun lounger, and various foam floats are stacked in one corner.

A private swim is so nice. I've longed for this for years. My parent's house had a private indoor pool I used to make full use of, but I had nothing to hide back then.

Here, I can get away with wearing next to nothing and feel the sun warm my skin through the crystal water. It's wonderful. It's freedom.

Scott wraps his bare, wet arms around my shoulders and kisses me. Deep and intense. It makes me wonder just how much privacy we have from our neighbours.

My question is answered before I ask it.

'Hello, lovebirds!'

That voice is too familiar. I pull back from Scott to see our neighbour.

I'm staggered when I see it is Dawn.

THIRTY-ONE

'I don't believe this,' I mutter.

'What are you doing here?' Scott stammers angrily. He wades away from me to face a serenely smiling Dawn.

'I know!' Dawn exclaims with a grin, flashing her bright teeth. They seem so much whiter beneath the Santorini sun. Has she had them redone?

'It's quite a coincidence, isn't it?' she continues, as though we have bumped into one another in our local supermarket, not well over a thousand miles from home. 'What are the chances of you two staying in the room next to mine? How funny!'

'It's not funny!' Scott snaps. 'You shouldn't be here. I thought you were going back to your flat?'

'I will. You can't expect me not to attend your wedding now, can you? Not since your parents cancelled, Scotty. I know Sam's guest list is sparse as well. I'll do my best to make the ceremony more busy, especially now that Libby and Dave have cancelled, too.'

Scott shakes his head. 'What?'

'Libby and Dave. They aren't coming to the wedding. They have decided to give it a miss.'

'How could they?'

'I called them earlier. I told them all about how badly you two have treated me. They couldn't in good conscience come to the wedding after they heard how much misery the pair of you have caused me. They told me they would time a bout of pretend gastroenteritis the day before they were due to fly out so they would have a plausible excuse not to go. So make sure you keep your phone handy for when they do. Maybe you could even arrange for them to receive a get-well card? I'm not sure how you want to play that one.'

Scott punches the water in frustration. 'You're crazy. I told you to forget all this. Go home, Dawn.'

'I'm not going anywhere. And you can't make me. My room is paid for. The hotel is happy to have a paying guest. That's all they care about.'

Dawn continues to smile. She has planned all this carefully. I can see she won't be moved. It's just such a shock to see her set up in the room next to us.

Something bothers me though. 'How did you know where we were staying?'

'Scott loves this village, don't you, babes? He has visited often. We had many a great time here.'

'But how did you know which hotel we would have the wedding at? And which room number?'

'Silly, Sam. Scott brought me to this hotel for our wedding day, didn't you, babes? Old habits die hard. I had a feeling he hadn't changed. As for the room number, the staff were more than happy to direct the chief bridesmaid to an adjacent room.'

Chief bridesmaid? Dawn is relentless. I thought she had given up. I can't understand why she is doing all this. Is this some desperate last-ditch attempt to stop the wedding? She must still be so desperately in love with Scott. Or obsessed—more likely that one.

It isn't working, of course. Scott doesn't look happy. He was expecting Dawn to appear as much as I was. His cheeks are flushing red, contrasting with the cool blue of the pool beneath them.

I have to admit the revelation that Scott is repeating the venue stings. 'This is where you and Dawn had your wedding? Why didn't you tell me?'

He shrugs angrily. 'It doesn't make any difference. Imerovigli is my favourite village, yes. I wanted to share it with you, that's all. There's nothing wrong with that. It's such a romantic place. Lots of people have their weddings here.'

I scoff. 'Not multiple marriages though. I thought this would be our special place.'

'You know what they say,' Dawn says, bouncing on her heels. 'Third time's a charm. Oh, wait. This is Scotty's second marriage. Sam, you'd better watch out for wife number three coming along! I wonder if he will meet her on your honeymoon?'

'That's enough!' Scott says, vaulting out of the pool. 'You need to leave.'

Dawn eyes the beads of water running down Scott's toned torso. 'I'm not going anywhere, babes. I'm staying for the wedding. You'll need me. It's going to be a quiet affair, remember? No mummy and daddy. None of your friends. Just Henry. Oh, and Sam's bestie.' She nods her head in my direction as she mentions Sara.

'I don't know what you are playing at, but you have gone too far,' Scott mutters to her. 'I want you gone.'

'I told you, I'm not going anywhere. It's your wife-to-be you should be kicking out.'

'Why's that?'

'Sam's been lying to you.'

My stomach contracts. What did she just say? I hope I'm hearing things.

'Of course, she hasn't,' Scott says, quick to come to my aid. 'Just stop all this, Dawn. I'm getting married in three days. I'm moving on. I want you to do the same. Go home while you still have your dignity.'

Dawn snorts. 'That's long gone, I think we

can all agree.' She tilts her head to the side in the annoying way she does. She looks politely puzzled. 'What I don't understand is why you are with Sam. She is lying about who she is. Did she tell you she changed her name?'

Scott pulls an appalled face and shakes his head. 'Of course she hasn't. What are you talking about? I demand you stop this insanity now!'

I open my mouth to say something, but I can't. It's like watching a slow-motion car crash. I'm in the middle of the pool, and Scott and Dawn are facing each other over the low wall, close enough to hug.

It's that battle of wills coming to the fore again. Scott has no authority over his ex-wife. She is a loose cannon. He may be all but free of her legally, but she is still wreaking destruction on our lives.

And she is about to deal another blow.

'Dawn,' I say, hating the pleading note in my voice. 'Don't. I don't know what you think you know, but—'

'I know everything! Sam Thorpe isn't your real name, is it? It's Holly. Holly Golding. You changed it. I found your deed poll hidden in your bedroom, along with many other things.'

My heart sinks. There were several occasions when Dawn could have found my file of documents. That thing was a goldmine of information. I should have hidden it better.

Wasn't beneath a pile of clothing at the back

of the walk-in wardrobe enough? I've always kept it safe, always worrying about someone finding it. It's an open book of my life for anyone to see. Sara has always said I've been too paranoid about it. People wouldn't be angry with me, she said. I never did anything wrong.

Dawn is the only one who has hated me enough to use this information against me. Adam could have given her a run for her money. But I think Dawn is taking her vendetta against me more seriously than my ex-boyfriend ever did.

She smiles gleefully now in the wake of her revelation. She isn't done, however.

'Did you also know, Scotty, that Holly here used to be an alcoholic?'

Scott shakes his head. 'None of this is true. This is nothing but a sad and desperate attempt to ruin my wedding day. I think you should leave us in peace, Dawn. You are in disgrace.'

A rush of gratitude floods through me. Scott believes in me so much. I wish I had told him the truth from the start.

Dawn points angrily in my direction with a wicked grin. 'Why don't you ask her then? I dare you, Scotty.'

Slowly, Scott turns and looks down at me. I'm still in the water and reluctant to leave it with an audience.

'Is any of this true?' he asks.

This isn't how I wanted this to come out.

I wanted to tell Scott in my own time. It was supposed to be the right moment.

Slowly, as though I'm bringing a hammer down on my head, I nod. 'Yes, it's true. My name isn't really Samantha. It's Holly.'

THIRTY-TWO

Scott blinks in the wake of my revelation. 'It's true?'

I nod. 'I'm so sorry. I wanted to tell you sooner.'

It's impossible to judge Scott's reaction. His face is a mask; his blank eyes belie nothing as he processes this fact. 'I don't know what to say. Why did you lie to me?'

'I didn't mean to.' My eyes are wide and imploring. I might even shed tears for the second time this week. 'It all happened so fast. I never expected our relationship to go this far, with a wedding. I've never been close with a man.'

Scott's eyes look watery now, too. 'Is it any wonder why if you lie to everyone you meet? Or is it just me you've deceived?'

'I never meant to deceive you! Everything just got out of hand so fast.'

'Are you after my money? Is that it?'

'No—of course not! I don't care about money.'

It strikes me as unusual that neither he nor Dawn have clocked the significance of my real name. That nugget and the scars on my arms don't add together to make four in their opinion? Maybe I'm not as infamous as I think I am.

'Please, let me explain,' I beg Scott imploringly. 'Then you'll see that how much you earn never mattered to me.'

'No,' he says quickly, looking around as though to ground himself. 'I need to get dressed. I'm going for a walk.'

'Good idea,' I say, wrenching myself from the pool. 'We'll both go. We can talk properly, in private.'

'No. I'm going alone.' He looks me up and down as though seeing me properly for the first time. 'Don't follow me. I need some time to think. I want to be alone.'

And with that, he storms towards the sliding doors of the hotel room, leaving me dripping beside the pool. I hesitate, wondering whether I should go after him.

Dawn may well have finally got her wish. Not because she sabotaged the guests, staged a break-in at our home, or blackmailed us into almost not being allowed the ceremony at all. But because of me and the fact that I am a liar.

I'm so stupid. I should have told Scott sooner. How could I even have thought of getting married when this secret was hanging over me? I've never let anyone other than Sara in on it. It's just in my nature to hide who I am.

Now it has cost me.

Dawn disappears for a few moments as I pull a towel around myself. She reappears with two glasses of amber liquid. She offers one to me as she knocks her own back. 'Drown your sorrows?'

I stare at the glass in her hands like she offers a water bottle after a marathon in a desert.

My mouth waters. Beads of condensation run down the glass. A rush of weakness makes my hand twitch.

I am thirsty, am I not? One drink won't hurt, will it? I've satisfied the conditions of the trust. My inheritance will be in my bank account within two weeks. There is nothing to lose.

Except for myself. I shake myself from my thoughts and look up to see Dawn observing me, her arm outstretched, proffering the glass of temptation.

'No thanks,' I say and head towards the hotel room. Scott is already gone. He must have left in a hurry. That's not like him. He usually likes to be composed, polished, and perfect. He must have still been damp as he pulled on a shirt and shorts and rushed out the door.

I pull on a long-sleeved floral dress and some sandals.

Something tells me to go after Scott, but I also want to respect his wishes. Although, what conclusion will he draw from what Dawn just revealed? I dread to think. I need to explain, say my piece. I wish Sara had arrived in Greece already. She could advise me.

I pull out my phone and video call her.

'Sam,' she says when she answers. She looks tense. The dark circles beneath her eyes are more pronounced than ever. 'I was just about to call you.'

'You were? Why?'

'I won't be able to fly out for the wedding. I'm so sorry, hun.'

'Oh.' Another fallen domino. There won't be anyone left at this wedding. Will the groom even turn up? I'm starting to think it will just be me standing at the altar, my white train blowing in the Santorini breeze, a gleeful Dawn the only figure in the rows of seats. 'What's happened? Are you all right? It's not food poisoning, is it?'

Sara shakes her head. 'No. It's Mum. She had a funny turn this morning.'

'How awful. Is she okay?'

'Not really.' The strain on Sara is worse than I've seen it. 'She woke me up at four this morning. She was wandering around the kitchen, trying to use the gas stove. When I turned on the light and approached her, she didn't recognise me at all. I mean, there have been times recently when she thinks I look too old to be her daughter. She still remembers the little girl I was, but this was something else. She couldn't even remember that I existed at all. She got hysterical. It took ages to calm her down. She thought I was an intruder. She was screaming, Sam.'

'I'm so sorry, Sara. Do you have any help with you? I can get someone over there. Let me help you.' I glance around me to check I'm not being overheard. 'My inheritance is almost in my bank account. It gets paid to me on the fifteenth.'

Sara shakes her head. 'Jill is with us now, so I could get dressed and get something to eat. But I can't just wash my hands of my mum, can I? She didn't do that when I needed care as a child.'

'You know this is different. Please, let me help. I'll send you some money to tide you over until I can get more.'

'Sam, I can't ask you to do that.'

'I know. You're too humble and all that. Just take it.'

'I have enough for care in the short term. The main thing is I can't stand to hand Mum over to someone else. This morning, she was so lost in her own head. I feel like I've already lost her.'

'I know what you mean. But you have to admit when you can't cope anymore. It's okay, Sara.'

She smiles back tears. 'Okay, thanks, Sam. I'll look into full-time care. Urgh. I can't believe I just said that.'

'You're doing the right thing. You've done your best. Patricia will understand that on some level. She knows you love her. It's not like you won't be able to see her anymore.'

Sara nods and sighs. 'I'm so sorry this is happening just before your wedding. What kind of friend am I?'

'Don't worry about that. I'm not even sure there will be a wedding anyway.'

'What? Why?'

I explain everything that has happened lately, including Dawn sabotaging the guests, setting herself up in the room next to ours and revealing that I had changed my name.

Sara frowns in concern. 'She's a nutter. Didn't I tell you? Does she know about the money coming to you?'

I glance over my shoulder again and push closed the sliding door that leads to the terrace. Dawn doesn't need any more ammunition.

'No. I don't think she does. She was playing on the angle that I was after Scott's money. She didn't correct him when he arrived at that conclusion.'

'That doesn't mean she doesn't know about your inheritance.'

'There wasn't anything in that file that mentioned the trust fund. It was all my supporting evidence. My change of name document, employment history, evidence of my sobriety.' I groan. 'She knows I was an alcoholic, Sara. She offered me a drink just now. I was so tempted to take it. To be honest, I almost did. I haven't felt like that since Adam.'

'Stay strong, Sam.'

'It's so hard. A bottle of vodka seems like it would take the edge off. It feels like everything has fallen apart.'

'Drinking is never the answer. It just causes more problems. You can't let Dawn win.'

'I think she already has. Scott won't talk to me. He just stormed out without me being able to explain the truth.'

'That wasn't right. He should have let you have your say.'

'He was upset. I've lied to him.'

'For good reason. None of what happened was your fault. What choice did you have?'

'I could have faced the music. As you said, I don't have to hide my scars. I should have been open with him to start with. I just never expected he would ask me to marry him so soon.'

'A cooling off period wouldn't do either of you any harm.'

I sigh. 'You thought it was too quick all along, didn't you?'

'You know I did. Don't worry about all this. If you and Scott are meant to be, then you will find your way. And if you don't, everything will be fine as well. I'll be here for you when you get back. Okay?'

I end the call after making sure Sara is all right, making her promise to get help for her mum. Part of me is tempted to fly back home and go down to Bournemouth to be with her, but everything with Scott is up in the air. Besides, Sara could tell what I was thinking and made me promise not to.

I flop on the large bed. After several hours of lying like this, I'm still alone. Scott still hasn't returned, even as the sun starts to set.

THIRTY-THREE

It's been too long, I think. Scott should have been back by now. We didn't do any sightseeing on the way through the village, so the place is still a mystery to me. Scott had a driver take us up here to check-in.

Tomorrow was supposed to be for exploring. My fiancé was going to show me the sights.

As a result, I have no idea where I'm going as I step out of the hotel. I follow the winding paths of Imerovigli, squeezing past tourists single file as I go. None of them are my fiancé.

Where is he?

A bride and groom are up ahead having their photograph taken by the glowing red light of the sun. The shots will be beautiful, I can tell.

Will that be me in a few days? Or will I be flying back to the UK alone?

As a teen, I'd spent years sitting on a beach alone in Bournemouth, wondering why everything bad happened to me. With my arms around my knees, I'd stare out at the endless rolling waves coming into shore. It was the perfect place to contemplate life.

Would Scott be doing something similar now? I could join him, and I would explain everything. He would understand and tell me everything will be fine. He would understand why I did what I did. It wasn't my fault, he would agree. We would sit upon the sand and watch the sunset together, just as we had done on our engagement evening.

But that won't happen. For one thing, I don't think there are any beaches nearby. We are high on a cliffside overlooking the rocky caldera.

Eventually, I'm forced to give up. It would have been a nice walk if my fiancé hadn't been missing, and I knew whether we would get married in a few days.

I return to the hotel alone. As I approach, I see my fiancé. Scott sits alone on the wall of the terrace where the hotel hosts weddings. In the glowing red sunset, with his strong jaw, shiny dark hair, and designer shorts, he looks like he is in a photograph for a glossy fashion magazine.

He stares out at the sea, oblivious to my approach. Only when my hand squeezes his shoulder does he look around in surprise.

'I'm sorry,' I tell him. 'I should have been honest with you sooner. Dawn was telling the truth about my name change. My parents named me Holly. I changed it when I was nineteen.'

'Why?'

'It's hard to explain. I'm not sure where to

start.'

'Because you're hiding something bad?'

'Sort of. But it wasn't my fault.'

'Come on. People don't change their name for no reason.'

'Some do.'

'Only if they have done something wrong. You've committed a crime, haven't you? That's why you're in hiding. Was it theft?'

'No! It's not that at all. It was my father. He committed the crime, not me.'

Scott still looks suspicious, so I explain. I tell him how my parents used to have rows—this much he already knows from our recent talk. Then, I describe how my mother was the catalyst for the event that ruined my life as I knew it.

I was sixteen when Mum got fed up with her husband's constant cheating and had a fling of her own. I thought for a long time that it was simply revenge. Tit for tat.

As I got older, I realised she was probably lonely. She was stuck in that big house all day, isolated and miles from anyone. I was young, but I remember how Dad didn't like her going out and having friends of her own. She didn't even have a job to escape to.

Dad's career as a professional tennis player provided the money to pay for our big home beside the sea. Mum was a homemaker, which is a full-time job in itself. Not that I was ever a handful.

I was a well-behaved child, back then anyway. It's only after what happened that I went off the rails and started dabbling in drink and heavier substances. That was the only thing that could push down the pain of what my father did one day, a few days after he discovered his wife's affair.

Why was it any different than him cheating? I'll never know. Perhaps he didn't like getting a taste of his own medicine.

Anyway, he took his revenge one winter's day. He took the shotgun he went clay pigeon shooting with and shot her right in the kitchen. Then he turned the gun to my baby brother in the next room, silencing his cries after the first deafening boom. He turned and came after me. I'd run upstairs in terror when I realised what was happening. Dad had gone crazy. That was all I knew.

I had to escape. I hadn't wanted to leave Mum or Theo, my little brother. I'd just heard Dad searching for me. His footsteps came closer, and I bolted. Stupidly, I ran up the stairs instead of out the door. I didn't think I would manage to release the locks in time. It was a split-second panic-driven decision. No teenager should have been put in that position.

Upstairs, I hid like a child under my bed—as if he wasn't going to find me there.

When my bedroom door finally opened, Dad brought the smell of burning with him. He had set fire to the house. He knew I had run upstairs. He was torching our life together and ending it all.

He just had one last loose thread to tie up.

After he threw the bedroom door open and stared inside, I thought it was the end. Especially when I heard my name, his voice made me shudder in horror.

'Holly!'

He had found me. I was convinced at that moment I was about to die. Then, after a few moments of staring into my apparently empty room, he turned away. His trainers trod along the plush carpet and out of sight.

He called out my name in the nursery instead. Did he think I was hiding in Theo's wardrobe or in the walk-in closet that held the spare packs of nappies, toys, and feeding paraphernalia?

Either way, I knew that was my moment. It was like an external force dragged me from my hiding place and down the stairs. But it was like stepping out of the frying pan and into the fire.

Literally.

The fire must have been set near the front door. Dad didn't make any mistakes in anything he did. He was an achiever. A winner, he always said. This was no exception. He wanted to make sure there was no escape.

I had two choices. Stay and be murdered by my father, or run through the flames. The door was locked; the chain was across. Dad made that a rule whenever we were at home.

This level of security would slow me down. Fire licked at the metallic trappings as I stared at them. That door was the only means of escape, however.

So I had to go for it.

That's how I got my scars. They remain on my forearms as proof I had to escape through fire to escape my father's murderous rampage.

THIRTY-FOUR

Scott's accusatory gaze has turned into shock and horror. 'You're Holly Golding,' he says slowly. The wheels in his head are turning. '*The* Holly Golding? Stephen Golding's daughter?'

'Yes. I'm surprised you didn't clock the name before. Dawn too. I'm the girl whose father snapped and shot his whole family and then himself. He would have killed me too if I hadn't managed to get away how I just described. I was the sole survivor of the tragedy.'

I can still hear the final boom ringing in my ears as I finally wrenched the door open. That shot told me it was over. I was the only one left.

Scott raises his eyebrows in surprise. 'Your family was all over the papers at the time. It was such a big story. It just didn't click when Dawn said it before. That girl and my fiancé are the same person.' He says this to himself as though trying to make the fact sink in.

I nod. 'I understand. It wasn't the way I wanted you to find out, believe me. I was going to tell you one day. I was just trying to find the right moment.'

'So, all that business with the wedding invites and not getting an answer...Where on earth did you send those invites?'

'I never sent them. I destroyed them after you saw me write them out.'

'So many lies, Sam.' He winces. 'That's not even your name, is it? What should I call you from now on?'

'Just call me Sam. It has been my name for so many years. I'm used to it. I wanted a normal life so much. That's why I invented estranged parents and siblings. I just wanted to look normal, like everyone else. That story being splashed all over the papers got me a lot of attention. I hated it. Everyone knew what had happened, both at school and college and when I walked down the street. The rumours spread so fast, even though my picture was never published. I'm lucky it wasn't the age of social media.'

I swallow. 'A lot of people knew who I was because of my father. He was well-known and liked in the community. People in the area loved having a celebrity neighbour. Whenever we went out, there was always someone who wanted his autograph or a picture with him. There wasn't any escape after everyone found out what he did. I hated the staring and whispering even years later. It was wherever I went. Every day. I couldn't go anywhere without constant reminders. The press was after me, too, hounding me to give an interview telling my side of the story. I ended up turning to alcohol to escape.'

Scott grimaces. 'That wasn't a good idea.'

'I know. I was stupid. And nineteen. I was an alcoholic for years. Until Sara managed to bully me into getting dried out, it took me a long time to listen to her.'

'You have a lot to thank her for.'

'I do. I'll never forget what she did for me. That's why I want to use my inheritance to help her.'

'Inheritance?'

I sigh. 'My dad was very wealthy from his tennis career. He earned a lot of money from tournaments and media appearances. He wrote an autobiography, too. The house was totalled after what he did. The insurance money paid out for it, and then there was his life insurance, too. It all amounted to quite a lot. I will inherit all of it in less than two weeks.'

Scott blinks. 'You must surely have had it already? Your father died years ago.'

'I made a lot of mistakes when I was younger. I told you. I was a mess. My uncle put the money into a trust until I could satisfy the requirements. He thought I was going to blow the lot and destroy myself. He would have been right.'

Scott looks out to sea. The sunset is reflected in his pale eyes. 'So you aren't after my money?'

'Of course not.' I reach out and take his hand, squeezing it. 'You know me. Our love is real. My name was different years ago. But I'm going to be changing it again in a few days, am I right? To Worthington-Hart. At least, I hope so. Can you forgive me for keeping this secret?'

Scott looks back at me and his characteristic smile spreads across his face. 'Of course, babes.' He wraps me in his arms and relief floods me. 'I can't be angry at you over this, can I?'

I hug him back, inhaling his peppery fragrance. It's then I realise that Dawn has been watching us from the terrace of the hotel, a drink in her hand.

Her expression is hard to read now that the sun has gone down. She turns when I catch sight of her and disappears back inside the building.

There isn't anything she can do to us now that Scott knows the truth and the divorce is finalised. Is there?

THIRTY-FIVE

It's the night before the wedding. My hen night is a quiet affair—or, at least, a lonely one. It turns out the last of Scott's guests did come down with a case of gastroenteritis after all. We get similar excuses from everyone else due to turn up for the wedding.

Only Henry has flown in from the UK for the ceremony.

Dawn obviously fed them lies as she did the night of the dinner party when several guests didn't show at all. When Scott asked them about it later, he surmised Dawn had headed them off when she answered the door with an excuse. From the sound of it, we guess that she told them the evening was cancelled while I was out picking up Sara from the station.

I video call Sara now at the bar I find in the village. We toast a virtual drink to each other. She has a glass of Prosecco, and I have sparkling apple juice.

After a while, though, she has to go tend to her mother. She tells me Patricia is moving into full-time care tomorrow, and it's her last night living with her daughter. Jill is there, too, supporting the pair. She has been Patricia's carer for years. It's the end of an era for all three women.

After the video call ends, I sip my drink and think of retiring to my hotel room. Fizzy drinks are a familiar companion in social settings when you can't drink alcohol. It's the only time I have them. I've lost count of the number I've had since meeting Scott.

My fiancé is out with Henry on his stag night. I can imagine it's quieter where they are. Henry turned up this afternoon in a similar suit to the one he works in. I smile at the idea of him letting loose on a bachelor party. The pair are probably talking business over wine somewhere, really going wild.

At least I don't have to worry about uncuffing my husband-to-be from a railing somewhere on the morning of our big day.

The door swings open, and I glance over to see Dawn enter through it. She is dressed similarly to me, in a cocktail dress. Only hers is far more revealing, of course.

I groan internally. Just what I need as I wrangle with last-minute nerves.

'Hiya,' she says brightly. 'Getting cold feet yet?'

'Nope,' I fib.

'Liar, ' she says, taking a seat on the bar stool beside me. 'All brides have the jitters, don't they? That last few hours of freedom when they wonder if they should do a runner.'

'That's not me. Maybe you should have listened to those instincts if you had them before you married Scott. Then you wouldn't be sitting here now.'

'True,' she laughs. 'I wish I had.'

She orders herself a martini and the same for me.

'I don't drink,' I tell her. 'You know that.'

She shrugs. 'If you can't have a drink on your hen night, when can you have one?'

'Never. It's called being teetotal.'

She wafts this notion away. 'Have some fun, Sam. Are we still calling you that, by the way? I didn't get a memo.'

'Yes. It's my name.'

'Only since you changed it.' She gives me a sideways glance. 'I googled you this evening. Your real name, I mean. I had no idea you were *that* Holly Golding.'

'No?'

'No, I honestly didn't. It makes sense now. The scars, the secrecy. I'm so sorry.'

'Yeah, of course you are.'

'I mean it. What happened to you and your family was terrible. I remember hearing about the story at the time. You must be scarred emotionally, too.'

I look at Dawn with a toughened expression on my face, expecting some kind of stinging punchline. But she looks genuine.

'I suppose I am, in a way. It wasn't easy.'

'I'm sure it wasn't. Is that why you changed your name? To get away from the stigma?'

'Yes. The press were obsessed with trying to get me to do an interview.'

'I bet. That's tabloid gold. I'm guessing they didn't give up easily.'

I shake my head. 'They tracked me down and bombarded me with requests. It would have ruined my anonymity nationally. Everywhere I went, there was a reminder of what had happened to me. I had to get away from it all. So I did. I changed my name and moved up north. I worked as a teacher, and then I met Scott. I thought I was going to live happily ever after. Then you came into the picture.'

Our drinks are set in front of us by the bartender. Mine sits in front of me temptingly. A cocktail stick of olives has never looked more appealing. Could I take a nibble without consuming the liquid? I refrain from licking my lips in front of Dawn. I don't want her to know how much I want a drink after recent events.

She raises her glass to me. 'I can only apologise for my actions. It just seemed so unfair to see Scott move on with someone else. I wanted...I don't know. I suppose I thought if I pushed hard enough, he might just snap out of this trance he has been in since he has been with you.'

'It's called love. '

'Yeah. Whatever you want to call it, Scott has had the blinkers on.' She nods and raises her glass. 'So, to a beautiful wedding tomorrow.'

I raise my glass and clink it against hers to humour her but return it to the bar, untouched whilst she sips hers with relish. 'Are you going to be at the wedding tomorrow? You technically aren't invited.'

'Be polite now. I told you I wasn't going to miss it. I can bulk up numbers.'

I snort. 'It's going to be a pretty cosy ceremony. 'The only guest we have coming is Henry.'

'What about your friend?'

'She can't make it. She has to look after her mother at home. She has dementia and is moving into full-time care tomorrow.'

'Oh, how awful. You really need me there, then. I'll make the seated guests more symmetrical.' She giggles, and I can't help but smile wryly, too. What's the saying? You have to laugh, or you will cry.

She recovers herself. 'I'm sorry I scared some of the other guests away.'

'I'd love to know what you said to Scott's parents to get them to decide against their only son's wedding, even if they are getting divorced.'

She swallows a gulp of her drink. 'You don't. They didn't take much persuading. You wouldn't benefit if they were there tomorrow.'

'Why do you say that?'

'Let's just say they are pretty fake people. I only saw them at my wedding, and that was it. Christmas and birthday cards would arrive when they remembered. Scott doesn't think much of family.'

'I admit he hasn't mentioned them much.'

'There you are then.' She sips her cocktail. 'You'll need me there tomorrow, if not only to hold your phone so Sara can watch you get married.'

I smile. Again, it's not with joy. How many other brides are like this on the night before their wedding day? 'I was thinking of placing my phone on one of the front seats, you know, so she can have a good view of proceedings.'

I crack up at how ridiculous this sounds. Hysterical tears form at the corners of my eyes.

Dawn throws her head back, too, in mirth and puts a hand on my arm. 'Oh no! Stop. You can't do that. I'll hold the phone for the ceremony. I'll get a tracking shot of you walking down the aisle. Who is giving you away?'

'Henry said he would do it.'

'Good old Henry.' She sighs and slides out of the hairpin, holding her casual waves back. 'Here. Have this.'

'What is it?'

'Something borrowed. I'll be expecting that back afterwards, mind. Or it won't count.'

I take it reluctantly, thinking it is some kind

of trap. Dawn seems pretty sincere for once, however. There is an air about her this evening, similar to how she was before we departed for Greece the other day. Tears seem not far from the corners of her eyes this evening.

She pulls one of the costume rings from her fingers and slides it across the bar to me. It has a sapphire-tone jewel. 'Here's your something blue,' she says.

'Thanks, I guess.'

She smiles at my reaction. 'You're welcome.' Then she looks thoughtful for a minute as she looks at me. 'I wish you weren't marrying Scott.'

There it is. 'Here I was thinking you were being civil for once. I thought you had accepted it now.'

'No, I don't mean that. I mean, I wish we could have been friends—proper friends, not just awkward interactions around my ex. I think we would have gotten along.'

'Really?' I'm not sure what Dawn means by this. She is a glossy, high-maintenance nightmare, and I'm normal-looking, down-to-earth. I can barely pull my hair into a ponytail at the best of times. I'm also actively shying away from the limelight at every opportunity. We couldn't be more opposite.

She smiles again. I have the feeling she has already had quite a bit to drink. Had she attacked the mini-bar in her hotel before arriving this evening? I know I was tempted.

'I mean, we were both raised with money,' she gestures. 'Your Dad was a tennis player, wasn't he? He must have made a fair bit during his career. My brother used to have one of the PlayStation games he was on. He chucked it after Golding's name was splashed in the papers for the wrong reasons. He said it creeped him out when he looked at it after what your father did. My dad was a hedge fund manager. That's where I got my inheritance. Dad was a heavy drinker, so my brother and I got our money pretty early in life. You and I probably had similar childhoods, too.'

'Maybe.'

'I mean it. Do you want to know why I've been so awful these past two weeks?'

I look at her in surprise. 'Why?'

'It's because you remind me of me. Back when I was preparing to marry Scott. I was so in love with him and excited about the wedding, here, of all places. It's just brought the past up. I walked away from Scott. It was my fault our marriage was over. I admit that. Just seeing you has made me realise what I've lost. It's been a real punch in the gut. I found it so hard to let go of what should have been mine, even though I was long gone before you showed up. I'm really sorry for everything.'

I nod slowly. 'I appreciate you admitting that. I'm sure it wasn't easy to say.'

'It wasn't. It's hard to admit eleven years

of your life have just turned to dust.' She closes her eyes and sighs deeply. 'That's all gone now, though. Like my inheritance. My brother's too.'

'Where did your brother's money go?'

She looks dreamy again. 'Warren invested it in some dodgy scheme. He lost everything. That's why he topped himself.'

Dawn shields her eyes with her palm all of a sudden. The bottom half of her face is contorted.

'I'm sorry. That's horrible. I know what it's like to lose a brother. Mine was just eleven months old when my father shot him. He was just a baby.' I put a hand on her back and rub gently for a few minutes whilst Dawn composes herself. 'Money isn't everything.'

Dawn laughs bitterly, dabbing at the corners of her perfect eyeliner with the heel of her hand. 'Only rich people say that. I asked you if you were a secret millionaire before, didn't I?'

'I don't know why you kept saying that.'

'I was right, wasn't I? You were keeping money hidden.'

'I wasn't. I won't even inherit for another few weeks.'

'How come?'

'My father's money was put into trust. My life was a mess when I was originally supposed to inherit. I had to fulfil the conditions before I saw a penny.'

The cogs whir in Dawn's head. 'That's what that file of documents was for? To prove you were responsible enough to receive the funds?'

'Yes. That's right.'

Dawn slides the glass of untouched cocktail towards me. 'So now you can drink to your heart's content. You've satisfied the trust. You can let your hair down. Enjoy yourself. It's just one little drink.'

Dawn downs another part of her cocktail. I watch her throat moving with each swallow as though I'm parched. I can only imagine how good the drink would feel coursing into my system. 'I guess one drink wouldn't hurt. Just this once.'

I don't have to finish the whole glass.

'Atta girl. Go for it.'

I'm right. The liquid warms me pleasantly as it goes down. I haven't reached the end of the glass before that tingling warmth spreads through the rest of me. Abstinence must have made me more sensitive to the effects.

That familiar buzzing feeling starts in my fingers and toes. Everything around me seems much more lively and friendly. Now I remember why I used to drink. It feels so good.

Dawn orders us another round of martinis. I protest, but she is pushing the glass into my hand.

'It's your hen night. Celebrate your last night of freedom!'

I take a sip of my new drink. This one is better than the last, amplifying the warmth in my body. It's okay to do this, I tell myself. It's only a one-off. I'm allowed one day off my best behaviour now and then, aren't I?

At the end of this glass, I don't argue with Dawn when she orders some tequila shots. She is all right, Dawn. I know what she means; we can be friends. Why didn't I realise this before?

'To lost brothers,' she says, raising her tiny glass. 'To Warren.'

'To Theo.'

The tequila courses through me faster than the cocktail. Now I'm really buzzing.

After the second round of shots, I tell Dawn that's enough with raised hands. Am I pleading? I stand up to leave, but I stumble.

She catches me and sits me back on my stool. 'You're not going anywhere just yet!'

My head spins. My face is in my hands; I didn't remember raising them. 'I think I've had too much.'

When I lower my hands, we have company. A handsome young man has joined us. I get a flash of dark hair and eyes. He can't be any older than twenty-five.

Dawn doesn't seem to notice this. She changes to flirtatious mode like a switch has been flicked, stretching herself across the bar like a lioness flaunting herself to a mate.

The man makes an unmistakable drink gesture to Dawn, his gorgeously thick eyebrows raised. She smiles suggestively. 'Yes, please. We'll both have a cosmo.'

She turns to me and grins when the man taps his card on the reader. 'Things are looking up.'

'I think we've had our fill, don't you?'

'Don't be silly. The night is just getting started.'

Dawn gratefully accepts her drink and sips it. The man tries to engage her in conversation, which is tricky as he doesn't seem to know much English. His intentions are pretty clear, however, as he lavishes attention on a beautiful and perfectly made-up Dawn. She is the attractive one, despite our age difference.

This guy barely glances at me, which is the story of my life.

THIRTY-SIX

My head pounds. I groan as I remember the night before. It comes back to me in flashes of euphoria and colours: Dawn putting an arm around my neck and giving me an affectionate squeeze, us downing shots, and later dancing in another bar somewhere. When did we decide to find another drinking hole?

It's a confusing tangle. Now I remember why I quit drinking.

I open my eyes and tentatively reach out in the bed. At least I've woken up alone. And this is my hotel room. I'm still dressed, although in the clothes I had on last night. Oddly, the long sleeves of my dress are rolled up.

I must have just flopped down atop the covers when I got in last night or this morning in the early hours.

Dawn must have done the same next door. I wonder if she was alone at the time. I honestly can't remember getting back to the hotel at all.

I hope she doesn't mention this to Scott. He likes the fact that I am strictly sober, praising me for it. I don't want to disappoint him on our wedding day of all days.

This thought jolts me. It's the big day.

I scramble out of bed and shower away any traces of last night, scrubbing my teeth twice. It's a good thing Scott stayed in a different hotel with Henry overnight; lucky he believes in the tradition of the bride and groom not seeing each other before the wedding.

Do I still smell of alcohol? I'm paranoid. I pull on a long-sleeve kaftan top and shorts and go down to breakfast. There, I drink a few glasses of juice in the sun at one of the outdoor tables. Any liquid is good. I've got until 4 p.m. this evening to flush any martini, tequila and whatever else I drank last night from my system.

I'm never going to slip like that again. With this thought, I glance around. I half-expect Dawn to appear and offer me the hair of the dog to go with my breakfast. I choose simple fruit and toast from the buffet, not wanting to risk anything else. The hangover mingled with last-minute nerves is quite a cocktail in its own right.

I spend the rest of the morning out in the sun on the private terrace of my hotel room. It's warm in the sun even at this hour. I glance over to Dawn's side of the wall a few times. All is quiet and still. The curtains are drawn behind the sliding doors. I wonder if it was her place or his last night.

There is still no sign of Dawn, as the photographer and hair and makeup artist knock on my door around lunchtime. I was expecting her to appear during these proceedings, as I have become accustomed to, especially now that we are sort of friends. Or is that why she is staying away? She has finally decided to give me some privacy, perhaps.

Funnily, I actually miss her presence. It would have been nice to have someone familiar in this room full of strangers. Better the devil you know and all that.

The stylist works wonders for my hair, pulling and shaping it into elegant waves that flow over my shoulders. I hand her the hair clip Dawn gave me last night and slip the blue-jewelled ring onto a finger of my right hand.

I'm so unused to having someone do my makeup for me. The photographer takes snaps during the getting-ready process. I feel like a celebrity. Not plain old Sam. I don't even miss my old name anymore.

This wedding is the start of a new beginning. It doesn't matter what name I started with; I'm going to be Mrs Worthington-Hart later today anyway.

Afterwards, we step out into the Greek sun to take various solo shots of me in my wedding dress—the last pictures of me as a single woman.

I'm directed onto some steps for a few snaps and then beside the main pool and various poses with the stunning caldera behind, all while the glorious sunlight beams down on us.

By the time all this is done, it's time for the ceremony.

Henry knocks on my hotel room door. He is, of course, dressed in an immaculate suit. This must be his special occasion version, which is remarkably similar to all his others. 'Ready to go, Sam?'

'Yes, absolutely,' I smile as I grab my phone and my wedding bouquet. I glance at Dawn's hotel room door as we pass. 'Have you seen Dawn today?' I ask Henry.

'No, I haven't. Finally, some good news, eh? Scott has kept me informed of the trouble she has caused. If she doesn't stop after we return to the UK, we can start legal proceedings against her.'

'I don't think that's necessary. She was with me last night. She had mellowed out a bit. I think she will be okay from now on.'

Henry gives something of an eye roll. 'Right.'

The stage for the wedding is beautiful. We are on the pure white terrace overlooking the caldera. The altar where a gorgeous Scott stands waiting has been decorated with fresh, colourful flowers. White ribbons flutter in the breeze. The sky is blue, and the weather is perfect. Barely a cloud in the sky.

Before we reach the beginning of the aisle, I video call Sara, and Henry seats her in pride of place on the front row for the best view. Then he returns and leads me down the aisle.

The ceremony is perfect. Scott and I say our vows and smile at each other excitedly. It's just like I imagined, apart from the lack of guests. We kiss as we are pronounced man and wife.

We've finally done it. Several times, it looked like it wasn't going to happen.

I'm now officially Mrs Worthington-Hart.

THIRTY-SEVEN

I wake up the next morning in marital bliss, naked and wrapped in Scott. I raise my hand in front of my face to look at my new wedding ring. I'm not a jewellery kind of girl, so it's weird that I have a ring on my finger. I guess I'll get used to it as I did with the engagement ring. The two take pride of place together on my hand.

This morning, we are checking out of the hotel and setting off for our honeymoon. Scott has chartered a yacht, and we are going to spend the next two weeks cruising around the Greek islands. I can't wait.

Scott takes our luggage down to our car. Again, I glance over at the door as I pass Dawn's hotel room. She didn't show up at the wedding, which took me by surprise. Twenty-four hours without Dawn. A few days ago, I would have counted that a blessing, as Henry had. Now, I'm a little worried. I get a funny feeling and can't express why.

I knock on her door. 'Dawn? Are you in there?'

No answer.

Maybe she didn't come back from her new friend's place, wherever that is? I don't even know the guy's name. Did he offer it?

The end of the night is a bit of a blur. I don't remember how I got back to my hotel room.

I knock a few more times but don't get a response. Then I notice something near the door handle. Blood.

There isn't much, but it's there. Now, the funny feeling intensifies. Whose blood is that? What if Dawn is hurt and alone in her room? What kind of injuries does she have?

I knock again, this time with more gusto. Still no answer.

I head down to the main desk downstairs. 'Excuse me. I think there might be something wrong with my friend, Dawn. She's in the room next to mine. I haven't seen her since Friday night. There is some blood on her door, and she isn't answering. I think she might be in trouble. Can you please check on her?'

Credit to the young receptionist, she is straight on the phone to hotel security. After a few moments, a security guard arrives. The receptionist explains the situation, and I follow him through the corridors back up to the hotel rooms.

He knocks a few times and concedes there isn't a response. He whips out a master keycard to get into the room.

The breath I braced myself with is exhaled

quickly. There is no sign of Dawn. There is more blood on the tangled bedsheets, however. Again, it isn't much. It's not crime scene levels, but it's noticeable.

All her stuff is in here. Makeup and toiletries are out in the bathroom. Clothes are on the chair beside the bed. The pretty cocktail dress she was wearing on my hen night is thrown over the back of the chair. There is more blood on that, too. She was here.

None of this sits right with me. Something bad has happened. I can feel it.

Scott appears, poking his head around the door. 'What's going on?'

'Dawn's gone missing,' I say.

'What are you talking about?'

'I haven't seen her since the night before the wedding.'

'That's a good thing. Certainly nothing to complain about. Are we going to go?'

'Don't you think we should find out what has happened to her?'

Scott groans. 'This is nothing but a last-ditch attempt to scupper our celebration, I'm sure.'

'I don't think so. I'm worried about her.'

'You're too soft. You are playing right into her hands. Come on.' He takes hold of my hand and leads me downstairs. 'The yacht is waiting. I can't wait for you to see it.'

'I can't. Dawn doesn't know anyone in

Greece. I think it's our duty to look out for her while she is here.'

'She wasn't invited,' Scott says flatly. It's her own fault if she has run into trouble. Besides, she likely hasn't. Dawn has probably picked some bloke up in a bar somewhere.'

I hesitate.

'Is that it? She met someone, didn't she?'

'Maybe.'

'See? What did I tell you? Like that night we left her behind at home. She quickly found herself a bed somewhere else to stay, or so she said, which speaks volumes about her state of mind. I'm sure she is having the time of her life in the village with a local hunk. Don't give her another thought. This is our time. Let's make it a trip to remember, what do you say?'

THIRTY-EIGHT

The honeymoon Scott has arranged for us is wonderful. It's like heaven as we cruise through the sapphire waters of the Greek islands on a sailing yacht. It's all blue skies, white sails, sunshine and sand. We stop here and there as we go, keeping ourselves busy below deck in between stops.

I hope our marriage stays like this. I want to bottle it for a rainy day. My life has never been more perfect.

My thoughts can't help but stray back to Dawn, however. Her sudden disappearance is uncharacteristic. As I sip a pear mocktail on the sunny deck, I think of the empty hotel room and the blood. What does it all mean?

'You're thinking of her again, aren't you?'

With the yacht moored beside another island, Scott takes a seat beside me. He slides his mirrored sunglasses up to sit atop his dark hair.

I want to deny it, but I know I can't. So I shrug. 'Maybe. It's just so odd. It's like she has vanished into thin air. That's not like her.'

'Don't complain. You wanted her gone. She

would have ruined our big day in one way or another. You wouldn't have wanted that.'

'No. She apologised. It's like she let her guard down in that bar. She was nice to me. She gave me gifts for the wedding. Something borrowed and something blue. I still have them in my suitcase.'

Scott pauses. 'Where exactly in your suitcase?'

'I don't know. The small compartment at the front.' I shrug. 'Why?'

'No reason.' He looks away. The horizon is reflected in his beautiful eyes and designer lenses. 'Just forget about my ex-wife. She is in the past. The future is all about us. Okay?'

I pause. 'Fine, but there are two possibilities, however. Either she is injured and needs help. Or if she does still have it in for us, I'm worried she is going to pop up when I'm least expecting her.'

'Don't worry, Sam. The hotel will take care of everything. You brought it to their attention before we left. They will handle the situation if there is one. You don't know Dawn as I do. It's either a trick she is playing to ruin our honeymoon, or she has forgotten about us and moved on with her latest fling. She had quite a few of those during our marriage. I lost count.'

A bright glare catches my attention from the nearest bit of land. I glance across and see a camera lens in the distance. A figure of a man holds a professional camera up to his face, aiming it at our yacht in the bay.

'What's he doing?' I say suddenly, feeling paranoid.

'Taking a picture of the boat. She is a beauty. Want another mocktail?' He takes my glass and disappears below deck.

I roll my eyes at his personification of the boat and turn my back to the man with the camera.

Photography isn't my thing. I have no idea what that lens can pick up from this distance. I have a bikini on. Having my arms in full view doesn't make for a great shot.

What does the man plan on doing with the photos anyway? He is wearing a wide-brim hat and sunglasses. He could be anyone.

I slip below deck, planning to come back up when the guy has got the shot he wanted of the boat if that's what he is into.

Scott has got the mocktail paraphernalia out. He is in the cabin where we sleep, however. He has my suitcase out, his palm flat inside the outer pocket.

'Hey,' I say to announce my arrival. 'What are you up to?'

He looks around in surprise. 'Nothing. I was just getting these.' He holds out his hand. In his palm is the hair clip and ring Dawn gave me before the wedding.

I blink in confusion. 'What for?'

'It's not the kind of souvenir we want for

our honeymoon.'

'What are you talking about?'

He shrugs. 'Sailors are superstitious, I guess. It's not good for you to be carrying omens like this around. I'll take them.'

'What on earth are you talking about?' I laugh. *Omens?* That isn't like Scott at all.

'I would feel better if they weren't on board.' He returns my suitcase neatly and moves past me up onto the deck. I follow just in time to see him launch the items of Dawn's jewellery into the sea.

'Have you gone crazy?' I ask him. 'I was supposed to return those to Dawn.'

'We aren't going to see her again. So don't worry about it.'

Something settles in the pit of my stomach. 'What makes you so sure we won't see her again?'

Scott sighs. 'Just drop it. I don't want to spend my honeymoon talking about my ex-wife.'

'But—'

'Please, Sam. That's the last I have to say on the matter.'

THIRTY-NINE

I don't know what Scott was thinking by throwing Dawn's possessions overboard. At that moment, I thought he had lost it. Aside from that little blip, however, he seems to be his usual perfect, wonderful self.

He is charming and treats me like a princess. If he had been acting out of character now, I might have been suspicious. But he is his usual self again. He can't possibly have done something to Dawn. Besides, he was with Henry. Dawn chose to leave the bar with that mysterious stranger on my hen night.

Didn't she?

I wish I could remember what happened. But as Scott said, he has known Dawn longer. The majority of mine and Dawn's interactions have been baffling and spiteful. Maybe Scott is right. She is pulling some kind of stunt and I'm falling for it. That's why we haven't seen her in over a week.

Today is my birthday. Scott moors the yacht at Katapola, Amorgos Island, and we venture onto dry land to explore.

My husband complains of a crushing headache, so we try to quickly find him a pharmacy. We wander through the narrow streets, passing whitewashed houses, colourful doors, and traditional shops selling local crafts and souvenirs.

Scott explains he has less intimate knowledge of this island than he does of Santorini. He explains that this visit is a first for him, as it is for me.

He looks very red in the face as I turn to him now. He pinches the bridge of his nose and sways on his feet. I steer him into a seat and find a small newsagent nearby to buy him a bottle of water.

'It could be a migraine. It's probably dehydration,' I tell him, handing the water over. 'I'll go and see if I can find somewhere that sells painkillers. Wait here and rest.'

I wander off alone and try to track down some paracetamol. It's actually quite nice to be alone. Married life has been wonderful so far, but I need to come up for air. It's nice to be by myself for a bit, even if it's just for a few minutes.

I find myself glancing behind me now and then. What am I expecting, the man with the camera and long lens? He was probably just a tourist. Scott says I'm being paranoid when I mention the incident. It wasn't an incident at all, really.

The streets are deserted when I look around. It's just the same tourists wandering back and forth, all hats, scarves, and sunglasses to protect against the blazing sun.

I finally manage to track down a pharmacy. It's small, and everything is labelled in Greek.

I ask the man behind the counter for some painkillers. He rummages around on the shelves whilst I stroke the ginger cat luxuriating on the counter.

That's when I catch sight of her. A woman in sunglasses and a hat. I turn around. Even below the accessories, I can tell who it is.

FORTY

'Dawn?'

'How did you know it was me?' she pulls off her glasses.

My mouth opens in surprise when I see blue bruising around her right eye. Her lip looks like it has been split, too. It's in the healing process.

'What happened to you?'

She shrugs. 'Rough date.'

'Are you serious?'

The man behind the counter places a box of paracetamol on the counter and looks at me expectantly. I pay for it and step outside with Dawn. She glances around nervously but seems satisfied she can turn and talk to me.

'Where did you disappear to?' I ask when we are back in the sunshine. 'I was worried about you.'

She snorts. 'So worried that you called off the wedding?'

'No,' I say guiltily. 'I didn't know where you were. I kept expecting you to turn up at the ceremony.'

'Anyone else in that situation might have

called the police or something.'

'I thought about it, but Scott said I was worrying about nothing. He said you went off with other men often, like the one in the bar.'

'I bet he did.' Her voice is bitter.

'What's that supposed to mean?'

'Scott did this to me.'

'What are you talking about?'

'How did he know I'd met someone in that bar? He wasn't there, was he?'

'No. I must have mentioned it to him...' I wrack my brain, trying to remember what I told Scott. He did seem to jump to the idea of Dawn meeting another man quickly.

'You didn't tell him, Sam. Scott had me followed. He paid that bloke to target me in that bar. I should have known better. The guy was barely in his twenties and looked like he'd just stepped off a hunks calendar.'

I stare at Dawn. She can't be serious. Scott wouldn't do such a thing. 'What did the man do to you?'

She crosses her arms. 'He assaulted me.'

'What do you mean?'

'Things were innocent enough in the bar. But after you left, he got aggressive. He forced me outside to the alley at the back of the bar. I won't go into details. But he made sure I got a good beating afterwards. He only stopped when some passers by interrupted him. Then he scarpered. I would have been killed if those other blokes on their stag do hadn't shown up.'

I swear. 'Are you all right?'

'Clearly not.' She points at the bruising on her face. She shows me more on her arms, fading to yellow now. There are marks around her wrist where she was obviously held down.

I stare at her injuries. 'What makes you think Scott paid that man to do this?'

'Because he did. I know him, Sam. It's what he does. He gets what he wants and doesn't let anyone else get in his way. In this case, it was me. He didn't want me interfering in the wedding, so he made sure I was out of the way for the big day.'

Dawn is talking nonsense. Scott is the last person to be involved in crime and paid hits, for goodness sake. He is simply my nice, sweet husband. 'It sounds very extreme. That bloke in the bar was probably just there to prey on female tourists. That's why he honed in on us. It must have been obvious we weren't locals. Scott wouldn't want to hurt you. He isn't like that.'

'Isn't he? You've known him for two minutes before rushing headfirst into marriage. You don't know what makes him tick. I'm not pretending I don't know exactly why he sent someone to kill me.'

I sigh. 'Why would you think Scott would want you dead?'

'Because he doesn't want to split the money with me.'

'That doesn't make sense. You both admit

you aren't getting much from the divorce.'

'Not that money, silly. Your money. Your inheritance. Scott and I agreed to share it.'

My breath catches in my throat. 'What?'

'It's the big day where that is concerned, isn't it? Your birthday. Have the funds been transferred into your bank account yet?'

'My inheritance?' I blink in confusion. 'I don't know. I haven't checked.'

'Well, Scott will be eagerly awaiting it in the next few days. He has been biding his time for ages. Mark my words. Your money is the only reason he married you. You still don't seem to realise.'

Dawn has made a mistake. She doesn't understand that I've only just revealed to Scott there is an inheritance. 'He hasn't mentioned the money at all. He never even knew about it until very recently.'

Dawn looks at me, almost with sympathy. 'He was already well aware. I'm sorry to have to tell you this. He has known all along.'

'He can't have,' I say, my voice rising with annoyance. What is Dawn trying to pull here? 'I didn't tell him.'

She laughs bitterly. 'Where there is a large amount of money, there are always parasites in the background. I saw the same thing with my Dad all the time. You think all those trust managers are squeaky clean, do you?'

'They have to be. It's their job.'

'Don't be so naive, Sam. When your uncle died, the trust was transferred to a new company, right? One up north.'

I hesitate. 'How did you know that?'

'Scott told me.'

'How. I only told him a few days before the wedding.'

'Yes, but Scott told me back in England. He told me everything about you, who you really were, why you had scars to hide. He knew all about the money, of course. He has contacts. A little birdie told him all about the trust that's been tantalisingly close all your adult life. Now, when you were likely to inherit, you suddenly get a marriage proposal that comes virtually out of nowhere. Coincidence? I think not. It was no accident that you and Scott bumped into each other in that coffee shop. He arranged the whole thing. He told me how he did it. He followed you, watched and waited until he knew your routine. You always chose to visit the same coffee shop after work. The one on Old Bury Road. It's near Ridgewood primary.'

I've gone very cold. For a moment, I forget I'm on a winding street beneath the Greek sun.

None of this can be true. My husband is wonderful. He loves me. He has done nothing but shower me in affection this whole time. Nothing.

We haven't had a single argument at all. I can't say that about any of my other relationships. Dawn must know this. She knows how wonderful Scott is as a partner. She is using it to her advantage, trying to make me believe this fabrication. I thought she had changed. I was obviously wrong.

'You're lying.' I shake my head and back away. 'You're just jealous of me and Scott. You said our wedding brought back memories of when you were going to marry Scott yourself. You're making this up.'

She groans. 'It's impossible not to feel jealous of the new wife. I admit that. But that isn't why I'm standing here telling you this. I've come to tell you that you are in danger now that you have married Scott. With no will and no children, he is legally the sole heir of your fortune. The money arrives in your account any day. He made sure you and he were legally bound before windfall day arrived. That's no accident. I can guarantee what he is doing right now.'

'What's that?'

'Scott is at this very minute preparing for your murder.'

FORTY-ONE

There is a silence between us as Dawn makes this declaration.

'You couldn't be more wrong,' I tell her firmly. This is the happily-ever-after I deserve after everything I have been through. No one will take it from me, no matter how elaborate the story.

Dawn tilts her head in that characteristic way of hers. 'Really?'

'Yes. We are a couple in love on our honeymoon. Scott has a migraine. I left him to find painkillers.'

'I can guarantee that he doesn't have a headache. He just wants you out of the way for a little while. He obviously needs to implement a part of his plan without you seeing. As soon as that money lands in your account and Scott knows it, your number is up.'

'Don't be silly. This is a typical honeymoon and nothing else. I think I would have noticed if Scott didn't really care for me. You're trying to split us up. That's why you are inventing all this.'

Dawn looks irritated by my reaction. Her

plan isn't going how she hoped. 'This is what I meant by you reminding me of my younger self, that naive girl preparing to marry Scott because she thought she was in love. I was so stupid. My fiancé love bombed me into not having any thoughts of my own, just like he has with you. He treated me like a princess. I could barely breathe. I couldn't see what he really wanted. My inheritance. It was common knowledge that my father had a drinking problem. He was a very wealthy man and didn't attempt to hide it. He had all sorts of parasites clinging to him. Addiction and money are a dangerous mix. They make you a target. Look at any Hollywood celeb.'

'This is crazy.' I turn my back on Dawn and her lies. 'I'm going back to enjoy my honeymoon. Please don't follow us anymore. Henry said he will start legal action against you if you don't stop harassing us.'

'I'm sure he did. He doesn't have a legal leg to stand on, though. Not now I know what he has done.'

I turn back. I should just keep on walking, but I'm curious to know how Dawn is trying to drag Henry into this.

'What did Henry ever do to you?'

'I have my suspicions. How do you think Scott found out about your trust fund?'

'I told you he didn't know anything about it until I told him before the wedding.'

Dawn laughs. 'You're in denial. Scott was

fed the information from Henry. Scott gets into a financial pickle, if you will, every so often. He needs someone to bail him out with a stack of cash. Men's fashion isn't as profitable as he would have you believe.'

'Of course it is. Scott is loaded.'

'That's what he wants everyone to think. His shop in the city is just a front, you know.'

Now Dawn really is talking nonsense, trying to make Scott out to be a criminal mastermind or something. I don't even know exactly what she is accusing him of to be honest.

'A front for what?' I ask exasperatedly.

'For a Ponzi scheme.'

A laugh bursts from me at this. 'Sorry, but that's just so ridiculous. Scott is so obviously into men's fashion.'

'He is—as a consumer. He keeps the shop running to make it look like he is an upstanding businessman. But he makes his money elsewhere. He gets investors to fund the so-called profits to other investors and so on. That's how he really makes his money. Think about it. Do you think one shop with an eye-watering rent makes enough money to buy a house like his?'

'You said your inheritance assisted part of his life.'

'Exactly. He only married me for my money too. We're in the same boat, you and me.'

'No, we're not. You're making this up. You just want to see us split.'

'Yes, to save you! You don't seem to realise the danger you are in.'

'I'm not.' I shrug, feeling irritated now. I just want to go back to my happy honeymoon. Everything was fine until Dawn showed up.

'Look,' I say. 'Scott's parents are wealthy people too. They might have helped out their son.'

'I can assure you they haven't,' Dawn smiles. It's like she is enjoying a private joke. 'Even if they did, do you think that would be enough for Scott's champagne lifestyle? You're smarter than that, Sam.'

I want to go back to Scott and continue the honeymoon from heaven I've been enjoying. I don't want doubts shadowing my trip and the rest of my married life. Dawn needs to let this out now so we can put this to bed.

It's my turn to cross my arms. 'If what you are saying is true, then why didn't you tell me in the first place?'

'I didn't know you had money when I first met you. You did a good job of hiding it.'

'Thanks, you keep telling me that.' I roll my eyes with more annoyance. 'Look, if you have genuine concerns then take them to the police. Let them deal with it.'

Dawn looks guilty at this. She glances around this way and that. 'I could. But that wouldn't help me get my inheritance back. We made a deal, Scotty and me. We would go fifty-

fifty on the money he got from you.'

'Why would he make a deal with you? That makes no sense based on what you have already told me. Why wouldn't he keep all the money for himself so he can guffaw his head off in his secret underground lair?' I laugh at the thought. Dawn's claims are becoming more elaborate by the minute.

'Because I threatened to ruin his wedding plans. He knew he needed to get you down the aisle and have a ring on you before that inheritance money landed in your bank account. That's why he was so determined to plough on with the wedding, even when I gatecrashed the lead up to the ceremony. When he knew I wanted money, he told me everything about you and what his plans were. I backed off after that. It was the day when you went off for your appointment at the trust. It was Jonathan you saw that day, wasn't it?'

'How do you know that?' I ask quietly.

'Because Henry has a son named Jonathan who works at a trust management firm in the city. They may have a different surname, but I assure you they are father and son. That's Henry's source of info. Henry Junior was handed your case after your uncle died. He knew everything about you. Including how much money you were sitting on. One-point-one million. Am I right? Scott knew everything about you because of him. He adapted his behaviour to seem like the perfect bloke. He made sure you would fall for him, fast. He did the same thing with me. Feels good, doesn't it, to be the only woman in the world with a gorgeous guy hanging on your every word?'

I pull the sleeves of my blouse down nervously. 'This can't be true. You've just found out who I am and have invented this. You've done your research on me and made some lucky guesses. It wouldn't have been hard to estimate my father's wealth. Anyone can look up a house price on Rightmove or the net worth of an athlete like my father, especially when his life was splashed all over the papers. You are clever, I will give you that. Maybe you did have a date gone wrong with that guy in the bar that night. I'm sorry, Dawn. I'm sure it was by chance, not because he was a hired hitter. It was bad luck.'

'You're in denial, Sam,' she says in a sing-song voice.

'No, I'm not. Your story doesn't add up. I can't trust you after everything. You have treated me awfully and done nothing but try and drive a wedge between me and Scott. Besides, if any of this was true, why are you stabbing Scott in the back now? You claimed you planned to split my money between you. So what changed?'

'Scott ordered me killed. That's what changed. Now I'm going to do everything I can to slam the brakes on the windfall he is, no doubt at this very minute, drooling over.'

I scoff. 'Again, you aren't dead. One thing Scott doesn't do is fail. He's an achiever. You must know that. Yet you are walking around just fine. If Scott wanted you dead, I'm sure you would be. Not that he is like that.'

'Hence the disguise and me laying low this past week. I'm making sure he doesn't succeed. I suspect the hired hunk didn't report back to say he failed. He probably did a runner with whatever he was paid. Scott thinks the deed has been done. So that gives me some advantage.'

I think of how Scott threw Dawn's jewellery into the sea. That was odd, I admit. Was he disposing of evidence after he thought his ex-wife had been murdered? Or rather, was he ridding himself of Dawn's memory after everything she has done to us?

'I can't trust you after everything you have done, every lie you have told. You have done nothing but manipulate me and Scott from the start. I just can't believe a word you say anymore.'

'Don't then.' She shrugs. 'It's your funeral. Scott will arrange for you to have a little accident on your honeymoon. Pretty easy on a yacht out to sea with no witnesses. He has already set the stage for a drowning. Did you notice the number of safety measures around your private pool at the hotel? I'll bet anything Scott told the staff you couldn't swim. It will back up his story if you accidentally fall off the boat on your honeymoon and drown.'

I think back to the life vests and what seemed like a pile of floatation aids around the pool. That was a little strange. Scott and I laughed about it at the time. Dawn had seen it all over her side of the wall, of course. Did she have the same measures on her side? I hadn't looked. She has had over a week to come up with this story that fits her narrative. I tell her this.

She shakes her head impatiently. 'Scott has it all planned out, I'm telling you. He will be flying home as a widow, I promise. What kind of funeral service do you want? Have you had the burial or cremation discussion with him yet? It's probably a downer on the honeymoon, I suppose.'

I stare into Dawn's eyes. Are her words laced with a threat?

I watch her as she adjusts her baseball cap. 'If Scott really was planning to marry and murder, then how are you still alive at all? Why didn't he kill you after he got your money years ago?'

'He didn't have to. He asked for the money and a plausible reason for needing it. Back then, I was too stupid to question it. I was happy to invest in our future together. He also didn't know when my father would die and I would receive the funds. He had to wait two years before pay day, it turned out. Besides, I served other purposes. I was his shiny accessory to go with his lifestyle. I can't say the same for you.'

I lift my chin defensively. Dawn is playing on my insecurities; she has lived with me and learned what they are. She knows how to play me. I refuse to let her see how much her comment cuts.

'Besides,' she continues, 'You're an only child, the sole heir. My brother got half of Dad's estate. Scott set his eyes on Warren's money, too. As I said, your husband gets what he wants. He doesn't fail.'

I roll my eyes. 'How could he possibly get your brother's money?'

'Far too easily. Warren was talked into investing in Scott's behind-the-scenes scheme. Scott promised guaranteed returns for doing nothing. It obviously was too good to be true, but Scott was believable. I'm sure you can relate. And Warren was greedy. Scott was my husband, which made him trustworthy on many levels. Warren didn't think anything of handing money to his brother-in-law. It wasn't like he was going to make a quick getaway with me as his wife.'

'What happened?'

'Warren was strung along for a good while. He believed in Scott. My husband was such a good salesman. Then Warren needed the money back. He had lost his job. He needed the money to pay his bills until he got back on his feet. Scott kept making excuses for why Warren couldn't just withdraw it. It sounded reasonable enough at the time. Then, my brother defaulted on his massive mortgage. His wife left him. Warren lost everything because of Scott. He was homeless. He became depressed and suicidal. It wasn't long before he had taken his own life.'

I blink and try to process this. Dawn looks sombre, haunted too. She certainly is good at acting.

She almost has me fooled. Almost. 'If that was true, then why didn't you do anything to help your brother? You still lived with Scott at that point. You surely had access to some money.'

Dawn swallows. She looks like she might be about to cry. 'I didn't find any of this out until I went abroad last year and visited Warren's ex-wife in Sweden. I had no idea Warren had invested his whole inheritance with Scott. The pair of them kept it a secret from me. Warren lied to me before. He told me it was just a small investment. Loose change, he had said. The bank statements I saw on my visit went back years. They didn't lie.'

Her eyes focus on me again after staring into the past. 'So that's what I want, Sam. Revenge. I want to take Scott down after what he did to my brother, to me. He sucked the best years of my life and sent me the bill. I need to get back at him. Especially after what happened last week with that bloke. I saw everything flash before my —'

I'm not quite sure what Dawn's everything flashed in front of because she slips her shades on hastily and disappears amongst a nearby guided walking tour. She is down a narrow archway and out of sight as I even open my mouth in surprise.

'There you are.'

It's Scott. I gasp in shock at his sudden appearance. Dawn's accusations are fresh in my mind.

'What's the matter?' he asks.

FORTY-TWO

'You found some, then?' Scott asks.

I blink in confusion. 'Found some what?'

He takes the packet of paracetamol from my hand and punches a few pills from the blister pack, downing them with a bottle of water.

'Yes, there was a pharmacy.' I gesture vaguely behind me. The quaint shop with the resident cat seemed like a long time ago.

'Are you okay?'

I open my mouth. I want to explain to Scott what just happened. A covertly dressed Dawn reappeared after her mysterious disappearance. She approached me and dropped a massive bombshell of wild accusations. *Dawn said you want to kill me, babes. Where can we get some Ouzo? It might take the edge off your migraine.*

Of course, I don't say anything like that.

It's impossible to know where to start to explain. I want time to process what Dawn has said before I filter it back to Scott. Or maybe I won't mention it at all. After the way he has been around the subject of Dawn since the wedding, I'm reluctant to say a word to my husband about his ex.

Dawn isn't a topic on the menu. Not if I want a peaceful life.

Then it occurs to me I haven't had a thought like that for a while. Not since my own disastrous ex. Controlling Adam had me keeping a mental list of dos and don'ts. I could never relax, always treading on eggshells.

Is that what is happening here? My fingers slip into my pocket for my phone. Sara is a fountain of advice. She can always help me see the wood for the trees, even on a cloudy day.

Before I even get the thing from my pocket, it starts buzzing in my hand. Is that thing happening where the person I'm thinking about is calling me first?

No. It's an unknown number.

A man's voice answers. British. 'Hello? Is that Holly?'

My insides run cold. I haven't been directly addressed by that name for years. 'Excuse me?'

'Holly? Holly Golding? Is that you?'

'Who is this?'

Scott stops sipping his water and stares at me. He raises his eyebrows questioningly. He mouths, *'Is everything all right?'*

The man gives his name and the newspaper he works for. He is a journalist.

Now I go hot and cold all over. 'What do you want?'

'Sam, is it these days? I've been researching

your story. I want to do an anniversary piece revisiting the events. It's been twenty years since you lost your family in such tragic circumstances. How would you like to tell your side of the story? Our readers might like to know what it was like fighting to escape from inside the inferno. That sort of thing.'

Suddenly, I'm lightheaded. Heat prickles the skin beneath my blouse. I need to sit down. Scott reaches out a concerned hand and supports my back. He steers me onto a low wall nearby, his concerned gaze on my face.

He mouths another question at me as he strokes my shoulders. *What's going on?'*

I finally pull myself together enough to speak into the phone. 'I'm sorry. I think you have the wrong number.'

The man on the line persists, insisting he has contacts, he has done his research, and all he wants is an interview. 'I'm not asking you to do anything right away. I understand you are on your honeymoon. The newspaper currently has a reporter and photographer nearby in Katapola on another story. I'm not asking you to hand the story to them. We can arrange something for when you get back to the UK. We can play this thing your way, no worries.'

'I'm sorry. I can't help you,' I say in a hollow voice that doesn't sound like mine. 'I don't know how you got this number, but you have made a mistake. Don't call again.'

My hands tremble as I end the call.

'What was that about?' Scott asks gently by my side. I'm so grateful for him. I've never needed him more. My honeymoon has taken a strange turn in the last fifteen minutes. I just want to slip back into bliss again. No Dawn. No reporters. I never expected to hear from the press again. Why would they hound me now?

Before I open my mouth to speak, I catch sight of a long camera lens pointing in my direction from beneath a wide-brimmed hat in the semi-distance.

Instinctively, my head turns, not wanting to be snapped. I think of the man photographing the yacht. The press has found me.

I stand up from the wall and hurry down the nearest narrow street.

'Sam?' Scott calls. He looks bewildered as he catches up with me.

I'm already looking for another exit. Where am I going in this unfamiliar territory? I'm a rat in a maze. This has been unexpectedly sprung on me. Throwing them off is the key.

What else can I do but run for cover?

'Sam, please!' Scott reaches for my arm. 'What on earth are you running from?'

'They've found me,' I mutter. My eyes dart around for an escape route. I need to get away, to think. All I need is to clear my head.

'Who has found you?' He looks at me with concern. 'No one can get you with me here, I assure you. I'll protect you. You've been acting strangely since the pharmacy. What's going on, babes?'

'I'm being followed by the press.'

'Press?' He looks around. 'Where?'

'A few minutes ago. There was a man with a camera.'

Scott relaxes at this. 'Sam, lots of people have cameras. It's a tourist destination. Look around. Everyone is taking a snap of something or other.'

He is right, of course. Phones and small compact cameras are in virtually every hand. But long lenses? Not so many.

Then I spot another one—an older man with a chunky DSLR camera and a large lens. It seems too big for a casual trip around a hot island in the sun—or does it?

I turn back to Scott. 'That was who was on the phone. Some reporter wants to do a story. He knew my real name.' I glance around me again, praying I'm being paranoid and nothing more. Some Ouzo sounds pretty good right now.

Or any kind of alcohol. I've never needed a drink more. I'd love to sit out in the sun with a cocktail or an ice-cold vodka, but I feel too exposed, as though anyone could pounce on me at any moment.

'I need to get out of here,' I whisper hurriedly.

FORTY-THREE

Scott looks at me as though I'm having a nervous breakdown, but he complies. He takes me back to the boat. I'm running on autopilot as he points out a rare bird at the dock, nodding and forcing a smile, pretending to be interested.

Inside, I'm fretting. How did the press find me? Who else knows about my new identity? Where on earth did that reporter get my number from? A whole bunch of people have had it recently in regards to wedding planning: Ellen at the dress shop, the photographer, the stylist, the hotel reception, and Scott's various drivers, to name but a few off the top of my head.

I can only hope lurking photographers haven't managed to sneak a shot of me. Can they print it without my permission? I'm well and truly an adult now, outside of child-protection laws.

Once we are far enough out to sea, Scott moors the yacht and brings me a glass bottle of sparkling apple juice from the fridge with some ice.

Do I even like this stuff? Right now, I want

vodka, wine, or some Irish cream—something with some burn to distract me from my whirring thoughts.

'Thanks,' I say, taking a sip.

'What happened back there?' He asks as he removes the cap off a bottle of beer; he tosses it into the sea, just as he had done with Dawn's things.

'I told you. Some journalist has found out who I am. Have you given my number out to anyone?'

'No one of consequence. Everyone wedding-related had both our numbers, just in case I couldn't be reached if I was at work or something.' He looks thoughtful for a second. 'So that means the wedding coordinator at the hotel, caterer, DJ, florist, photographer, stylist. There are probably loads more. Why? Do you think they leaked your number somewhere?'

'I don't know what to think right now.'

Scott nods and slips his hand into my pocket. I look at him in surprise for a moment until he slips my phone out.

'What are you doing?' I ask him.

'Switching this off. If you think the press has somehow gotten hold of your number, they could have hacked you. If you leave it switched on, they could be tracking you.'

'Oh. I need my phone, though.'

'Of course. When we get to the next island, we will try to find someone to check it for malware, just to be on the safe side.'

'That's a good idea,' I say with relief. I expect Scott to hand my phone back, but he slips back inside the cabin and returns without it.

'Just in case,' he explains. 'I don't want our private conversations overheard, do you?'

'Can bugged phones pick up audio even when they are off?'

Scott shrugs. 'I think so. I've heard all sorts of stories. Best not to take chances.'

I nod. 'Who do you think leaked my number?'

Scott frowns. 'I can't imagine anyone to do with the wedding being involved. Those people were professionals. I wouldn't have hired them otherwise. Besides, how would they have known who you really are? I certainly haven't told anyone. It hasn't been possible. I've been with you the whole time.'

I blink, Dawn's accusations earlier coming back to me. 'Apart from the night before the wedding and most of the wedding day.'

'Yes, apart from that.' He smiles and takes my hand. He pushes up the sleeve of my floral blouse and plants kisses carefully all the way up to my elbow, avoiding my scars. 'It was torture being away from you for so many hours. It was the first time apart we have had since before we were dating.'

He is right, I realise, as I think back. Since Scott and I started dating, we haven't been out of each other's company for more than a few hours or so. I haven't stopped to breathe.

'Is that healthy?' I ask out loud.

Dawn said something along those lines, too. Was it the same for her in those blissful first few months of her relationship? Hadn't it also been the same for me and Adam? He was wonderful until the day I moved in with him. Then the switch flipped. The mask was whipped off. He showed his true colours after that.

Scott laughs. 'What do you mean?'

'I mean…I don't know. Did we really think about getting married before we dove in?'

The smile slips slightly from my husband's handsome face. 'What are you saying?'

I stand up and shrug. What am I saying? I'm still jittery from what happened on the island. I rotate my shoulders a few times as I pace back and forth.

'I don't know. Maybe I am happy.'

Why is my mouth still making noise? I need to stop, take a breather and not say anything to ruin my honeymoon. We are supposed to be happy. It's only downhill after the wedding, isn't it? That was the case for my parents and Scott's, too, it seems. The same goes for Dawn.

Why did she leave Scott again? I struggle to piece it together. How do I separate fact from fiction when I've had so much thrown at me from both sides?

Scott's ex-wife left for another country.

Sweden, if you believe Dawn. She went off the rails after her brother's death. Scott admitted that himself, so that must be true. He didn't say what triggered those events. Could there be a speck of truth in what Dawn has told me?

Or is she still the psycho-ex trying to mess with my mind? She has admitted she is jealous of the sturdy relationship I have with her ex-husband.

'Are you saying you didn't want to get married?' Scott stares at me in confusion. 'You could have fooled me. A week ago, you looked like the happiest bride on earth. I have the pictures to prove it.'

I look at him sharply. 'Prove what?'

Dawn's voice sing-songs in my head. *Silly, Sam. Scott has set the whole thing up. The stage is set for you to have an accident.*

'That you were happily married to me.'

'Why would you need evidence of that?' I ask defensively, thinking of Dawn's accusations.

Scott gets up with a smile and puts his hands on my hips. 'So we can show our grandchildren, of course.'

'Oh. Right.'

He scrutinises me. 'What happened at the pharmacy earlier?'

'Nothing.'

'Are you sure? You started acting strangely before you had that phone call. Did you have a run-in with someone else?'

I shake my head, not wanting to rock the boat, so to speak. Then I realise I feel like I'm having a conversation with Adam, not my lovely new husband.

Forget that. I'm not treading on eggshells again. I promised myself I wouldn't. Life is too short for that nonsense.

'Actually, I did meet someone,' I admit. 'I ran into Dawn.'

Scott's beautiful eyes widen. 'Are you serious? I thought she was gone.'

I watch him as he moves over to lean on the railing of the yacht. I can't see his face, but he looks devastated by this news.

'It shouldn't be that much of a surprise,' I tell him. 'You knew Dawn was in Greece. She was in the hotel room directly next to ours. Is it that much of a shock if she shows up on our honeymoon?'

'I really thought she had left…She was gone the night before the wedding.'

'With the man from the bar?'

'Yes. I just figured she had hooked up with a guy and given up on hounding us.'

'How did you know Dawn had met someone?'

'You told me.'

I think about this for a second. Adam so often used to gaslight me. I will not let it happen again. I know what is real. 'No, I didn't.'

'Sam, you did. I remember. How else would I

know?'

'Exactly.'

'Excuse me?'

I shake my head, not wanting an argument. Dawn has succeeded in driving a wedge between myself and my husband, one way or another. I need to get this off my chest so we can move on. 'Dawn says you hired someone to meet her in the bar. She says he tried to kill her after she was assaulted.'

He blinks. 'So?'

I pause. 'What?'

'So what if Dawn accuses me of yet another thing? She always made wild accusations when we were together. All the while, she was treating me like shit, cheating on me at every opportunity. It was humiliating. I had a really tough time.'

Scott winces. 'The years with her were some of the darkest in my life. I was upset when she left, actually, because I was disappointed I wasn't the one to end things. I guess I took my vows too seriously. Now, here I am, all these years later, having to explain to my new wife just how crazy my ex is instead of enjoying my honeymoon. We only get this time once, Sam. You wonder who handed your number to a journalist, use your imagination.'

'I'm sorry,' I say quietly.

'Dawn has done nothing but try to split us up and cause as many problems as she can. I thought she was in the past. I can't believe you would believe any old story she makes up about me. It's very distressing, Sam. Maybe I'm the one who should be wondering if I did the right thing? Especially when it turns out you have been lying to me about who you really are since we met.'

'It was Dawn,' I start quickly. 'She was the one who revealed my real name just before the wedding. She did everything to split us up. I was wrong to think she could have been telling anything other than lies.'

'Were you planning on telling me the truth ever?'

'Yes, of course. I was just waiting for the right moment. I would have told you sooner. I wanted to, believe me. When I ran that errand before we left the UK, it would have been a good time. If we had been alone without Dawn that day, then I would have told you everything.'

'Why that day?'

I take a deep breath. This should have been happier news. 'My inheritance is coming through shortly. I already told you it was in a trust fund all these years until I got my life sorted out. Remember that day I went and ran that errand? That was the day I visited the trust and proved I met their conditions for receiving the funds. That was the same day I wanted to tell you everything. The money is everything, from the insurance payout on our family home to Dad's life insurance. It's quite a lot, over a million. The money should be in my bank account within the next few days.'

Scott is quiet as he contemplates this. 'So you were never after my money then?'

'Of course not. That's not why I'm with you. You know that.'

He softens at this, and I take this as my cue to wrap my arms around him.

'I love you,' I tell him. 'I'm sorry. I wasn't accusing you. I just had so many doubts after what Dawn said. She can be convincing.'

'Now you know a little of what I went through with her. I meant it when I said the decade or so with her was a dark time for me. I never knew where I stood with her or what she was going to do next. You've seen just a snippet of how she used to behave. It was like I was being what she wanted me to be. I could never relax or be myself. Something innocuous would set her off, and she would find a way to punish me.'

'That sounds familiar. I had a relationship like that.'

My husband sighs. 'You can feel so trapped, can't you? I thought I had broken free from her when she walked out one day. Then she came back, just when I was moving on with you.'

'She won't win. I will not let her get to us again. She can't get to us on this boat. When we get back home, she won't have a right to the house either. We can put her behind us if we stick together.'

'That's all I wanted all along.'

He kisses me, and I return the gesture with interest. It isn't long before my blouse is slipped over my head. I relish the freedom and privacy of being alone above the gentle Greek waves. The privacy is liberating in the red glow of the sunset.

We are far enough from the islands that even the longest lens couldn't reach us. They can't capture how we return to our honeymoon activities with enthusiasm.

FORTY-FOUR

After Scott and I have made up after our slight disagreement, we enjoy the remnants of the sunset together. Scott serves us a candlelit dinner at the table on the yacht's deck. Despite his lack of kitchen skills, he manages to rustle up a special dinner of grilled fish and herby salsa.

After a dessert of honey cake, Scott whips out a beautifully wrapped gift and hands it to me.

'I had almost forgotten it was my birthday,' I say as I thank him and start tearing open the shiny paper.

Inside is a small velvet gift box. I think of the expensive diamond jewellery Scott has showered me with. There is something more rustic inside. It is a handmade ring with a roughly hewn semi-precious stone inside.

'It's the colour of the sea here,' Scott says. 'I thought it would be a nice souvenir from Katapola. When you look at it, you'll always remember our honeymoon.'

'You got this here?'

'Yes,' Scott smiles. 'I picked it up earlier from

a little shop selling handmade gifts. I had to fake a migraine to get it. Sorry.'

His words immediately catapult me back to Dawn's comment about Scott faking a headache so he could sneak off and do something subversive. I wonder if she knew he was buying jewellery for me and used it to her advantage.

'You like it?'

I love it,' I say, slipping it on a finger and admiring it. 'It's beautiful. You are right. It's the perfect reminder of our honeymoon.'

'You definitely like it then?'

'Yes. It's gorgeous. I love handmade stuff more than commercial pieces. I adore blue jewels, too. It's probably my favourite piece of jewellery you have got me.'

'Wonderful,' he grins. 'I'll take the rest back to Cartier when we get home.'

I laugh and bat him playfully. 'I didn't mean it like that.'

'Well, with a one-point-one million windfall, you should be the one treating me.'

My smile falters slightly. Did I tell Scott exactly how much I inherited? I don't recall.

Scott steps back inside the kitchen to fetch more drinks. Now that the sun has gone down, I start to shiver. The sky is strips of gold and red between powdery purple clouds; the wind is starting to pick up.

I get up and open the deck box to retrieve a blanket to wrap myself in. But I stop dead. My insides run cold. There is a gun nestled atop the bundle of blankets.

Scott appears at my side and freezes, too, a glass in each hand.

'What's this?' I ask him, horrorstruck.

He shrugs. 'Just in case.'

'In case what?'

'I don't know. It can be dangerous at sea. It was Henry's idea, to be honest. He handed the thing to me on the morning of our wedding. Some friends of his were almost taken hostage during a sailing trip once. And what with this Dawn thing, it just seemed like a good idea to have some security.'

He sets the drinks down and slides the blanket out from underneath the gun. He seems unwilling to touch the weapon with his bare hands.

I turn to him. 'You wouldn't shoot Dawn, though, would you? I mean, she has done some strange and intrusive things, but she is still a human being.'

'I told you, you don't know Dawn like I do. She is unpredictable.' Scott wraps the blanket around my shoulders. 'Underestimating her might be the last thing you do.'

FORTY-FIVE

Once twilight hits, Scott takes me below deck to the bedroom cabin. It's obvious what is on his mind, but I'm feeling distinctly unsettled. I pull away from his kiss.

'What's the matter?'

'I don't know. I guess I'm not happy about there being a gun on board. You can imagine why I don't like them. They remind me of my past.'

Scott scoffs. 'Don't worry about it. I will only use it for an emergency.'

'What if there isn't one?'

'That would be great.' He shrugs and trails his mouth down my neck. Normally, I would be melting into him at this point, but I'm just not in the mood right now. There is too much on my mind. I'd really like some time alone to process everything.

There is no solitude to be had on this yacht. It's smaller than I imagined it would be; I'd expected Scott to splash out for this trip.

As a result, I was distinctly underwhelmed when Scott pointed out this vessel in the marina in Santorini. Is it true what Dawn said about

Scott running low on funds?

This yacht is perfectly lovely. Its white sails and graceful curves won't have come cheap.

Was I anticipating a crewed megayacht? Not exactly. Maybe a captained catamaran would have been better, albeit more expensive? A crew would feel welcome right now. It's just Scott and me out at sea alone. The isolation is screaming at me.

Should I let Dawn's words affect my opinion of my new husband? They've crawled into my brain, either way.

Scott is still the same man I met and fell in love with, isn't he? Dawn has done too much to spite us for me to take her accusations at face value. I would be crazy to believe her now when she has existed these past few weeks purely to rip me apart from Scott.

I'd have liked some processing time, just so I could settle this thing in my head and focus on enjoying my honeymoon.

If it hadn't been for that call from the journalist, I wouldn't have rushed back to the yacht in such a hurry. Maybe a solo walk around the island this afternoon would have done me good?

My husband hasn't married me for my money, I tell myself. He didn't even know about my inheritance until I told him.

Okay, says a little voice. So how did he know the exact amount?

Maybe it was a lucky guess?

I groan inwardly. My thoughts run in circles, eating their own tails.

Scott pushes me down onto the bed as his mouth works lower. He tries to ease my legs apart but meets with resistance.

He sighs with frustration and rests his hot cheek on my bare knee. 'Forget about the gun, Sam. I told you it wasn't my idea. Henry handed it to me and made me promise to keep it close by. He didn't give me a choice, okay?'

'It's not that.' I sigh. 'How did you know how much I am inheriting?'

'What?'

'You knew the exact figure. I never told you how much it was. So how did you know?'

'What are you talking about? You told me it was over a million earlier. That's all I know.'

I shake my head as I remember our conversation. 'No. I didn't tell you how much it was. I just said it was over a million.'

'Right,' Scott says slowly. 'One-point-one is over a million.'

'So is one-point-two or one-point-four. Or one million and change, and so on. There are lots of numbers that would fit. You said the correct figure earlier, so matter-of-factly like you already knew.'

'Okay.' Scott pauses as he looks at me with his pale eyes. I have the sense he is weighing up options. He sighs. 'So I knew about the inheritance.'

I'm stunned into silence for a few moments. I was right. Dawn was right. Scott already knew about the money.

FORTY-SIX

I'm in shock for a few moments. 'What do you mean you knew about my inheritance?'

He shakes his head. 'I found out just before you told me. You see, I was in shock when I learned the truth about you.'

'When was this?'

'A few days before the wedding. When Dawn told me you had lied throughout our entire relationship about who you were—she told me you had even lied about your real name—I was upset. I called Henry and talked to him about it. I wasn't sure if I still wanted to marry you after you had deceived me so much.'

A jolt of annoyance stabs at me. 'It wasn't that much of a deception. Sam *is* my real name now. It's legally been mine for years before I met you. I wasn't exactly lying to you.'

'Right, of course.'

'So, how did you find out about the money?'

'Henry told me. His son happens to work at the trust your inheritance is held with.'

My mouth falls open. 'Jonathan. He is Henry's son?'

My husband thinks about this for a moment and nods. 'Yes, Jonathan, that's right.'

I'm outraged. 'He can't divulge private information about clients! It's supposed to be confidential.'

Scott shrugs as he looks away. His lips start caressing my knee, moving upwards. 'Don't worry about it. Henry only told me to assure me everything checked out with you.'

I place a hand on Scott's shoulder, stopping him. 'What do you mean "checked out"?'

'Just that you weren't simply a teaching assistant and nothing more. You were the daughter of a wealthy tennis player.'

My voice rises as fury bubbles in me now. 'What difference does that make?'

'Well, for one thing, it proved that you weren't after my money,' he murmurs against my leg.

'You supposedly knew that all along, didn't you? You were happy to accept me as a teaching assistant in the first place. You were happy with me for who I really was, or so I thought. That's why you asked me to marry you. You wanted us to be together. Why would that change all of a sudden? I shouldn't have to financially prove myself to marry the man I love!'

Scott groans in frustration. 'You are taking it all wrong. Just relax.'

He pushes my shoulders back onto the mattress, but I resist. There is a flash of anger in his eyes, something I haven't seen before. 'Sam, what's this all about?'

I take a deep breath and voice the thing that I've been doubting since I met Dawn earlier today. 'Scott, did you know who I was? I mean before Dawn revealed my identity?'

Scott's eyes narrow on me for a moment too long. It's like he is weighing up his options again. That's all the answer I need.

The air is heavy between us with this realisation. He knows I see through him.

I put a palm to my forehead and stare at the cabin ceiling. 'I can't believe this.'

'It's no big deal,' Scott says quietly.

I look back at him. 'How long have you known?'

My husband seems caught in the headlights now. He shakes his head and licks his lips as he casts around for an answer. 'A while, I guess.'

'How long? How did you find out? Was it through Henry?'

'No,' he says quickly. Too quickly. 'I came across your documents by accident one day. They were under the bed.'

Now I know he is lying. I never kept the documents there. They have always been at the bottom of the walk-in wardrobe since I moved in. Scott would have had to go snooping very well to have found them.

I watch Scott closely. 'You just told me Jonathan told his father the figure I'm inheriting.

Is that how you found out about the money in the first place?'

Scott shakes his head. 'It's nothing like that. I found out accidentally. That's all. Stop fretting about all this.'

Scott is reminding me of Adam and the way he used to dodge questions he didn't like. He would shrug them off and want to slip beneath the floorboards like a cornered ant.

My insides have turned cold. It's much more likely what Dawn said was the truth. Henry told Scott about me ages ago. What else was she right about?

Dawn's accusations seem plausible all of a sudden. *Money makes you a target, Sam,* comes Dawn's sing-song voice in my head.

'I need some air,' I say suddenly as my heart hammers with fear. It suddenly feels much more claustrophobic in here. It was bad enough already; the walls of the cabin are practically touching the double bed. 'Maybe we should head back to port.'

I pull myself up on my elbows and roll onto my side. I'm about to swing my legs from the bed, but Scott puts an arm in front of me to block my way.

'Don't go,' he says firmly. Scott's defined muscles are flexed, and his eyes are intense. 'I love you, Sam. You can't leave me.'

'I'm not leaving you. I just want some space. I need some time to think. Alone. It's impossible on this boat.'

'It's late. Where are you going to go in the dark?'

'I don't know. I just need some air. Some breathing space. Please, Scott.'

'There is all the air you want in here.' His voice is flat in a way that terrifies me. As I look back into his grey eyes, I realise he has no intention of taking the boat back to Katapola, no matter how much I ask. 'This is our honeymoon. We are supposed to be having a good time.

Scott rolls me onto my back and is on top of me before I know it. He kisses me and I find myself stiff and barely responsive. I just want off this boat, but Scott's hands are forceful as they succeed in pulling my shorts down at last.

It's just the two of us out here on the sea in the dark of the Greek night. I'm too scared to move.

I'm frozen beneath him as he pushes into me. It's such a contrast to all our other encounters when Scott has been gentle and tender. Now, I'm rigid with terror.

The toughest thing to deal with is the notion that I should have listened to Dawn.

FORTY-SEVEN

I stare at the dark ceiling of our cabin for many hours; the breathing becomes slow and rhythmic from Scott beside me. His bare torso rises and falls gently.

If only I could sleep as soundly as my husband. Wouldn't it be nice to pretend last night had been a simple nightmare? I don't think I'll ever fall asleep beside him again, not now that I know the truth.

How many days have I got left on this boat with him? Will my spouse push me into the sea and leave me to drown? Maybe he won't take any chances. He could simply shoot me before pushing me overboard. It wouldn't be much of a fight.

I dread to think what sort of animals live beneath the waves out here. Are there sharks in this region? No one would ever find my body with the incriminating bullet hole. Yes, that's the most likely option; I shiver at this realisation. Dawn was right.

Why didn't I realise this sooner? Oh, I remember; Dawn behaved like the classic psycho ex-wife who didn't want her husband to remarry. Why didn't she just come straight out with the truth when she had me alone? She had plenty of chances before the wedding. I guess I will never know.

Now, I am trapped. I will bet anything that Scott was the one who handed that journalist my phone number. That was the call that made me run from the island. My husband would have been able to guess how much I feared the press finding me. He knows I'm a private person who hates the limelight.

Panic flutters in my chest. Despite what Scott might have told the hotel, which provided numerous poolside floats, I can swim perfectly well. There is no way I feel confident that I would make it back to the shore from this distance, however, even if I weren't shot.

How on earth do I get out of this one? I turn my head and stare around the dark cabin for my phone. I can't remember where I left it.

Then the memory comes back to me with a wave of dread. Scott took my phone under the pretence of thwarting hackers and snooping press. He switched it off, too, so there is no chance of hearing it vibrate with calls or notifications.

He has played me so well. Was the journalist even real? The man was a voice on the end of the phone. If Scott paid someone to kill Dawn in the alley behind the bar, it is not unlikely he could have paid others to play parts, too.

I need to get out of here. I want to think about something other than what he has planned next. There is no way I'm hanging around to find out.

The problem is, I'm even trapped in the bed. Scott's heavy arm is trailing over my shoulders as though on guard while he is asleep.

Holding my breath, I try shuffling from beneath it. I take hold of one of his thick thumbs and lift his arm gingerly off me.

It works. But then Scott murmurs and shuffles in his sleep. For a horrible moment, I think the arm will come back up and trap me again. My husband turns the other way and settles again.

After a nerve-wracking few moments, I have made it off the bed. Grabbing my clothes from yesterday, I slip from the cabin on tiptoes and feel my way into the kitchen.

A wave sends me slamming into the kitchen units faster than I expected as I hastily pull on my shorts. When I glance back, I expect Scott to come charging from the room, disturbed. But the door remains shut and still.

I grab hold of the worktop to steady myself and start silently rummaging through cupboards. I don't dare turn a light on, so I'm feeling my way around instead. The sky is barely lightening outside.

I can't find my phone. My heart sinks. Did

Scott throw that overboard, too, as he had with Dawn's jewellery?

What do I do now? Can I sneak into the cockpit and attempt to take the boat back to Katapola? Even if I figured out the controls, wouldn't the engine wake Scott?

I have barely taken two steps towards the pilot's seat when I hear a bang. My knees hit the carpet hard, and I clutch at my chest, feeling for the bullet wound.

FORTY-EIGHT

I can't believe I've been shot. Scott must have come at me from behind. My breath comes short. It's still completely dark as I clutch at my chest, gasping for air.

It's like the bullet my father loaded into his shotgun for me has found me at last. I dodged it when I was sixteen. This time, I'm not so lucky.

I'm on my knees as I stare at the pale carpet, which remains cream. No blood spatter ruins the luxury plush. Not like when Dad shot Mum.

Then I realise I feel no pain beneath the adrenaline. My limbs shake, but only from flight or fight. The bang came from elsewhere, I realise, as logic catches up with my wild thoughts. It shook the whole boat.

Maybe we hit rocks? Or land? Perhaps Scott failed to secure the boat last night because he had other things on his mind. We might have drifted back to the island. My heart leaps at the thought, and I quietly hurry out onto the deck.

My mouth opens in shock when I realise the truth.

There is another boat. A smaller yacht, one

without sails. The dark figure on its deck reaches out and grabs hold of the rail of mine and Scott's vessel.

Even in the dim light of the emerging sunrise, I recognise the shape and form of the figure. The long flowing hair in the wind is too familiar.

It's Dawn.

'Hey!' she hisses, looking up to face me. Her features are indistinct in the darkness. 'Climb over here, quick!'

I'm so pleased to see another person out here in the isolation of the sea that I could cry in relief. I'd thought it was all over. I thought I was a goner, especially just now with the jolt of the impact.

My bare feet find their way onto the side of the deck. The gaps in the railing seem precarious in the dark, but I don't care. I'm getting out of here. I would jump on board an inflatable kayak right now if that was what Dawn had turned up in.

I'm sidling along when there is another bang. This time the sound makes me scream out loud. My ears ring.

There is no doubt this time that it was a gun.

FORTY-NINE

Dawn jumps back onto her vessel. For a split second, I think she has been hit, thanks to the speed at which she moves.

Then I realise it was either a warning shot or a miss as I turn around. Scott appears behind me on deck. He has a t-shirt on now and is pulling up his shorts with one hand. In the other, he holds the gun from the deck box.

'What's going on here?' he shouts, his voice filled with fear. 'Get down from there, Sam. You will fall.'

I can't help but scoff at this. 'You just fired a gun at me, and now you are concerned for my safety? Yeah, right.'

'Don't be fooled,' comes Dawn's voice. She is once again standing upright on the other boat, her hands doing something behind her back. 'Scott doesn't want you to escape, that's all. He doesn't care about your safety.'

Scott sounds outraged. 'What are you talking about?'

'Don't play stupid. Let's not pretend you didn't tell me exactly how you were going to dispose of your wife on your honeymoon. After you promised to share the money with me, of course. You had it all planned out before you bumped into her on purpose in that coffee shop. Didn't you, babes?'

My husband shakes his head in the dim light. 'I don't know what you are talking about! You're crazy, Dawn.'

This is said with so much conviction and heart that part of me melts for him. Maybe this is a big misunderstanding, after all?

I want there to be a reasonable explanation for everything and for Dawn to remain the villain. It was so much simpler that way. No such luck, however.

Dawn takes a tentative few steps forward, raising her arm. She holds a flare gun and aims it directly at Scott. 'I'm not the crazy one. I'm not fixated on taking people's money and leaving their lives in tatters.'

'Aren't you? Then what are you doing here? I thought you wanted to claw your money back?'

'I did,' Dawn smiles. Her white teeth gleam in the gloom. 'We agreed that was how it was going to happen, after all.'

'Did we?' Scott calls. 'Why the past tense? What changed?'

'I've never killed anyone. My conscience is clear. I'd ideally like to keep it that way.'

'Then what are you doing here in the middle of the night aiming a weapon at my wife and me on our honeymoon?'

'I'm trying to stop you from destroying someone else. I'm stopping your little scheme and saving a woman's life at the same time.'

'Really? It doesn't look like it. If anyone were to see this scene now, they would think you are the jealous ex-wife coming to take her revenge on the newlyweds.'

'It doesn't matter,' Dawn shrugs. 'No one will see this. Sam is going to board this boat with me, and we will go back to land without you. You can stay here and cry over the money you have lost because your wife has walked out on you when she realised the truth. You only married her for her money—she knows that now. The game is up.'

'You are talking rubbish, as usual, Dawn. But if money was my motivation, I haven't exactly lost, have I? Sam's inheritance arrived this afternoon in our joint account. I get at least half by default. So I don't need to kill anyone. Not that I would want to hurt Sam. She is my wife. I love her.'

Scott's words should be reassuring, but something isn't right.

'Bullshit!' Dawn shouts. 'You were only ever after her inheritance. Don't listen to his lies, Sam. He wants your money, and he wants you dead! If I leave you alone with him, then you won't ever make it home. I can assure you of that.'

I turn to Scott. 'What do you mean the money landed in our joint account? I arranged for it to be paid into my personal account.'

Scott glances at me. 'You can't have. I got a notification from our joint account earlier. I'm definitely not imagining all those figures in my account, Sam.'

'*Our* account,' I correct him.

'Right. Anyway, you must have made a mistake when you filled out the beneficiary form. Your mind was elsewhere. Probably on your imminent wedding.'

'No, I didn't make a mistake. I specifically gave my personal bank account details. I didn't know when I was going to tell you about the money at that point. I wanted to leave my options open for the perfect moment. There is no way I handed over our joint bank account details that day.'

'You are absolutely right, Sam,' Dawn adds. 'Scott has undoubtedly arranged this with Henry's son, Jonathan, at the trust. You filled in the forms correctly, I'm sure. Then Jonathan made sure that cash landed in Scott's account instead. Don't let Scott gaslight you into thinking you made an error. You know the truth, don't forget it.'

'It's so trivial either way!' Scott snaps. 'What difference does it make? Just admit you made a mistake, Sam.'

I hesitate. Did I fill in the forms wrong? I

was a wreck before that meeting at the trust.

'Don't listen to him,' Dawn urges. 'If you do, then how is this any different than still being with Adam? You've been burned before by an abusive shit. Don't go down that road again. Get away now. Come with me.'

I turn to Dawn. 'How do you know about Adam?'

'She knows too much about you, doesn't she?' Scott answers quickly. 'She is obsessed with you. Dawn was the one who revealed your real name before the wedding, remember? She thought it would put me off marrying you. She made our life hell. Do those that sound like the actions of an innocent woman to you?'

Dawn laughs. 'Says you, babes! Scott had a file on you, Sam. Long before you even laid eyes on him in that coffee shop that day you met. He engineered your supposedly accidental meeting. He spilled his coffee on the two of you on purpose. I only know about the abusive relationship with Adam because I overheard you talking to Sara about it at the train station when you dropped her off. Don't let a man like that win. You are with one again now. A wolf in Armani clothing! He only wants you to finance his lifestyle. Scott's Ponzi scheme needs some more capital to keep it afloat and keep everyone thinking he is a successful businessman. Henry found the perfect solution and handed you to him so he could put his plan in place. Henry will get his cut, too, at some point. Don't let them get away with it. Come over onto this boat now.'

'Don't listen to her, Sam!' Scott shouts imploringly, his dark hair ruffling in the wind. He squints at me in the light of the sunrise. 'Stay here with me where I will keep you safe. If you get on Dawn's boat, she will kill you. She will push you off and leave you to drown in the deep water. Even a strong swimmer would struggle to make it to shore from this distance.'

I hesitate.

'Oh, Scotty. Is that what you had planned for her? Very well thought through, that notion, isn't it? It's pretty hands-free, too. You never liked to get your hands dirty, did you? Come on, Sam. Time to go. I'm aiming right at Scott. If he tries anything, I will shoot.'

I look nervously between the gun-wielding pair. The last thing I want to do is come between them. They are locked onto each other as they have been before, only this time, each is armed with more than simple glares. Which one of the couple is more dangerous? Who is the liar?

'I thought you weren't a murderer, Dawn?' Scott calls sarcastically.

'I'm not. Not like you.'

'I haven't killed anyone.'

'You caused my brother's suicide by stealing his inheritance, just like you did mine. His life was ruined because of what you did. You as good as killed him. His blood is on your hands whichever way you look at it.'

'Warren was a willing investor. He knew there were risks.'

'His wife said you promised him guaranteed returns.'

Scott laughs. 'There isn't any such thing! Warren understood that. He obviously sold his wife a pile of lies so she wouldn't argue about the investment. There is always a risk with anything.'

'It doesn't matter now,' Dawn snaps. 'Your new wife will get away from you, and I will make sure you don't see a penny of her money. Come on, Sam. What are you waiting for? Climb aboard.'

I put my hands to my face in distress. 'I don't know who to believe.'

Dawn groans. 'Believe me! I'm trying to help you here! I'm your only friend right now.'

'You should trust your husband!' Scott calls, giving me a desperate glance away from Dawn's weapon. 'I'm trying to protect you from my crazy ex-wife! You would have to be insane to go anywhere with her after everything she has done to us. She sent you threatening notes, made it look like we were burgled and tried to sabotage the wedding at every turn. She has treated you appallingly—you know all this. Don't believe a word she says!'

Dawn interjects. 'Scott set all of that up! Yes, I was upset with you for taking my place at first, but I never wanted to harm you. Those notes weren't intended for you either, not that it was me writing them at all!'

'What do you mean?' I ask her.

'Someone else was sending those notes to Scott. I clocked it as soon as I looked at one. Obviously, I knew I wasn't the sender, even though it was fun at times to allow you to believe I was. None of the envelopes had an addressee on, did they? Scott used that to his advantage to leave you to believe I was sending you those messages. It was too easy. They just kept coming through the door, even when I was elsewhere.'

I let out a breath of confusion. 'If you didn't send them, then who did?'

'Someone with a grudge against Scott. My best guess is someone heavily invested in his dodgy investment scheme. Perhaps someone who wants their money back too soon after handing it over? They might realise by now that they have been duped. Scott has taken money from the wrong person, if you ask me. They aren't taking the theft lying down, not like my brother and I did. The messages were getting more ominous every time, weren't they? "*You were warned. Don't try to hide from me*". I wouldn't want to be in Scott's shoes when they catch up with him and he can't pacify them with your inheritance.'

Scott is shaking his head wordlessly.

Dawn continues. 'It sounded like they didn't

like Scotty disappearing to that hotel with you. Maybe they thought he was giving them the slip. That was just a happy accident, and that message arrived after the fake break-in. It made it sound like I was upset about being left alone in the house. Scott must have taken it from the doorstep when he got back and put it upstairs. The cleaner then found it and handed it to you. I can see from how the notes were worded you might have thought it was me. But no. It wasn't my style, even if Scott planted that printer in my room during the supposed break-in.'

I blink. 'Planted it?'

'Yes, it was all set up. Scott is good at that sort of thing. Attention to detail, he calls it. I didn't even have a laptop with me. I'm not sure how I was supposed to be printing notes without a computer. That old printer I found smashed in my room wasn't even the type that could be connected to a phone. Goodness knows where he found it.'

The sun has fully risen now. Scott's dark hair and pale face are becoming clearer. He looks contemplative as he continues to aim the gun at Dawn, who aims straight back just as determinedly.

'You aren't denying any of this,' I say to Scott.

'I shouldn't have to—you know me. I'm your husband. This is all lies.'

I cross my arms across my chest. 'Not all

of it. You lied about not knowing who I was. You said you knew nothing about the money at first. It also looks like you have arranged for my inheritance to go into the wrong bank account. That's serious. It proves how involved you are. Then, on top of that, you have people sending you threatening notes because you have scammed them out of money. I had no idea you were running a dodgy investment scheme.'

'That's not even the half of it,' Dawn snorts behind me. 'Wait until you hear about his parents.'

'What about them?'

'They're dead.'

FIFTY

'What?' I gasp in shock. Marty and Katherine? How can they be dead? Scott was on a video call to them not all that long ago.

Horrorstruck, I expect Dawn to reveal that their murders were part of their son's plan. Has Scott arranged for another inheritance to come his way? I can't imagine how he could expect to make that look natural, inheriting so much money all in one go.

'You'll never get away with all this,' I say to my husband.

He swallows. 'Away with what?'

'You killed your parents. Were you after their money, too?'

Scott bursts out laughing. 'Don't be ridiculous. They were dead to me long ago, just not physically, as far as I know.'

'What do you mean?'

In the golden glow of the sun, it's obvious Scott is shaking with rage. 'My mother was a drug addict who hardly noticed I existed. I barely knew my father. I haven't seen him since I was five.'

Dawn nods, realisation spreading across her face. 'So that's where Marty and Katherine come in! I've been wondering for a little while why you did it, Scotty. Ever since I found out.'

'That doesn't make any sense,' I say slowly. 'Your parents video called from Egypt.'

Dawn snorts. 'Looked more like Rhyl, from what I could see. As I said, Scott loves a good set-up. Conning people is what he does best.'

I look between them with exasperation. 'Will someone please tell me what you are talking about?'

Scott looks ready to burst into tears and refuses to look at me at all. I feel a tug for him again, but since he is holding a weapon, he doesn't look all too approachable. I get a chill from seeing him with a gun.

Dawn answers me instead, 'Remember how you asked me how I got Scott's parents to cancel their wedding invite? I told you you didn't want to know. I'll tell you exactly how now. They were paid actors. Marty and Katherine. Those aren't their real names, by the way. Those people you saw on the video call aren't a married couple.'

The last bit of breath I was holding is forced from me with this revelation. 'What are you talking about?'

'They work for an agency. Scott hired them to attend the wedding. Then I paid them to cancel that invitation and say I was their favourite of Scott's partners, just for fun. It turns out they will work for the highest bidder. What a laugh! I could have told them to do or say anything, and they would have done it. If only I had more funds, I could have had some real fun. A five-minute video call was all I was willing to shell out for, however. They were the pair that showed up to my wedding with Scott, you know. For years, I believed they really were Scott's parents.'

There is silence as this declaration is made. Scott doesn't deny this. He stares seethingly at Dawn.

I ask the obvious question. 'How did you find out they were actors?'

'It was Warren's wife. She always said how handsome Scott's dad, Marty, was. By chance, she spotted Scott's so-called father in an advert for cat food. She said she didn't know he worked in acting. I told her he didn't. Marty was a retired army officer—supposedly. When he wasn't luxuriating at his country manor, of course.'

Dawn nods, the sun illuminating her bright green eyes. 'That was another thing. Scott loves to brag about his parents, who live in a country estate with three acres of land and forest. I never once got invited over there for Sunday lunch. Not in eleven years of marriage. That was odd.'

She laughs. 'I never did get a satisfactory explanation. It was always, "Oh, my parents are renovating the manor." Or "They are out of the country for a while on some expensive holiday." There was always some excuse for why I could never see this beautiful house and grounds Scott wittered on about. That's because it doesn't exist. Scott's parents were never wealthy, and they certainly aren't Kathy and Marty. The actor's names are Dave and the other is Michelle. You can look them up on the agency website.'

Scott's reticence on the surprise video call from his supposed parents comes back to me. The conversation was stilted. He had seemed unwilling to even answer the call. At the time, I couldn't understand why.

I turn to him now. 'You hired fake parents? Why?'

He has gone bright red. 'I told you. My real ones are dead to me.'

'That's because they don't fit in with his rich and successful image,' Dawn offers. 'He loves telling people he is the son of an elite couple from Harrogate and is the heir to their fortune. So he changed his name by deed poll to something that fitted the bill. It adds to the image, doesn't it?'

Dawn shrugs. 'Who wouldn't feel safe handing their money over to a promising investment opportunity with Scott? If they knew he was the son of a druggie and goodness knows what, it might make them think twice before parting with their life savings. He wouldn't have got a penny from Warren if my brother knew the truth—I'll tell you that for nothing! Scott is just one big facade. He takes and gives nothing real back. I've learned that the hard way.'

'Shut your face!' Scott's posh accent has slipped now. I can't quite place what might be his real one underneath as he jabs his weapon at Dawn aggressively.

'Okay, Scotty. We are leaving, anyway. Aren't we, Sam?'

'No,' Scott says firmly. 'You aren't going anywhere.'

'You can't stop us. No way can you shoot us both and get away with it. It isn't believable we both drowned on your honeymoon.'

'No?' Scott asks with a strange smile that doesn't suit him. It somehow disrupts the angles of his usually symmetrical face. One of his hands has slipped into his pocket, and he presses his phone to his ear, still unblinkingly staring at Dawn. His trigger finger is still at the ready. I wonder if he would dare pull it. Can the man I love be a killer?

'Hello? Henry, it's me,' Scott says hurriedly in a low voice. It's like he doesn't want Dawn and me to hear his conversation. There is nothing but the gentle lapping of the sea where it kisses the sides of the boats. We hear every word.

'Yes, I know what time it is! I'm in the middle of a fucking disaster here! It's Dawn. She has shown up making all sorts of wild accusations. She told Sam I'd married her for her money and Sam believes it. Dawn is trying to convince her I'm going to kill her. What do I do?'

Dawn and I exchange a glance. The pleading note in Scott's voice says a lot. It sounds like he is begging Henry for help. Is our current fate in the hands of Scott's solicitor back in England?

'I can't do that,' Scott says quietly after a few moments, muttering into the phone. 'There are two of them. It will never work. I understand that, but I can't...Yes, I will. Of course. You can count on me. You know that.'

Dawn glances at me again. She looks more anxious as Scott hangs up the phone and pockets it again.

'So what did old Henry say?' she asks politely with a smile. 'Are Sam and I sleeping with the fishes tonight? Or has your trusty solicitor come up with a magical legal solution to get you out of trouble?'

Scott smiles calmly. 'You need to lower your weapon, Dawn. Are you really planning on shooting me? You won't get a single payment from the divorce if I'm dead.'

'I won't get anything if I'm at the bottom of the sea!'

'That's not going to happen.'

'Like hell, it's not! You aren't getting out of this one, Scotty. So you might as well just let me and your new wife go. I told you that you can't kill us both and make it look like a tragic accident! No one can get out of that kind of trouble so easily, no matter how rich they are. No one will believe you.'

'What people will believe is that my jealous, crazy ex-wife has latched onto my new wife and I. Henry will back that up, so can lots of people, even Sam's best friend. I can tell everyone there was a struggle. Say, for instance, Dawn, you shoot Sam—you will both fall into the water and drown before I can recover either of you. That certainly would be a tragic twist to the honeymoon, wouldn't it?'

'You can't do that,' I tell him firmly as I shiver again.

'No?' Scott shakes his head. 'Apparently, I'm capable of quite a few things. It sounds bad, doesn't it? When you hear it all laid out like this, I mean.'

He laughs and looks to the glowing horizon as if wanting someone to share the joke. Dawn takes the opportunity to strike.

As Scott looks away, Dawn pulls the trigger on the flare gun.

FIFTY-ONE

Scott's lapse in concentration costs him. Dawn launches a flare right at him. He jumps out of the way and literally hits the deck.

I scream as the flare misses him and fizzes and smokes in the sea.

Scott is quick to retaliate. It all happens in a few seconds, but I witness everything as though time has slowed down.

Scott rolls over and aims at Dawn, who has used her single shot and is now unarmed. My husband locks onto his target, who seems frozen in terror all of a sudden, and squeezes the trigger.

'No!' I scream in horror. I launch myself at Scott. I don't even realise what I'm doing until it's happening. One moment of panic and I've thrown my weight at him to stop him from killing Dawn.

The shot fires. The sound reverberates through my body. My ears ring. The sound of the sea suddenly becomes distant.

Then Scott's body slumps beneath me, the fight gone out of him.

If I hadn't heard the bullet hit the water

with a splash, I would have thought Scott's head or torso had taken it. It takes me a few moments to realise he hasn't been shot. It's like my husband is a puppet; the animator abruptly stepped out to lunch.

'What happened?' I whisper in horror and confusion as I reach out for the side of Scott's face. My fingers find a wet patch in my husband's hair. When I slide them out to look at them, they are stained bright red.

'No,' I whisper. 'No! No! No! Scott!?'

I scramble around, trying to feel for a pulse. My hands are shaking so badly; I can't tell if it's my trembling or my own terrified heartbeat I can feel beneath my fingers. It's even beating in my throat.

I scramble away and throw up over the side of the boat on trembling knees. The last remnants of the late-night supper I shared with Scott sink into the deep blue water.

When I find the strength to turn back, I see Dawn. She has come over to our boat and carefully checks Scott's pulse.

'He's dead, isn't he?' I ask her quietly as I remain slumped in the corner.

After a moment, she nods, staring down at Scott's crumpled form. 'It wasn't your fault, Sam.'

A hysterical laugh bursts from me. 'I killed him. I must have hit his head when I jumped on him.'

Dawn nods and gestures to a smear of blood

on the otherwise pristine white side of the deck where Scott's head must have struck.

I swear as I burst into uncontrollable sobs. 'What am I going to do?'

She shrugs. 'I guess you are going to prison. Come on over to my boat. I'll get you back to Katapola. We can go to the police station together. I will tell them what happened so you don't have to. You don't look in any condition. I'm sorry to have to tell you this, but Greek prisons aren't very nice. I just thought I should warn you.'

I stare at her in disbelief. My stomach twists again, threateningly. 'I can't go to prison abroad. Or anywhere. I didn't mean for any of this to happen!'

'I know. Maybe they will be lenient on you. The maximum you will get is a life sentence. But it could be as little as two to ten years. You never know.'

Life in prison. That's where my mind gets stuck.

Dawn keeps on talking, but I can't hear her. My dream honeymoon has taken an abrupt turn into a trip from hell. My husband is dead. His blood is on my hands. The best case scenario is he killed me for my money, that tainted inheritance that I only received because my parents' lives were cut prematurely short. Now, the worst outcome is that I will spend the rest of my life in a Greek prison.

The thought is unimaginable.

'Ready to go?' Dawn sighs. 'We can't leave him here like this. It isn't right. Just looking at him is freaking me out.'

She is right, of course. Blood pools around Scott's dark head even as we look at him. I can't bear to face that direction. The reality is hitting me hard. At least his eyes are shut.

I've killed my husband. I'm going to prison. My life as I know it is over.

I look up at Dawn pleadingly. 'I don't know what I am going to do.'

She steps over Scott gingerly and comes to crouch beside me. 'I know. This is hard. I didn't expect this when I arrived here. The flare gun was just a deterrent. I didn't think I would have to use it. I knew he was going to shoot when he pointed that gun at me, so I couldn't lower my weapon. We got locked onto each other and neither of us could back down.'

'Why?' I shake my head, trying to understand everything that has happened. 'Why didn't you tell me the truth about Scott sooner? Then none of this would have happened!'

'I told you, I didn't know you had any money to start with. I asked you if you were secretly rich. Remember? You denied it. Then later on Scott wanted me to back off making your lives a misery. While you were with Jonathan at the trust, Scott told me you were about to inherit a fortune. If I bided my time and let the wedding go ahead, he would share the money with me, he said.'

I swallow down sour liquid. 'So why didn't you do as you were told?'

'I'd already hired the fake parents for the video call. It was all arranged before Scott's revelation about you.'

'But why did you turn up in Greece? You didn't have to do that. Scott didn't look pleased to see you.'

Dawn nods and looks sombre for a moment. 'I know. That wasn't part of the plan. I told myself I wanted to keep an eye on Scott, make sure he wasn't going to trick me out of the money. Deep down, I couldn't let him go through with it. I didn't want your blood on my hands. I feel responsible for Warren's death. If I hadn't fallen head-over-heels in love with Scott then Warren would still be alive. I didn't want anything else like that on my conscience. It's hard to live with knowing I could have done things differently for a better outcome. So that's why I stopped Scott this time.'

I shake my head but don't know what to say. 'I still can't believe Scott did this. I believed he loved me. I'm such an idiot.'

She takes a deep breath. 'I felt the same way too when I realised. At least you lost a few months and not a decade. Scott was a piece of work. You know that now, too. Why did he have a gun in the first place? Your whole relationship was just a sham. He didn't love you. I'm sorry. He just wanted you for your money. Now, he will destroy your life if you let him.'

'What do you mean, "if I let him"? It's all over. What choice do I have?'

Dawn glances over at Scott's immobile form before she answers. 'I hate Scott. He ruined my life and stole my money. As far as I'm concerned, he killed my brother. He can't take your money now, but he can take your freedom. I'd hate to see him win after all. I can help you.'

I'm shaking uncontrollably now. 'How?'

She glances back at her ex-husband again. 'No one will know what happened here. Not if we clear up the evidence. You could be the one to inform the authorities that your husband had the accident, instead of him telling them it was you. Scott has set everything up in your favour here when you think about it. The hotel knew there was a non-swimmer staying in one of their rooms. You could just say they misunderstood which one of you it was. He has hired this yacht and sailed it out to sea with no witnesses, other than those who saw a happy couple on their honeymoon. It's the perfect set-up to get away with murder out here.'

Something clicks in my brain, and I realise what Dawn is proposing. 'No. I can't do that.'

'Scott was going to do the same thing to you if I hadn't shown up. You know that. He had no qualms about throwing your body into the sea like a piece of trash.'

My stomach lurches again. 'Please, don't.'

'You should take a leaf out of Scott's book and use the situation to your advantage. Don't let him steal anything more of your life, as Adam did. You have the chance to walk away from this. Because of me, you are still alive. Let me help you keep your freedom, too. It's the least I can do.'

The newly-risen sun illuminates the golden highlights in Dawn's hair. She crouches over my collapsed form like an angel offering support. Who would have imagined she would become my hero?

'I can't do this,' I whisper.

'I'll help you,' she says in a gentle voice. 'I just need some extra support getting his body into the sea. Okay? One step at a time.'

She pulls me to my feet, and I'm shaking violently as we tread closer to Scott's body.

Dawn takes the top end, and I take Scott's feet. His body is still warm as we groan, pull, and shove his weight along the deck. I can't believe I'm doing this.

Several times, I feel like throwing up again or running below deck to hide from this horrible activity. This is the worst thing I have ever had to do. It tops having to run through raging fire as a teenager, knowing full well I'd be scarred for life.

We both groan as we finally get Scott to the back of the boat.

'Just one more shove,' Dawn pants.

Then I hear another groan. It's not mine, and it's not coming from Dawn either. It vibrates beneath my fingers as they rest upon my husband's chest.

Scott is still alive.

FIFTY-TWO

My eyes widen in horror, and I freeze. Dawn stops shoving now, too, and watches Scott as he makes a feeble movement and groans again. His confused eyes come to focus on his ex-wife's face.

The edges of Dawn's mouth are tensed as I glance sideways at her. Is she smiling?

She makes a final push before I can react. There is a horrible splash.

I scream and grab fistfuls of my hair as I stare frantically into the water. 'He was still alive! What have we done? We have to get him out of the water!'

'No. We don't.'

'We have to take him to a hospital. He might still be okay!'

'If he survives he will go after you again. He won't stop until he has your money and you aren't around to tell the tale!'

'That doesn't matter!' I look hurriedly around the deck. There is a life buoy on a nearby railing.

Dawn watches me as I unhook it and

prepare to throw it in the water. 'You don't want to do that, Sam. Scott will destroy you if you save him. He has no loyalty. Not even to his parents, his only flesh and blood. What will he do to the woman he has known for mere months if you threaten to expose him? He ordered me killed for threatening to get in his way. Do you think he will let you live when you know the full extent of what he has done and planned?'

I hesitate. I know Dawn is right.

'Scott will take everything from you. That's not right. Even if you don't want your money, you could give it to a good cause. I bet Sara could do wonders for her mum with that kind of wealth. It could set them up for life and easily pay all the care costs. Patricia could have the best. Doesn't she deserve that?'

I stare into the blue water with my arm looped around the life ring. There is no sign of Scott. Bubbles come up and break the surface. Has he already sunk out of my reach?

'You said there was no pulse,' I say quietly.

Dawn shrugs. 'I couldn't feel one.'

I look up at Dawn. Scott's ex, my unlikely rescuer. I can't tell what is going on behind her beautiful eyes, and I'm not sure I would want to.

FIFTY-THREE

Once we are seated on the plane, I'm in a cold sweat. There are wet patches under my arms, and I'm all jittery. How did I manage to get through airport security in this state? I'm a wreck.

Dawn keeps smiling beside me. 'She's a terrible flyer!' she keeps telling everyone. 'She never can get used to it.'

This is my first time with a conscience quite this guilty. I was convinced throughout the boarding line that someone from security was going to drag me off to a holding room at any second.

In my plane seat, I glance around, wondering if the Greek police will catch up with me before the plane takes off. Or the press. The last thing I need is for my new identity to be blown at a time like this. I analyse the man nearest us. Could he be the staff member the journalist on the phone said was in Greece? Or was that all part of deception set up by Scott to keep me in hiding aboard the yacht? I'll never know.

'Relax. You are looking suspicious.' Dawn is calm and composed in the seat beside me as the engines finally roar into life.

She skim-reads a magazine as though we have just returned from a girl's weekend in Tenerife.

You wouldn't guess we have disposed of the body of my new husband or intensely cleaned the deck of the yacht to remove all evidence of what happened aboard. His phone was crushed and soaked in bleach for good measure before being thrown overboard with him.

It all seems like a blur now, as though it all happened in a dream. Except I swear that I catch a hint of bleach as I turn my head. I must be imagining it. The numerous showers since then must have washed away any trace of acrid cleaning product.

I glance at the faces of the people around me. People are returning from their holidays, not a care in the world. Are we really getting away with this? Should we?

'Sam,' Dawn warns. You couldn't be any more conspicuous if you tried. Watch a movie or something. Take your mind off things.'

I stare at her. 'I can't just forget what happened. How can I? I'm a newlywed travelling home without her husband.'

'Think yourself lucky you are the widowed one. Had the tables been turned, it would have been disastrous for you.'

'Lucky? I feel anything but at the moment.'

'Scott would have been doing the same thing had his plan succeeded. Except he would have been laughing all the way to the bank. He would have sat in his seat on this plane, thinking of all the things he would be doing with your money. Maybe you should, too.'

I scoff and stare out of the window as the runway becomes smaller and fades into the distance. All I can think of is that last exchange with Scott, the one held at gunpoint. If he was everything Dawn said he was, why hadn't he pulled the trigger sooner?

I voice this quietly to Dawn when I am satisfied no one is listening.

Her response is snappy. 'I told you we won't discuss that now we have left Greece.'

I shake my head. 'He didn't exactly admit everything on the yacht. Why didn't he just come out with the truth if he was guilty?'

Dawn looks up from her magazine again. 'I don't believe this. Scott didn't deny anything either. You saw him. He was like a rabbit caught in the headlights. I ruined his plans. If I were in your shoes, I would never stop saying thank you. I saved your life, Sam. Never forget that.'

I turn away again so Dawn can't see my tears of grief and regret. She isn't overly sympathetic to my pain of losing Scott. I guess she lost him a long time ago and has come to peace with it.

She puts down her magazine in the empty seat beside her. 'While we are on the subject of your gratitude, we can discuss plans for moving forward. It saves time when we get home.'

'What are you talking about?' I wipe my eyes on the sleeves of the hoodie I've set up camp in the last few days.

'My inheritance. Now, banks won't allow you to simply transfer the whole lot to me in one go, so you will need to make several payments.'

'Several payments?' I repeat blankly.

'Yes. When you make that sort of transfer, your bank will call you and run through a series of questions for security. You need to tell them that we are good friends and you are giving me a cash gift to start my own business. Tell them it's a high-street salon. That sounds straightforward enough. You say you have seen the premises in real life, and my business plan is solid. Tell them you are satisfied everything is in order. We have been friends since school, and you trust me completely. Have you got all this? You are staring at me like I've got two heads.'

'I don't understand.' This has to be a joke, right? How many times have I had this thought about Dawn, and it turns out she is deadly serious?

'What is not to understand?' Dawn tilts her glossy head. Her hair is perfect, not an inch out of place, her makeup, too. She is so composed after what we have done it is scary. 'I need my money, and you are going to give it to me. Understood?'

'No, it's not. You said you wanted to stop Scott. That was your motive for helping me.'

'And it would be a poor reward to leave your rescuer with nothing, wouldn't it?'

My mouth opens in shock. 'I didn't think you needed a reward.'

'Think again. Nothing is free in this world. I learned that a long time ago, *Sam*.'

The emphasis on my new name leaves me with a sinking feeling. 'What will you do if I refuse to hand the money over?'

'I'm sure you can use your imagination. I might get creative. Or I can simply turn up at a police station and tell them what happened on the boat. I will tell them you became paranoid and were convinced your new husband was after your money. I will explain how you flew at him in a rage and cracked his head on the side of the boat. I may not have been as thorough as you thought with the bleach. I may have left some specks here and there. I know exactly where too, and I can direct a forensic team if I need to.'

I shake my head in disbelief and answer back in a shocked whisper. 'But you were there too. It was your idea to move his body. He wasn't even dead before he hit the water!'

Dawn smiles serenely. 'Your bloody fingerprints were everywhere they shouldn't have been as you moved your husband's body.

Mine were nowhere, I made sure of it. His murder has your name written all over it. If you don't want to spend the rest of your life in prison, then I suggest you do everything I say.'

New tears burn my eyes now. On top of losing my husband, I'm being blackmailed.

'What about Sara?' I say after a few minutes as Dawn picks up a new magazine. 'She and her mum need that money.'

'Oh, Sam. You are making me sound like a monster. I only want five hundred thousand. You can keep the rest. Donate your share to your friend. There should be enough to cover the care costs. It might be good for you. That money seems tainted, doesn't it? You can't possibly hold onto it yourself without feeling a little bit ghoulish after everything that has happened around it.'

'That's nice of you to think of Sara,' I say sarcastically. 'I thought a conscience would be a foreign concept to you.'

She smiles. 'I told you, I'm not the villain. Everything I am today is because Scott made me this way. I used to be nice, you know.'

I snort. 'Yeah, right.'

'I still am to a certain degree. I'll prove it to you.'

'How?'

'I'll give you a full two months to get your things out of my house. After that, I will resume ownership when you sign the deeds over to me.

The house will be yours now that your husband has passed away. It will no doubt be heavily re-mortgaged, but I will take care of that. As for where you will live, I know a cute little flat coming up in Crumpsall. That's your neck of the woods anyway, isn't it? It's where you were living when you met Scott. You have visited my place already, haven't you? You even spoke with the landlady when you were snooping, I'm told.'

She smiles again and lifts her shoulders at my look of surprise. 'So don't worry, Sam. When you move out, it should feel like home sweet home.'

FIFTY-FOUR

I feel ready to give up when I slide the keys into the lock at the house and open the front door. Once again, I catch sight of the engagement and wedding ring combo on my finger. For pretences, I'm still wearing them. I get a horrible feeling every time I see them next to my skin; I can't wait to be rid of them. As a widow whose husband tragically drowned on our honeymoon, I can't be seen to remove them just yet. I'm officially in mourning.

Stepping over a pile of post, I set my suitcase down in the large glass entrance hall. Dawn passes me, carrying her magenta one straight upstairs.

For some reason, it seems futile to take my things to the master bedroom, not when it turns out I'm not allowed to stay here for much longer.

Through the open gates, I catch sight of a dark vehicle in the street. A figure is inside behind tinted glass. I have the feeling of being watched. I lock the door firmly behind me and stand in the familiar entrance hall. Everything looks different somehow.

This is the home I shared with Scott. My time here is now limited. It's like the countdown to the next phase of my life has begun. Dawn has it all planned out. I'm to sign over ownership as soon as I can and move out. At the same time, I have to hand her half my inheritance in incremental payments. I've never felt more helpless.

Dawn looks at my despondent body language as she trots back down the staircase. 'It could be worse, Sam. You could be at the bottom of the Greek sea. Thanks to me, you still have the rest of your life. I saved you, remember?'

'Sure.' I collect the pile of envelopes and junk mail gathered in the two weeks since we left. I sort it into important and advertising. It is hard to believe that something as normal as junk mail exists after the horrific time I've had abroad.

Amongst the chaos are several familiar-looking envelopes. I stare at the familiar ones as I tear them open one at a time.

You should have listened,
Scott. Now you will pay.

The second one isn't any better.

All we wanted was the money.
Watch what happens next.

Dawn is piercing the film on a ready meal as I enter the kitchen and drop the notes and junk mail into the bin.

'More of those threatening messages, eh?'

I nod. I still don't know who the sender is, but I know their intentions aren't good. Are the threats real or hollow? What kind of people did Scott get tangled up in with his dodgy investment scheme?

At least this proves Dawn isn't behind them since she has been stuck like glue to me for the past week. She was telling the truth. That's something, I guess.

*

Weeks later, Dawn and I are eating lunch together. She demanded I cook her an elaborate pastitsio, a Greek lasagne with added pancetta. This dish was served at our pre-wedding dinner party; the irony is not lost on me. She does these little things to remind me why I have spent the last few weeks pouring money from my account into hers.

Afterwards, Dawn goes to the master bedroom ensuite for a long soak in the bathtub. She missed using it, she says; I have been relegated to the smaller guest room at the back of the house. Dawn has emptied the contents of my wardrobe in here. Now I'm the one living from bundles on the carpet. I can't be bothered to sort any of it out since I'm not here forever as I once thought.

Dawn leaves me with an extensive amount of dishes whilst she goes to luxuriate with the expensive bath products Scott used to buy from France. The little bottles and jars used to come in on regular subscription. I suppose that needs to be cancelled, along with a load of other things that come with the admin of the end of someone's life.

There is still so much to do.

This is what my life has been like since we got back. I have been fated to run around after Dawn while trying to shut down Scott's affairs, and I am still working full-time at school as a teaching assistant.

It seems I will be in that job for the rest of my career. Dawn decided she wanted my inheritance in its entirety after all, rather than the half she initially demanded. It turns out Scott was up to his eyeballs in debt on the house, and Dawn argued she needed the extra funds to pay it off. It makes sense, she said. Since Warren's half of the inheritance was absorbed by Scott too.

That means I am left with hardly anything. I'm back to square one, minus the rich husband I thought I was marrying.

Not that it was ever about the money for me. I thought I was going to be the wealthy one in our relationship, enjoying the fruits of my father's successful tennis career. He owed me for ruining my earlier years and literally scarring me for life. I was once excited to tell Scott the news of my inheritance. It should have been a more positive announcement.

So much for helping Sara with her mother. I still haven't explained everything to my best friend. I'm not sure how to go about it, certainly not over the phone. I don't want to incriminate myself further.

At least this arrangement of being Dawn's slave is not forever. I only have a few payments left before Dawn has everything she asked for. The change of ownership on the house will also be completed in the next week or so.

The doorbell rings. I rub my soapy hands on the dish towel and go to answer it.

My stomach drops in horror when I see who it is.

FIFTY-FIVE

It's Henry at the door. He stands there in one of his characteristic suits, looking stern.

'Can I come in?' he says after a few moments where I stare at him in fear.

'I guess so.' I glance up the stairs as I shut the front door behind him. How long will Dawn be in the bathtub? I need her here now.

I don't feel safe alone with Henry. Didn't he tell Scott to finish Dawn and me over the phone when we were on the yacht? I couldn't hear his side of the conversation. Who knows what was said?

Henry seats himself at the breakfast bar and turns to me stiffly. I stand by the windowsill, where there are heavy terracotta plant pots. It's the only thing out on the kitchen surfaces that would work as a makeshift weapon in a hurry. It turns out head injuries are pretty dangerous. Scott's cost him his life, in a way.

'So,' Henry says after a moment of awkward silence. 'You've returned home from your honeymoon without your husband.'

'Yes.' I slip back into the story I told the

Greek police repeatedly. 'He had an accident on the yacht. Scott slipped and went overboard. The waves were too strong for him and he had hit his head during the fall. He wasn't a good swimmer.'

Henry raises his eyebrow at this. He has known Scott for years and likely knows this part isn't genuine, but he doesn't argue. 'Yes, the police informed me.'

Henry nods after a silence. 'So that's how it happened, was it? A head injury? That's how you killed Scott?'

'I didn't kill him. It was an accident. He fell overboard and drowned.'

'Do not lie to me!' Henry has the air of a strict headmaster, and I'm in his office after school. 'I know what you have done.'

I stare back at him fearfully. 'Are you going to the police?'

'No. I don't believe in punishing people for the sake of it. A good friend of mine has lost his life. There isn't any point in throwing away another. Scott wouldn't have wanted that.'

My lip trembles at this, and a hot tear runs down my cheek. 'I'm so sorry.'

Henry nods stiffly and looks out the glass of the patio doors. 'That sounds like an admission of guilt. You aren't to talk like that from now on. If anyone asks you about your husband's accident, you tell them it is too distressing to talk about. Change the subject. Do you understand?'

No, I don't understand any of this, but I

nod. Why did this have to happen to me? I take a tissue from the dispenser nearby. 'Why are you helping me?'

'He isn't,' comes a bitter voice that makes me jump.

Dawn is striding into the kitchen, looking furious and covered only in a towel she has fastened around herself. 'Henry is only protecting himself. Anyone would report you to the police for the murder of a *good friend*. So what are you up to, Henry? Protecting yourself? Your son, too? He had a part to play in all this, too, didn't he? Jonathan, isn't it?'

'I have no son.'

'Of course not. I know he works at the trust fund management company. He was the one who leaked Sam's info to you and Scott so you could each get a share. Was it you who found me too? The daughter of a rich businessman who stood to inherit the fortune early due to her dad's obvious drinking problem—that was me. Did Scott come up with the info on me alone, or was that you?'

'I have no idea what you are talking about.'

'Of course you don't. While I've got you here, I'm curious about how Scott got into the business of conning people. Was it you, Henry? Did you find some intelligent, disadvantaged boy with rubbish parents and take him under your wing? Is that how it went? It sounds like it from everything I have found out. You were partners in crime together. I guess you won't be taking a cut from this project, though. Bad luck.'

Henry stands and smooths the front of his suit jacket down. 'I advise you to keep your wild conspiracy theories to yourself.'

'Of course I will. They won't leave this room. I won't tell another soul the truth. Neither will Sam. We can all live happily ever after now, can't we?'

'Is that right?'

Dawn nods. 'I think so. You can leave us in peace now that your little plan is thwarted. It would look too suspicious if anything were to happen to Sam or me. I have plans set up, you know. If anything were to happen to me, my solicitor would know what to do and what to tell the police. You won't get away with it, not even with all your law knowledge, because I've been studying too, Henry. I've started the process of becoming a solicitor. Remember when I said I was between jobs? It's my new career.'

'Is that so? Well, it's time for me to leave.'

'Don't ever come back,' Dawn calls after him.

I follow Henry to the door so I can shut it behind him. Mentally, I make a note to change the locks, but then I remember I won't be living here for much longer.

Henry steps outside and turns back to face me. 'I would be careful with the woman in your house. She is dangerous.'

I nod. I'm still not sure who presents the most threat to me. Henry, or Dawn. 'I'll bear that in mind, but I'm leaving this house soon. She wants me to sign it over to her.'

There is understanding in Henry's eyes. 'I see. You are planning to do so without question, are you?'

'I don't have a choice,' I say flatly.

'There are always other options. I'm not your solicitor, but I can help you if you choose to hire me.'

'For a certain fee, I suppose?'

He nods.

I scoff. 'There is no way I'm hiring someone who suggested to Scott he should kill both Dawn and me on that yacht.'

Henry frowns. 'You are very much mistaken. That wasn't what I suggested at all. I simply told Scott to be careful. Dawn was and is delusional. She continues to come up with wild stories to suit her narrative. They have grown increasingly dangerous and damaging throughout her marriage to Scott. I see she hasn't given up now that he is dead. She seems to be your problem now, however.'

He drops his voice. 'I must warn you, though, that Dawn was diagnosed with a personality disorder early on in her marriage to Scott. I'm not sure if Scott told you this.'

'No,' I say slowly, wondering if this is another trick. 'He didn't.'

He nods. 'Dawn became hard to manage. Scott tried his best with her over the years, but it often backfired on him. His wife would always twist and turn things around to suit her wants and needs. She had relations with so many other men, but Scott didn't part ways with her. He wanted to abide by his vows until the day she dealt the final blow by walking out on him without a single word of goodbye.'

I stare at my husband's solicitor and friend. 'Are you saying she made everything up about Scott? You would say that now, wouldn't you? You are only covering yourself. Dawn is right. Look, I won't tell anyone about what happened. I just want to be left alone.'

'Well, if that is your goal, you are housemates with the wrong woman. And I must say that Scott's love for you was real. It would be a tremendous disservice to pretend he was anything other than besotted with you. He was so looking forward to a happy and long life with his new wife.'

I cross my arms across my chest. The seeds of doubt are sprouting in my mind. Why didn't Scott shoot me when he had the chance? If he had planned to murder me on our honeymoon, he had plenty of chances. He could have pushed me overboard so many times. What was he waiting for?

'Out of all of Scott's acquaintances, I knew him the best. He was excited about the future with you in it. There is no way what Dawn is accusing him of is true. Believe what you want, but you must know that your love was real.'

With this, Henry smiles sadly and turns on his heel.

'Wait!' I call after him. 'What do I do about Dawn? She is taking everything from me.'

Henry sighs. 'As I said, there are always options. Did Scott not have any dangerous enemies to whom he owed money?'

'Yes, so?'

He shrugs. 'I wouldn't want to be the one holding all of Scott's wealth alone in a big house that enjoys so much privacy.'

With this, he turns again and strides away down the driveway and out of sight.

The dark car that has been lurking intermittently is back again. The figure is inside as usual, watching behind tinted glass.

I glance down and see my suitcase beside the door where I left it in the entrance hall weeks ago. A capsule wardrobe. I still haven't unpacked. Perfect for a quick getaway, it turns out.

I slip on my shoes, reach out, and wheel my waiting suitcase down the driveway. As I step out onto the pavement, the car's engine starts, but I raise my hand to tell them to stop.

It's important that I speak with them. I know by now they must have been the one responsible for hounding Scott, their messages are getting more and more threatening.

They must be desperate to get their money back, so I will tell them exactly who has the funds to pay back Scott's debt.

THANKS FOR READING

Did you enjoy The Big Day? If so, please consider taking the time to write a quick review on Amazon or Goodreads. It really does help other readers find the book! :)

Also, if you would like to get news & be the first to know when my next book gets released, then visit my official website and enter your email address. It is only used to make sure you are the first to know this kind of news!

www.RuthHarrow.com

MORE BOOKS BY RUTH:

In Her Footsteps
You're All Mine
In My Wake
Dear Sister
Just One Lie
The Silent Wife
The Victim
The Guilty Girl

Printed in Dunstable, United Kingdom